A NOVEL

Lucy

A Novel

Lucy

Ellen Feldman

 W. W. Norton & Company

New York • London

Copyright © 2003 by Ellen Feldman

For information about permission to reproduce selections from this book,
write to Permissions, W. W. Norton & Company, Inc., 500 Fifth Avenue,
New York, NY 10110

Manufacturing by Courier Westford
Book design by Charlotte Staub
Production manager: Julia Druskin

Library of Congress Cataloging-in-Publication Data
Feldman, Ellen, 1941–
   Lucy : a novel / Ellen Feldman.— 1st ed.
      p. cm.
   ISBN 0-393-05153-6
1. Rutherfurd, Lucy Mercer—Fiction. 2. Roosevelt, Franklin D.
(Franklin Delano), 1882–1945—Fiction. 3. Triangles (Interpersonal
relations)—Fiction. 4. Roosevelt, Eleanor, 1884–1962—Fiction.
5. Presidents' spouses—Fiction. 6. Social secretaries—Fiction.
7. Presidents—Fiction. I. Title.
   PS3572.I38 L83 2003
   813'.54—dc21
                                                    2002010093

W. W. Norton & Company, Inc., 500 Fifth Avenue, New York, N.Y. 10110
www.wwnorton.com

W. W. Norton & Company Ltd., Castle House, 75/76 Wells Street,
London W1T 3QT

1 2 3 4 5 6 7 8 9 0

For Stephen ∾

❧ I am grateful to the following individuals, libraries, and archives for permission to quote from their materials.

The Franklin Delano Roosevelt Library, Hyde Park, New York

The Wilderstein Preservation Archives, Rhinebeck, New York

The Oral History Collection of Columbia University, the Reminiscences of Florence Kerr

The descendants of Lucy Mercer Rutherfurd

The descendants of Anna Roosevelt Halstead

A NOVEL

Lucy

~ 1947

"It is a story which reminds us of the code of another day, of the complexity of human relationships, of the human problems of statesmen bearing the heaviest responsibilities and of the capacity of mature people to accept the frustrations of life and, perhaps, to make of frustrations a sort of triumph. Eleanor Roosevelt, Franklin Roosevelt, and Lucy Mercer all emerge from the story with honor.

And, if Lucy Mercer in any way helped Franklin Roosevelt sustain the frightful burdens of leadership in the Second World War, the nation has good reason to be grateful to her."

◦ Arthur M. Schlesinger, Jr.

ᴇ Prologue

We had turned our chairs so the sun was behind us. It slid over our shoulders and glinted off the hollow circles of our wedding rings. Our spectator pumps—Violetta's brown and white, mine navy blue and white—made parallel imprints in the grass, which was as short and springy as the haircuts of the still-returning war veterans.

The boys were coming home. The big stone house behind us that had echoed for too long with the fluty voices of women and the reedy shouts of children would thunder like a full orchestra again. The girls would stop looking at their babies with anxious eyes, willing them not to grow another inch before Daddy came home. They would stop staring in the mirror with faces set against the damage time might do before a husband walked in the door. The boys were coming home. It would have been mean-spirited to dwell on the men who would never return.

I'd had my life. More of it than I deserved, Violetta was thinking that afternoon, though she didn't say as much. She didn't have to. We were sisters. We spoke in fragments. We communicated in code.

She was right. I'd had more than my share. Each morning I awakened to a fresh realization of how much I'd lost. That day

3

I'd been trying to recall the deep buoyant timbre of his voice, but the harder I strained to hear, the quieter the world grew. You can carry a photograph close to your heart. You can write your soul out in letters. Every man at the front and woman left behind knows that. But a voice evaporates into the past like a wisp of smoke. I'm not talking about his public voice. People were always sending him recordings of his speeches and fire-side chats. He never wanted to listen to them. What I missed now was the private tone, the conspiratorial laugh, the exu-berant cry of *Grand, isn't it grand.* All I heard was silence, though the shouts of the children splashed around us in the buttery light that slanted across the nine-hole golf course—nine holes as long as you played some of them backward—hit the lake, and shattered into a spray of diamonds.

I adjusted the umbrella tucked into the wrought-iron arm of the chair to keep off the sun, a vain old lady of fifty-five coddling a complexion there was no one left to caress. Across the lawn that was green as legal tender, one of the children detached himself from the group and came hurtling toward me on short fat legs, tipsy as a drunk careening out of a bar. That was when Vio spoke.

"What was your secret?" she asked.

The question didn't surprise me. For years I'd been seeing it in people's eyes, hearing it in their voices, sensing the dis-paragement it implied. You're not a great beauty, despite the complexion that has made you vain. Your hair was thick and auburn before it began to gray, and your eyes blue, but not so thick and auburn or so blue as to cause a stir. Eleanor had masses of hair that went from red to gold depending on the light, and her eyes were the color of a robin's egg, and just as defenseless. Years ago some man—not Franklin, that wasn't Franklin's style—had compared my voice to dark velvet, and people said I dressed well, considering that I'd had no money when I was young and other constraints later, but with all due regard to Richard Strauss and perhaps Verdi, men do not fall in love with a voice, and only other women and French couturiers care about a woman's clothing. I could make him laugh, but many people could do that. Certainly I was no great wit. According to my friend Elizabeth Shoumatoff, who was painting his portrait that day at Warm Springs and can't resist telling anyone who asks about it, and some who have the discretion not to, I'm not even very bright. Poor Elizabeth. I never guessed she was so eager for the spotlight. So perhaps she's right. Perhaps I'm not very bright. That only brings me back to the question. What was my secret? they want to know. What special charm did I possess, what tricks did I have up my sleeve, what wiles did I use to attract the greatest man of our time and hold him until he died, not in my arms as gossip has it, but close enough? Even my sister, whose resentment I'd never suspected until that moment, couldn't resist asking. She was twisting her wedding band around her finger as she spoke. "What was your secret?"

The child weaving toward us took a tumble, and I was out of the wrought-iron chair and across the lawn in seconds. I had no intention of answering Violetta. The reply would only make her more angry. I'd invited her to stay as long as she wanted. I'd tried to make it sound as if we were two girls together again, though we both knew we were two women alone.

There was another reason I didn't answer Violetta. She wouldn't believe me. No one would. The secret was too simple. It was so simple that sometimes I couldn't help hugging it to me with greedy pleasure like a miser hoarding gold.

But there were other times, even after all these years, when

I saw things differently. Then the question was not how I'd held him, but how I'd lost him. There were the letters, of course, but the letters were merely the excuse. How many had there been, a dozen, fifteen, twenty? A handful, literally, enough to fill the span between thumb and fingers as Eleanor lifted them from the overseas bag. When I'd posted them, one after another, they'd been white with hope. But I imagine them as they must have looked when she took them from the suitcase, tied with one of the velvet ribbons I'd worn around my throat in those days, spattered with mud, waffled by rain, and crushed from being shoved into his bag among the heavy woolen uniforms, and sinus medications, and dozens of other letters from his mother and his children and his wife. He threw away nothing.

He'd been foolish to carry them that way, tied in a ribbon that sent a message as clearly as one of his navy signal flags, though I would have hated it if he'd tossed them into his suitcase with all the other letters. Still, what had he been thinking, to pack them where anyone could find them? I know what the psychiatrists would say. I may be a vain old lady, I may not be a mental giant, but I am not an antiquated ninny. I'm familiar with the theories of Dr. Freud. I've heard the younger generation talk. They would say that Franklin wanted the letters to be found. The idea is ludicrous. Franklin had no desire to be caught. He was simply sure of his own invincibility. He was convinced there was nothing in the world he couldn't do. Certainly he never dreamed he wouldn't be able to walk off a ship on his own legs and unpack a bag with his own hands.

Eleanor unpacked for him. "The bottom dropped out of my own particular world," she told one friend and then another, and the friends told their friends. Elizabeth Shoumatoff is not the only one eager for the spotlight. But as the world knows, Eleanor went on. She had supporters who closed ranks around her. She had children to raise. She had a husband to find her way back to. "I can forgive but not forget," she also told friends. Eleanor always did have a penchant for undressing in public.

My position was more precarious. I had no husband, no children, no army of supporters eager to circle the wagons around me. I'd had the hope of those things, and I'd thrown it away. Perhaps that's the real question. Not how did I hold him or lose him, but how did I find the courage or the audacity or the sheer recklessness to risk him?

It's hard to understand from this vantage point how much of a chance I was taking. We live in a different world, built on broken rules, crowded with giddy inventions, dedicated to unstoppable progress. I see young girls racing around in short skirts and long trousers, and boys speeding after them in fast cars, and couples carrying on in public as we would not have dared in private, and I'm happy for them. But we inhabited a universe bound by convention and stalked by consequence. When we were told that a lady did not take a chair a gentleman had just vacated for fear the upholstery retained some of his heat, we gave the recently emptied seat a wide berth. When we were told a kiss might lead to pregnancy, we turned our faces away from temptation. Thanks to Vio's nursing studies, I was fairly sure a man's body warmth was not contagious and a kiss did not lead directly to motherhood, but I could not get over the suspicion that both acts, and a good many others, were bound to end in some form of disaster or damnation.

Vio and I had to be doubly careful. A man might marry a tarnished heiress. An exemplary man, the kind I wanted, might marry a young lady whose parents had been imprudent

enough to squander their fortune. But who would marry a girl
with feckless parents and a frayed reputation?

Marriage, of course, was what I was after. That was what
love was about. I burned to yield to a man, but one who
belonged to me. I was made for happiness, not sacrifice. That
is why I cannot understand where I found the courage to do
what I did. Guts, the boys coming home from the war call it.

The girl who risked the only future she could imagine is a
stranger to me now. I look at the old photographs and recognize the face she wore, but I can't feel her pulse. I remember
the handful of good evening dresses she rotated, but I can't
hear the hope that rustled in the silk as she dressed for dinner.
I recall the first time she danced with him, but the hair on the
back of my neck doesn't stand on end as it did on hers when
she saw him coming toward her across the ballroom. That girl
with nerves running too close to her skin and senses rubbed
raw by expectation is a stranger to the woman I have become.
But sometimes when I'm not thinking about that girl at all,
when I'm reading a book or sitting in the garden or worrying
about Violetta, the book and the garden and my sister fall
away, and for a moment so ephemeral it is gone almost before
I am conscious of it and I am left with only the ache of another
loss, that girl steals up and slips into me, and I know what it
was like before the bottom dropped out of Eleanor's particular world, and mine.

❧ 1914

✍ One

"Lucy was gay, smiling and relaxed . . . with a rich contralto voice, femininely gentle where Mother had something of a schoolmarm's air about her, outgoing where Mother was an introvert. . . . Though she was a paid employee . . . she was listed in the Social Register in New York as well as in Washington, a lady to her fingertips."   ✍ Elliott Roosevelt, *An Untold Story*

The sky stretched over the city, gray and menacing as a battleship, though that is not the analogy I would have made that afternoon. The war was months in the future. A generation of men who would die in disillusion still believed in God and country. A generation of women still acquiesced to men. Children obeyed parents. Everyone deferred to his betters. Everyone believed there was such a thing as betters. Archduke Francis Ferdinand was still alive. True, an obscure Serbian nationalist was dreaming of assassination, but dozens, perhaps hundreds, of unhappy young men were hallucinating self-sacrifice and glory, and most of them would do nothing about it. There had been two Balkan wars in as many years, but someone was always fighting someone else in that vague area of shifting borders forty-eight hundred miles away. I was probably one of the few Americans who knew where the

11

Balkans were, and that was only because, thanks to the generosity of Papa's aunt, the Countess Heussenstamm, Vio and I had spent a year at a convent school in Melk on the Danube, where the daughters of Austrian noblemen and American patricians, dressed in dirndl skirts and embroidered blouses, polished their catechism and their wifely virtues. Certainly no one believed the United States would go to war over anything that happened in the Balkans. The afternoon I set out from the Decatur Apartments where Mama and Vio and I were living, there were many who insisted the world would never go to war again. At a recent dinner, I'd sat beside a gentleman—an extremely eligible gentleman, heir to an extremely respectable fortune, Mama had pointed out—who'd spent a good part of the evening explaining that since it was a proven fact that modern warfare did not pay, bankers would not finance it, and therefore it could not happen in the twentieth century. The gentleman was deep-thinking as well as rich.

But I was not concerned with war that afternoon. My heels tapped a rapid staccato beat as I made my way down Massachusetts Avenue in my brand-new hobble skirt. I had no patience with dowagers who insisted that clothes, like wine, should be aged in a cool dry place for at least a year before being broken out. Nonetheless, I was regretting my new skirt that afternoon. You couldn't hurry in a hobble, or if you tried to, you ended up mincing along with tiny teetering steps and looking foolish. According to a doctor at Violetta's hospital, the reason men liked hobble skirts was that since the limbs couldn't move in them, everything else did. I thought the comment, and the fact that he'd made it to Vio, scandalous. In fact, he'd said legs, not limbs. The more I thought about the way the doctor had talked to Vio, the more certain I was that I was doing the right thing. I had to find a position. I could not let the burden of supporting us fall entirely on Vio. But I could not imagine touching strange skin or ministering to anonymous bodies. I had no more enthusiasm for sitting behind a metal desk in a long line of metal desks in a government office. I could hear the din of the typewriting machines. I could see the sleeves of my soft shirtwaist disappearing into ugly paper cuffs.

As I turned into DuPont Circle, a young woman clutching a sheaf of pamphlets to her black-frogged coat held out a leaflet. Washington was full of people trying to convince other people to stop whiskey leaking from wet counties to dry, or outlaw baseball games on Sunday, or protect young women from the white slavers who were supposed to be lurking around every corner. I had no desire to spend an afternoon standing under a leaden sky in DuPont Circle trying to convert strangers to my opinions, but I was curious why someone else would, and took the pamphlet she held out to me. As soon as I glanced down at it, I realized my mistake. Bold black letters demanded the vote for women. I should have guessed as much from the cut of the girl's coat. Woman suffrage was becoming fashionable. In New York, Mrs. O. H. P. Belmont, formerly Mrs. Willie K. Vanderbilt, had marched up Fifth Avenue for the vote. In England, ladies with names out of DeBrett's and girls who ought to be preparing for their presentation to the king were chaining themselves to fences and forcing gentlemen they'd dined with only the week before to send them to prison for it. But from what I'd heard, Mrs. Franklin Roosevelt did not strive to be fashionable, and I did not want to walk into her house wearing my convictions on my sleeve, especially since I wasn't sure they were my convictions.

I was in favor of the vote for women because it really would mean an end to war. What wife would send her husband off to battle, what mother her son? But I was also susceptible to my own mother's arguments against it. Mama insisted that the more like men women became, the less desirable men would find them. I wasn't sure I could afford the vote.

I don't mean to suggest I was opposed to progress. I thought front-closing corsets, for example, were a splendid step forward. Lacing old-fashioned stays had been as logical as buttoning a coat in back. It was surprising no one had come up with the idea sooner, but fortunately Mr. Goddard finally had, or so his magazine advertisements claimed, and now women could dress themselves without the help of a maid or a mother or a husband. We had been liberated. Some people, many of them doctors, said that in the interests of a sound body and healthy constitution, women ought not to wear any corsets at all, but I thought that was going too far. If anyone had told me that in a few decades I'd trade my corsets for a scrap of elastic called a girdle, go out in public with several inches of calf showing through sheer stockings, and encourage younger women, in the interest of patriotism, to forgo even the nylons in favor of leg makeup, I would have blushed to my hairline. That afternoon I was still offended by the doctor's comment about hobble skirts.

"Did you leave the room?" I'd asked Violetta.

"We were changing a dressing, Lucy."

I pictured Vio and the doctor, who was no gentleman, at the patient's bedside. I thought again of Mrs. Roosevelt. Mrs. Cowles said her niece required a social secretary, but wasn't sure she wanted a social secretary. As I turned onto N Street, I crumpled the pamphlet for woman suffrage and shoved it deep into my purse. It was a lucky thing that I did. Later I found out that at the time Eleanor was still vehemently opposed to woman suffrage. Franklin won her over, but only after the

flamingly beautiful suffragist Inez Mulholland perched on his
desk in the New York State Senate to convert him to the cause.
Franklin loved that story, though Eleanor always insisted he'd
come out in favor of the vote for women two months before
Miss Mulholland climbed on his desk to win his support.

I was abreast of the brick house now, not the one I was
headed for, but the one I'd left behind, and determined not to
look at it. My head swiveled toward it.

The black numbers I used to trace with a finger still ran
beside the front door, 1761, but now gold draperies hung in
the windows like sunlight in the winter-gray afternoon, and
the paint on the front door was red and shiny as lip rouge. I
told myself it was garish, but I felt as if I could toast my chilled
hands and feet on the warmth the house gave off. Mama had
hated living there. It was so much smaller and meaner than
what she'd been accustomed to. But Papa had come back to
us in that house, and it had been perfectly cozy for a family of
four.

A shadow drifted across the window, a stranger moving
around our front parlor. Only it was no longer ours. I probably wouldn't even recognize the room. The massive silver tea
service that went back to the Mercers who'd founded Mer-
cersburg would be gone, and someone else's ancestor would
hang over the mantel. I could still see Papa standing beneath
the portrait of Charles Carroll, the only signer of the Declaration of Independence richer than George Washington.
Though Papa and Mama believed that talking of money, even
thinking of it, was vulgar, certain exceptions were permissi-
ble. I didn't want to think of Papa standing beneath that gilt-
framed ancestor. A few days earlier, I'd seen him beneath
another portrait, and the memory still made me cringe.

I'd taken the streetcar out to the Chevy Chase Club for a

luncheon, and as soon as I came through the door, I spotted him across the big hall, though he was slumped in a chair half hidden by a potted palm. I stood staring at his face, stubbled with a day-old beard, and remembering the sensation of his smooth freshly shaved cheek as he bent to kiss me before walking out of my life each afternoon and evening. His head was sunk on his chest, which rose and fell as his lungs took in the palm-scented air and let out what I knew would be, if I got close enough, the fetid afterscent of brandy. Even from a distance, I could see the spots on his dingy shirtfront. Perhaps it was the sight of Papa facing the world in soiled linen that made me do what I did, for in spite of everything I loved him. Vio and I both did. Even Mama still had moments when she succumbed to the memory of his charm. But that afternoon I turned and started around the other side of the room. Years later I would be called immoral for acts which were not, but no one ever blamed me for what I did that day at the Chevy Chase, which was.

I dragged my eyes away from the house and continued down the block to the address Mrs. Roosevelt had given me. Even if I hadn't once lived on the street, I would have recognized 1733. I'd seen it, all America had, in the rotogravure section of the papers. When Mrs. Roosevelt's uncle, Theodore Roosevelt, had become president in the wake of Mr. McKinley's assassination, he hadn't wanted to hurry the widow out of the White House, so he'd stayed with his sister, Mrs. Cowles, at 1733, and it had become known for a short time as the Little White House. But now Mr. Theodore Roosevelt was off somewhere shooting animals and stirring up wars, and Mr. Wilson was in the real White House, and Mrs. Cowles had rented 1733 to her niece, whose husband, Mr. Franklin Roosevelt, had come to Washington as assistant secretary of the navy. As I started up the steps, I wondered why the wife of a government official would resist having a social secretary. I could not imagine what kind of woman Mrs. Franklin Roosevelt would be.

I pushed the bell and heard it ring on the other side of a door that was painted white rather than lip-rouge red. A moment later it swung open, and beyond a maid in a gray afternoon uniform, I glimpsed an entrance hall so like the foyer of the house we'd lived in down the street that I still visited it in my dreams, only unlike the stylish foyer of my memories, this one was impossibly cluttered. Coats and hats and motoring dusters and mackintoshes hung on a large walnut hall stand, almost obscuring the long oval mirror at its center. Umbrellas and boots in a dizzying array of sizes were scattered around and beneath it. In the corner a dog leash hung from a baby's carriage. A worn-looking golf bag was propped against the wall. The disorder gave off an enviable air of permanence taken for granted.

I told the maid Miss Lucy Page Mercer was here to see Mrs. Roosevelt. She took my coat, hung it over a woman's duster, and led me down the hall. The doors on either side were closed, but I knew what lay behind them. The house would be built on the same plan as the one down the street, a jumble of boxy rooms, piled on top of and spilling into one another through heavy double sliding doors.

The maid stopped in front of an open door. "Miss Lucy Mercer, m'um," she said and backed away.

The woman at the desk looked up, and I gazed across the room, and though Eleanor Roosevelt and I had never met, we recognized each other instantly.

She rose and came around her desk. I stepped into the room. We stood facing each other. Our blue eyes met at the same level. I was relieved. I'm a tall woman—statuesque, Mama liked to say—and it would have been awkward if Mrs. Roosevelt had to look up to her social secretary.

We were dressed almost identically, though her shirtwaist had a high lace collar, while I wore a dark velvet ribbon around my throat. The ribbon was intended to set off my complexion. I was also trying to make my lace collars last until I could buy more. Our serge skirts were the same navy blue, though hers was not a hobble. For the second time that day I regretted that mine was. I wanted to be stylish, but I didn't want Mrs. Roosevelt to think I was frivolous. The waist of her skirt was a hair's breadth thicker than mine. I didn't find out until later that she was pregnant—*enceinte*, as we said in those days. The condition didn't sound as intimate in another language.

She held out her hand to me. "Miss Mercer, I am so glad you could come." The words escaped from her mouth like a flock of small birds flying out of a cage, fluttered upward, and beat their tiny wings against the ceiling. I was surprised. I'd thought I was the one who was nervous.

She asked if I'd care for tea. I'd already noticed the tray in a corner. I said I would. As she led the way toward the table, the steel-gray sky beyond the window split, and a shaft of watery winter sunlight trickled in.

"What a lovely room," I said. I was trying to ingratiate myself, but I was also sincere. Though the furniture was heavy and the room dark, the sunlight seeping into it at that moment struck me as a good omen.

She looked around and frowned. It was only then that I noticed the dust hanging suspended in the thin stream of light. Later, I'd learn how she worried about Franklin's sinus infections. Later, I'd worry about them myself.

We sat facing each other across the tea table. She lifted a pot in one hand and cup and saucer in the other. The china, an iron-red Chinese tree pattern, had a patina of use as well as age. It was exactly the kind of china I intended to pour tea from in my own home.

She handed me the cup and saucer and said Mrs. Cowles had spoken highly of me, and I told her how much I admired her aunt. Like the observation about the room, the statement was calculated, but not insincere. Mrs. Cowles was a dark-skinned, plain-faced woman, cursed with a curvature of the spine so severe it made her look as if she were wearing a small pillow on her plump shoulders. But once she began to talk, or listen, which is a more exceptional art, the deformity became invisible. She was clever, and fearless, and boundlessly energetic. People said if she'd been born a man, she, rather than her brother Theodore, would have been president. There was another reason I admired Mrs. Cowles. She'd married late in life, long after her family and everyone else had given up hope. Unfortunately, she'd married the gruff and intimidating Admiral Cowles. I couldn't decide whether Mrs. Roosevelt's aunt was an inspiration or a cautionary tale.

The conversation turned to other mutual acquaintances. We knew the same people, who they'd been before their marriages, and where they stood in the vast tangle of aunts and uncles and cousins who insisted on marrying one another generation after generation, because after all who else was there? The longer we talked, the more certain I became that the arrangement was perfect. Mrs. Roosevelt required a social secretary. I knew Washington society. I was at home in this house. And I liked her. I could easily imagine inhabiting her life. Wasn't the ability to do that part of a social secretary's job?

Eleanor seemed more reserved. I thought it was because, as

her aunt had warned me, she was reluctant to hire a social secretary. Later I would realize there was another reason as well. All her life Eleanor craved affection. And whenever she found it, she distrusted it. I know what you're thinking. She had good reason to distrust me, but not then, not yet. My admiration for her was immediate and genuine.

As we sat drinking tea from the old Canton china I coveted, talking about a variety of things that did not matter because we were both too well mannered to mention what did—her need for help, mine for money—a girl of eight or nine bounded into the room. Her white woolen stockings bagged about her knees and ankles, and her long blond hair, held with a large blue bow, was a mass of tangles, but she was a lovely child, and she interrupted her complaint about James, who I gathered was her brother, and Dicky, who appeared to be the dog, to allow her mother to introduce her as Anna and to shake my hand and tell me how pleased she was to meet me. After Anna left the room, I complimented Mrs. Roosevelt on her daughter. Once again, I was trying to ingratiate myself, but I was sincere. Anna Roosevelt reminded me of the daughter I intended to have someday.

Mrs. Roosevelt looked uncomfortable, as if she appreciated the comment but did not want to take credit for the girl. I asked about the other children, and she told me there were two younger boys, James and Elliott. She didn't mention Franklin, Jr., the son she'd lost. Only later, when I knew her better, and only rarely, did she speak of him. "He was the biggest and most beautiful of my babies," she said once. "I should not have left him so much in the care of a nurse," she told me another time.

I brought up the recent bill declaring a national holiday in honor of motherhood. Mother's Day, it was called. I didn't understand how the government could legislate sentiment. I was offended at the idea of wireless companies selling stock messages to people who were too unimaginative or lazy or hard-hearted to write their own. But Mrs. Cowles had said her niece needed a social secretary because she was the wife of a government official, and I wanted to show her I was *au courant* with government proceedings.

"I'm sure the men who run the country know far more than I do, Miss Mercer." Her voice fluttered somewhere near the ceiling again. "But I cannot help thinking that if they were really interested in helping mothers, they would do something about our mortality rate in childbirth, which is twice as high as that in any other civilized nation. At least it was when I worked at the Rivington Street Settlement House in New York. Of course, that was before I had children of my own and had to give up going into the slums. As my husband's mother pointed out, I could not risk bringing infection home to the children."

The echo of regret in her voice surprised me. She had a daughter and two sons. How could she miss the contagious babies and beleaguered mothers who'd depended on her for medical advice and milk and kindness?

There was a sound of children scuffling in the hall. A woman told them to stop. A man asked the woman when Mrs. Roosevelt wanted the automobile brought around. Mrs. Roosevelt excused herself, stood, went to the door, and told the man to bring the auto in twenty minutes. I did not have much time.

For a moment I thought of throwing myself on her mercy. You may not need a social secretary, I would tell her, but I need employment. Vio ministers to strangers, and sits up late into the night sewing her uniforms, and subjects herself to overly familiar doctors. A distant relative, who in deference to our dignity refuses to reveal her identity, sends a monthly check through a Boston attorney. I must find a way to do my share. If I'd said that, Eleanor would have engaged me on the spot. She was irresistibly drawn to those in need. She longed to give. But I did not know that at the time. And I had my pride.

"You can see how cramped we are, Miss Mercer," she said when she returned. "My husband calls it living cheek-by-jowl."

I said nothing, though I was thinking that life with a husband and children at 1733 was not nearly as cramped as existence with Mama and Vio at the Decatur Apartments.

"There are the children, and their nurse, and a governess. Four servants live in, and the chauffeur and others come in for the day to help with the cooking and cleaning and laundry. I can't imagine where we'd find room to work."

I smiled.

"My husband and his assistant Mr. Howe are constantly in and out."

I nodded.

"And the official duties are not really so onerous. I should be able to fulfill them. A wife ought to be able to do whatever is necessary to help further her husband's career."

Now I understood why Mrs. Roosevelt was reluctant to hire a social secretary. She would not shirk her duties. She would not turn over to a stranger the obligations she had assumed as a wife.

"But isn't that the point of a employing a secretary, Mrs. Roosevelt? To give you time for more important matters by seeing to the menial tasks, like calling lists?" Mrs. Cowles had said calling lists were her niece's biggest worry. She simply could not keep up with them.

Eleanor frowned. "You have a point about the lists, Miss Mercer. I never dreamed there would be so many calls. I make between ten and thirty every afternoon. On Mondays I call on the wives of the Supreme Court justices, on Tuesdays of the members of Congress. I will never understand why my New York representatives move so frequently. I feel as if I am always climbing stairs in strange hotels and out-of-the-way rooming houses."

I nodded and said nothing. It was not my place to explain that most congressmen could not afford to set up additional households in the capital, as Mr. and Mrs. Roosevelt had. I did not even want the knowledge to show on my face.

"On Thursdays it's the wives of senators," she went on, "and on Fridays of the diplomats. On Wednesdays I either call on the wives of cabinet members or am at home to the same ladies. Sometimes I can't help envying Cousin Alice. Mrs. Longworth says she has too much interest in the political questions of the day to waste her time calling on people who do not figure importantly in them. She also says she does not like to be bored." Mrs. Roosevelt shook her head again. "As if anyone does."

I knew the stories about Alice Roosevelt Longworth. The whole nation did. "I can control Alice or I can run the country," her father was supposed to have said when he was in the White House. And though the more recent rumors about her and Senator Borah were not supposed to reach my innocent ears, I suspected what was meant when people called her Aurora Borah Alice. I'd also heard she did a wicked imitation of her cousin Eleanor, and if I'd heard that, I was fairly sure Mrs. Roosevelt had too. I decided to risk it. I would show Mrs. Roosevelt whose side I was on. Some women require that, though I wasn't sure she was one of them. Years later, when the little girl with the wrinkled stockings and tangled hair was a grown woman and her mother turned on her because of me, I would realize how right my instinct had been, but at the time I was taking a terrible chance. Mrs. Longworth was Mrs. Roosevelt's cousin. I was a stranger.

"And if paying calls on government wives were suddenly forbidden," I said, "Mrs. Longworth would be racing around town calling on every political wife in sight."

There was a moment of silence. I waited. The room held its breath. Mrs. Roosevelt smiled. Her smile was a revelation, though she didn't know it. She thought it revealed her unfortunate teeth. She had no idea it exposed her unexpected spirit.

"I see you know my cousin," she said, then stopped as if she too had gone too far. "Of course, Mrs. Longworth is wonderfully clever, and unlike me, she's extremely knowledgeable about political matters." She hesitated. I waited again. I couldn't nod or even smile. Agreeing with her about her cousin's political acumen would mean acquiescing to her own lack of it.

"But she does not pay calls, Miss Mercer, and I must, and you are right about the interminable lists. So if you are free three mornings a week, perhaps you would come and help me with them, and invitations, and heaven knows what else is in store for us."

The paper cuffs fell from my wrists. The knowing laugh of Violetta's doctor, who was no gentleman, died. I told Mrs. Roosevelt I would be delighted to come in three mornings a week and help in any way I could.

There was one thing more. We both knew it, and we both dreaded it. We were of a world where ladies did not discuss money, even if they had to think about it all the time. They might deign to mention wages to an Irish maid or a colored cook, but they did not haggle with other ladies whom they were likely to meet socially in other people's houses. Nonetheless, Mrs. Roosevelt and I had to talk about money that afternoon.

"We were thinking," she said, and now her voice beat its wings against the windows as if desperate to escape, "of a salary of twenty-five dollars a week."

I felt the color creep up my neck and onto my cheeks like a rash. "That is acceptable," I said.

It occurred to me on the way home. Everyone knew twenty-five dollars was the sum Mr. Henry Ford had announced he would pay each and every worker on his assembly line for a five-day week. When I'd read about it in the papers—and I hadn't been able to help reading about it, because headlines had screamed of the revolutionary idea, and labor leaders had debated it, and editorials had lamented its deleterious effect on workers' characters—I hadn't dreamed it had anything to do with me. But now I couldn't help wondering if that was where Mrs. Roosevelt had gotten the sum. The idea was ridiculous, of course. I had noticed the news articles because I had to earn my living, but why would the wife of the assistant secretary of the navy be concerned about the working-men on Mr. Ford's assembly line?

1916–1917

⪻ Two

The front door swung open, the floorboards sang under his shoes, and the house swelled with his presence. *Bully,* he liked to say, and *dee-lightful, tickled pink,* and *Grand. Isn't it grand!*

"Hello, Babs!" he called now, and his voice, big, resonant, caressing as the navy cape he'd later take to wearing, floated down the hall and encircled the two of us. We were working side-by-side in the comfortable, cluttered room overlooking a small garden with a rose arbor on the edge of bloom.

Two years had passed since I'd sat here drinking tea with Eleanor, whom I still called Mrs. Roosevelt. In Sarajevo, which many Americans could now locate on a map, a Slav nationalist had pulled the trigger. The archduke and his wife had died. Half a million young men were dying at Verdun. In a month and a half, twenty thousand British soldiers would die in the first day of fighting on the Somme, a hundred thousand before the battle was over. The numbers should have put matters in perspective. They only made the war more incomprehensible.

There were happier developments. Hobble skirts were out. Hemlines were up. Corsets were smaller. War has a way of shrinking clothing and unlacing restraints.

"Hello, Babs," he called again and was in the room with us before the words died. "And the lovely Miss Mercer," he said when he saw that I was there too.

The-lovely-Miss-Mercer, as if it were one word, was another of his expressions. I knew it was a joke, but I also knew that he wouldn't say it if he didn't think there was a kernel of truth in it. Women look at their less attractive sisters and compliment them on their luxuriant hair or fine complexions or sunny smiles. There is always one redeeming feature. But only a heartless man would tease a girl about being lovely if he did not think she were, at least a little.

There was a note of surprise in his voice when he pronounced my name. I was not supposed to be there at that hour when the last rays of afternoon light were slanting through the windows, glancing off the disarray of family photographs and nautical prints, rare books and stuffed birds, stamp catalogues and ship models, the whole motley clutter of possessions that Eleanor was always moving from house to house in New York and Albany and Washington. I was fond of that room, though I couldn't have said why. It was not aesthetically pleasing. The wallpaper was muddy, the walnut furniture gloomy, the carved mantelpiece heavy over worn tiles. It was what Mama, who had worked as an interior decorator during one interlude of reduced circumstances, would call haute respectable. I had worked with Mama briefly, and I loved beautiful things, but I also had a secret affection for haute respectable.

I didn't even mind the clutter. It gave the room character, his character, because the prints and books and stuffed birds and catalogues belonged to him. Franklin was a passionate collector. He was always joking about being in debt to dealers of one sort or another. I was surprised. It was bad enough to speak of money. I couldn't imagine joking about owing it. I still can't.

"Miss Mercer," he went on, "haven't you heard of the fifty-four-hour law for women and children? It was one of the first bills I put through when I went to Albany."

Out of the corner of my eye, I saw Eleanor look up from the letter she was writing, frown, then go back to her task.

"But this is the District of Columbia, Mr. Roosevelt. Your New York State laws don't apply."

He laughed, and I preened, and across the room Eleanor's pen went on scratching.

"And I was just about to leave," I added, though I hadn't been. I had no engagement that evening and was in no hurry to return home to the apartment at the Decatur. Violetta had left for a Red Cross hospital in France, and now there were only Mama and I. We pretended to keep each other company. In fact we rarely met. She dwelled in the past, when she had been the most beautiful woman in Washington, a sought-after heiress in London, a flamboyant young matron in Cairo. I was concentrating on the future by keeping up a hectic schedule of lunches and teas and dinners and dances, when I wasn't with the Roosevelts at 1733 N Street. I frequently stayed late, as I had that evening, and even returned to the house after I'd gone home, as I had one night when I'd first come to work for Eleanor.

She and the chicks—that was another of Franklin's expressions; he called the children the chicks—had been away, but Franklin had come back to town to attend a reception for

Latin American diplomats. He'd had Albert, the chauffeur, call to see if I would come in to fix things up for him. I'd tidied the sitting room, and sorted the mail, and arranged for the cook to make him a light supper. He'd been wonderful about it, joking that it was fortunate I hadn't had an engagement that evening, and teasing me about my efficiency, and acting as if I were doing him a favor instead of my job.

Mama had been furious. "You were not employed to air the dog and wash the baby!" she'd said when I finally returned home. Poor Mama couldn't forgive the world for the hard times on which she and both her daughters had fallen. The fact that she hadn't been pushed, but had flung herself head-long, only made her feel the injustice more acutely.

The night I'd come in to fix things up for Franklin had been some time ago. Now, when I returned to the house after dark, it was usually to fill an empty place at the dinner table, because someone was ill, or the party was short a woman, or there were thirteen at table. Franklin was superstitious. Some-times the invitation arrived for no reason other than Eleanor's kindness. I was an unmarried young lady. Franklin and Eleanor entertained many eligible gentlemen. I always ended up beside one of them, though neither Eleanor nor I ever men-tioned the matter, not even while we were drawing up the seating arrangements.

Franklin stepped into the room and stood looking down at me. I was sitting on the worn Turkish carpet, surrounded by piles of invitations and lists and letters. Both Mama and Mrs. James, as Franklin's mother was known, disapproved of floor-sitting, but Eleanor and I were gleefully, if secretly, contemp-tuous. We had work to do, and the only place where we could spread out sufficiently to do it in that cramped house was on the floor.

As I sat there that afternoon gazing back up at Franklin, I felt as much in his shadow as if I were one of the chicks. He loomed over me, tall, narrow of body but deep-chested, neatly buttoned up in his well-tailored English suit. His shoes were English too, Peel, and dusty from his walk to and from his office in the State, War, and Navy Building, which was just across from the White House. A gold watch chain ran from one pocket of his waistcoat to the other. It reminded me of the shiny ribbons that had bound the gifts of my precarious childhood.

Above the high, stiff collar, his features were chiseled; the lips narrow but not ungenerous, the nose finely modeled, the eyes set deep beneath dark brows. His light brown hair, which was retreating slowly but inevitably, leaving twin half moons on either side of his high forehead, lay close to his head, the result of the bowler hat he'd left on the stand on his way through the entrance hall. In another month or so he'd change to the straw boater with the striped ribbon around the crown. I preferred the boater. It made him look more insouciant, though insouciance was not a trait I thought I admired in a man. I preferred reliability, which in those days we called character.

His eyes, the cloudless blue that promises a clement day, continued to gaze down at me through a pince-nez. He was nearsighted and wore the pince-nez instead of eyeglasses because Theodore Roosevelt, who was his distant cousin as well as Eleanor's uncle, wore a pince-nez. Cousin Ted also said *bully* and *grand*. Cousin Ted had been assistant secretary of the navy too. He'd also been president.

Franklin tossed back his head as if to get a better perspective on me. It was a characteristic gesture, which some people saw as a sign of arrogance. They thought he was looking down his nose at them. Later, when he had to look up from a wheelchair, many of the same people would see the same toss of head as an expression of defiant hope.

He bent to reach for one of the piles of papers that circled me like a fortress, and I inhaled the scent of shaving soap, and tobacco, and wood-paneled rooms where men met among themselves, without women. I had no desire to infiltrate those rooms, but I liked the manly aura of them that Franklin gave off. I also caught the faintest whiff of whiskey. If I'd recognized it, Eleanor must have too. We'd both been schooled in the scent at our fathers' knees, though that was something else we never mentioned.

"The lovely Miss Mercer is bringing order from chaos," he said as he lifted a letter from one of the piles near my foot.

"While Mr. Roosevelt is an expert at reversing the trend," I answered. Perhaps I shouldn't have. If I'd been more retiring, or more demure, I would have turned away from his teasing. But I've always had a phototropic disposition. I can't help turning to sunlight.

Franklin laughed and waved the letter in the air as if he'd snared a prize, and I shook my head in mock disapproval, and Eleanor's eyes snapped up from her work. "Now, Franklin!" Her voice fluttered somewhere near the ceiling. "Don't get things out of order, Franklin. Don't bother Miss Mercer, Franklin. Don't, Franklin, don't."

But he did. He couldn't help himself, just as he hadn't been able to keep from embellishing the story about the fifty-four-hour week. I didn't know how he'd exaggerated. Perhaps he hadn't been the one to put the bill through. Perhaps he hadn't even been for it until he'd held his finger up to the political wind. Even then I sensed he was a brilliant tactician. But I knew from Eleanor's frown that she remembered exactly where he'd stood and what he'd done. Eleanor was a stickler for facts. Franklin was a raconteur. I admired her scruples. Who would not? But I enjoyed his stories.

"Have you read this, Miss Mercer?"

He was gazing through his pince-nez at the letter he'd taken from the floor. It was from a naval wife thanking Eleanor for one of her many kindnesses. "They've buttered my missus. They've buttered my missus on both sides."

His clean-shaven, fair-skinned face cracked open, easy as an egg, and a smile broke over us. Eleanor couldn't help herself. The frown evaporated. She beamed back at him. There wasn't a doubt in my mind she forgave him the exaggeration about the fifty-four-hour bill, and the whiskey on his breath, and his harmless teasing of her secretary, who, she must have known, had the sense not to take him seriously.

ᴇ Three

"I had painfully high ideals and a tremendous sense of duty
entirely unrelieved by any sense of humor or any appreciation of
the weaknesses of human nature."   ᴇ Eleanor Roosevelt

"One of the central problems facing anyone dealing with
Franklin Roosevelt's personal history is just what made him the
man he became."   ᴇ Joseph Alsop (a distant cousin of FDR)

I remember what I was wearing that evening. Women
always remember what they were wearing when their lives
start or stop, as if a well-cut coat can contain a swollen heart
or spotless linen whitewash shame. It was my second-favorite
shirtwaist, pale lawn with a lace-trimmed jabot. I remember
the silver dinner gown Eleanor changed into too. It rippled in
the light of the gas lamps. I even recall the stain on Mr. Howe's
tie. It looked like the Cheshire cat's grin. And I can see the
small cotton bandage on the soft flesh where Franklin's thumb
met his palm. The Sunday before, he'd played thirty-six holes
of golf. He was putting in long hours for the war effort, but
he still found time for golf. He would always find time for
golf, until he could no longer play, then he never mentioned
the game again.

Europe had been at war for almost two years. Predictions that it would be over by the fall harvests, Christmas, the first unthinkable anniversary had all proved wrong. America was not yet a belligerent, but it was a beneficiary. Washington, a sleepy southern town so heat- and malaria-plagued that only a short while earlier the British Foreign Office had listed it as a hardship post, was turning into a world capital. Representatives from France and England were braving the U-boat threat in the Atlantic to buy American ships and shells and uniforms and bandages. Dollar-a-year men and government girls and workers with eyes on the main chance were crowding into rooming houses and hotels and apartments. I heard stories of salaries twice what Mrs. Roosevelt was paying me and saw young women surging through the city in expensive hats and the new shorter skirts they were showing in Paris, and envied the styles, but I had no desire to leave the house on N Street. It wasn't because of Franklin. I admired him. I planned to marry someone a good deal like him. But I saw him at a distance, on the other side of Eleanor.

She and I organized relief, and served on committees, and knitted for Allied soldiers and Bulgarian women and Russian children. There was no getting away from the war. The newspapers were full of it.

BRITISH SMASH 7 MILES OF FOE'S LINE,
TAKE 2 TOWNS AND 2,000 PRISONERS
FRENCH JOIN ATTACK, TAKE 3 TOWNS

Column after column told of Allied gains. There was no mention of Allied losses. The English had cut the single cable linking American and German communication, and British intelligence thought Allied casualties would have a discouraging effect on American support. Franklin must have known the cable had been cut, though he didn't talk about it at the time. He wanted to keep supplies going to the Allies, and realized that though Americans had a soft spot for underdogs, they preferred to back winners. He was also working for preparedness at home, and knew Americans would be more willing to build ships and train men if they thought the ships would never be sunk or the boys shot at.

The night I was wearing my second-favorite shirtwaist, Franklin returned home from the Navy Department a little after six. His arrival was always an event. The door flew open, and his voice filled the house, and the air in the room where Eleanor and I were working quickened. His vitality could be frightening, but only if you tried to resist it. If you didn't pull against it, if you didn't try to tame it, if you gave yourself over to it, it was thrilling.

Louis Howe, the assistant Franklin had brought down with him from Albany, was usually in Franklin's wake, but that evening Mr. Howe didn't turn up until a few minutes after Franklin. He and Eleanor and I were in the back parlor when I heard the front door open and caught the aroma of Sweet Caporals.

"The bell, Mr. Howe," Eleanor muttered, "the knocker. This is not a public way station. This is our home."

I don't think she knew she'd spoken. Frustration made her indiscreet.

A moment later Mr. Howe materialized in the doorway. His head was too large for his slight body. His black eyes were forlorn holes in his face, one of the four ugliest faces in New York, he used to say, and the comment always saddened me, because it was obvious he was only making it before someone else did. In those days I could still muster sympathy for him. Evidence of his lunch, of several meals, stained his suit and shirt and left a memorable mark on his tie. A cloud of smoke hovered over him like an improbable halo. A Sweet Caporal drooped from his mouth. I had never seen him without one. Franklin used to joke that only those who'd seen him asleep had.

"Good evening, Mrs. Roosevelt," he said and broke into a fit of coughing.

"Good evening, Mr. Howe," Eleanor chirped. I knew that voice. The more she resented Mr. Howe, the more scrupulously she behaved toward him. "Do you think you should see a doctor about that cough?"

"I once saw a doctor, Mrs. Roosevelt. He gave me two months to live. That was ten years ago." He swung his dark pockmarked face to me. "And the lovely Miss Mercer."

I looked up from my work and smiled, though I didn't like the term in his mouth. It lost its innocence. I think that was why I came to hate Mr. Howe. Not because of what he did, but because of what he was. Louis Howe was a man without innocence.

He turned to Franklin. "Evening, boss," he said, though they'd parted at the Navy Department only a short while earlier. He stepped into the room and insinuated himself into a chair. "After you flew the coop, the secretary got the heebie-jeebies again." Mr. Howe's language always seemed to be at war with his voice, which was deep and distinguished. He had a passion for amateur theatricals. "Couldn't stop worrying about the Naval Reserve. Wanted me to hold his hand and tell him how democratic—small *d*—it's going to be. Not just your old sailing buddies from Groton and Harvard, but volunteers from all over."

"How many times do I have to tell him?" Franklin asked. "The Reserve will be strictly democratic. Small *d*. I've already included several Yale men."

Mr. Howe's laughter was sharp, and when I looked up, his face was twisted in a sardonic grin, but his eyes gave him away. His eyes, as they lingered on Franklin, were indecent with love.

Franklin stood, crossed the room to a carved walnut sideboard, and opened one of the cabinets. "What you need, Ludwig," he said, using one of the nicknames he was always bestowing, "what our friend, the secretary, would benefit from greatly if he weren't such a dyed-in-the-wool dry, is a cocktail." He took out the silver shaker and several bottles and pulled the cord of the servants' bell.

I bent my head over the checks I was sorting, but out of the corner of my eye I saw Eleanor lift the gold watch that swung from a diamond-encrusted broach pinned to her shirtwaist. Once, when I'd admired the piece, she'd told me Mr. Roosevelt had designed it himself and given it to her as a wedding gift. Then she'd added that it was far too grand for her. She looked down at it now and frowned, and I knew what was coming.

Don't, I pleaded silently as I went on sorting the checks. Don't spoil his pleasure. Don't make yourself unhappy. But she did. She had to.

"I'm not sure you have time for a cocktail, Franklin. We're dining out."

The temperature in the room plummeted. This must be what the new air-conditioning I'd read about would feel like. I understood her fear. Though we did not discuss our fathers, I knew about hers. In that world, we all knew about one another, and said nothing. I'd even heard about the time her uncles had gotten so drunk they'd taken out their hunting guns and begun shooting at her from a window of her grandmother's house in Tivoli on the Hudson. And by then I'd met her brother Hall, a handsome young man who wore doom the way Franklin wore promise. Perhaps there's some truth in what people say. Perhaps a weakness for alcohol does run in families, like blue eyes or baldness, at least in the male line, though it seems strange that it might. One always has the choice to say yes, I'd love one, or no, thank you, I'd rather not. But there was no history of weakness in Franklin's branch of the family. And even if there were, it clearly did not run through him. He liked a cocktail in the evening. He enjoyed drinking in the company of other men, especially after a Harvard victory at football or crew. And he loved mixing drinks. It occurred to me once, though that was much later, that he enjoyed mixing cocktails as much as he did drinking them. I can see him behind the big desk in the oval study pouring and stirring and shaking until we were all drunk on the dexterity and joy of the performance. Certainly, the attraction couldn't have been the drinks. Mr. Howe always complained that Franklin's Haitian Libation, as he called one particular favorite, tasted like fruit punch intended for the kiddies. When the chicks were no longer children, they'd insist the old man didn't know the first thing about making a martini.

"Nonsense," Franklin said and rubbed his hands together in anticipation. "We have time for one. At least one." His smile, inserted between deep parentheses on either side of his mouth, was white and hard and cold, but it wasn't directed at Eleanor. It took in, or rather kept out, the world. Even I felt the chill, though I wasn't the one who had stepped between him and his pleasure.

Eleanor opened her mouth, then closed it. Her eyes blinked. She looked as if she were clenching her teeth. It was a heartbreaking display of a woman at war with herself. But Franklin, who had his back to the room as he began pouring whiskey into the shaker, missed it. She stood and crossed to the door. "In that case, Franklin, you and Mr. Howe have your cocktails, and I'll go up to read to the children and hear their prayers before bedtime."

She hadn't said don't. She hadn't carped that he'd already had a cocktail. She'd tried a way around, but he'd recognized the ploy and sidestepped it. I wondered if all marriages were made up of endless negotiation and subterfuge. I was sure they didn't have to be.

"Tell them I'll be up in a minute," he said. "As soon as Ludwig and I have our cocktails."

The ice melted from his grin. On the rare nights when he got home in time, he loved to romp through the nursery, tickling and kissing and asking over and over, "Are you snug as a bug in a rug, snug as a bug in a rug?" And the chicks giggled and wriggled and screeched with pleasure. Eleanor read to the children and heard their prayers nightly, but Franklin's more infrequent bedtime visits were the ones they waited for. It wasn't fair, but neither was it Franklin's fault.

He finished mixing the cocktails, bestowed one on Mr. Howe as if he were a priest anointing an acolyte, and told him they'd go into the front parlor so the lovely Miss Mercer could get her work done. The old parquet groaned as they made their way down the hall, but there was no scrape of casters. They hadn't bothered to close the heavy sliding doors.

"You can joke about it, boss, but it ain't funny," I heard Mr. Howe say. "Gussie Gardner's going around quoting those figures, and telling people where he got them."

"Of course Gardner's telling people where he got them," Franklin said. "I told him he could. They carry more weight coming from the assistant secretary of the navy than from the honorable gentleman from Massachusetts."

Two years earlier I would not have known what they were talking about, but since I'd come to work for Eleanor, I'd begun to follow the news more carefully, especially the political news that involved Franklin. There was nothing untoward about my interest. The mere mention of someone we know always catches the eye before a major news story about someone we don't. Besides, following Franklin's public life was part of my job. Since his infancy, Mrs. James had carefully wrapped, labeled, and stowed away for posterity her only child's locks of hair and lost teeth, frilly dresses and outgrown shirts, baby rattles and every scrap of his writing. Mama said that Mrs. James regarded the detritus of her only son's life with the same reverence the newly minted millionaires she used to decorate for viewed their Titians and Tintorettos. But I admired the tradition and didn't mind helping Eleanor continue it by clipping accounts of his public appearances. I'd recently cut out several articles about the figures Mr. Howe had just mentioned.

Franklin had testified before the House Naval Affairs Committee. He'd done a superb job. You don't have to take my word for it. The article I clipped from the *New York Herald* is probably in Franklin's lovely new library at Hyde Park. He explained to the committee that while the navy had indeed gained efficiency in this administration, technical studies showed that other navies had enlarged and improved more rapidly, so that relatively we were now less strong than we had been. The U.S. Navy, he said, ranked no higher than third, behind Britain and Germany, and might even be fourth after France. He quoted admirals and cited investigations and spewed numbers. He was dazzling.

"The numbers are right, Ludwig," Franklin said now. "All you have to do is—"

Mr. Howe cut him off. He was the only one in that house who would. "You don't have to convince me, boss. I believe the numbers you gave Gardner. But the secretary's convinced the situation ain't as bad as it looks. He's got numbers to prove it just like you do. And his numbers are the ones he gave when he testified before the committee. Now, Josephus Daniels is a fine old southern gentleman, but no man, not even a southern gent, wants his assistant going around contradicting him in public."

"You worry too much, Ludwig. The secretary's crazy about me. You've heard him say so yourself. 'The minute ah laid eyes on Franklin Roosevelt back at the national convention of the great Democratic Party in nineteen hundred and twelve, it was a case of love at furst sight.' " Franklin's drawl was a perfect imitation of the secretary's. His demeanor would be too. I knew because I'd seen him do his impersonation. He'd bow his head, and shuffle his feet, and yank at an imaginary string tie. It was grand. Everyone said so. Everyone except Eleanor. She thought Franklin's performance was disloyal. I could see her point. But I couldn't help laughing at his impersonation.

"Save it for your friends at the Metropolitan Club," Mr. Howe said. "Who, incidentally, won't be able to help you this time. You've got the Roosevelt name. You've got the la-de-da friends like Gardner and his father-in-law, Senator Lodge. But this is politics, boss, not a cotillion, and the secretary is holding all the cards. He's got the president's ear. He's got the party's support. And he's got the approval of that great repository of all wisdom, 'the American people.' Only a man who didn't like being assistant secretary of the navy and wanted to go back to shuffling legal papers at Carter, Ledyard, and Milburn would go up against that trio."

I know it's hard to believe now, but there was a time when

Franklin's future was not written in stone. He always acted as
if he didn't have a doubt. It wasn't merely a matter of ambition, though heaven knows he had plenty of that, but of des-
tiny. He knew God had a plan for him. Mr. Howe, however,
believed that God helped those who helped themselves, and
let the devil take lesser mortals who were lazy or stupid or
prone to impolitic gestures such as subverting superiors who
had the president's ear and the party's support. Eleanor worried about Franklin's conduct too, and not merely because it
verged on disloyalty to Mr. Daniels. She wanted her husband
to do well. She was even more eager for him to do good. She'd
fretted over the newspaper accounts that had compared the
testimonies of the secretary of the navy and his assistant.

"I only hope Franklin is right," she said one morning when
we were working in the back parlor.

"He must be," I answered. "The paper says he is."

I leaned over her shoulder to point out a line in the *Herald*
article I'd just clipped. "He showed that in the short time he
has been Assistant Secretary," the *Herald* had written, "he has
made a most complete study of the problems of naval defense."

"But what if he's not?" she insisted. "What if the secretary
is right, and what Mr. Roosevelt calls preparedness is merely
provocation? What if getting ready for war simply drags us
into war? What if the president succeeds in negotiating a
peace between Germany and the Allies, and we've spent the
resources that might go to feeding children and building hospitals and clearing slums for ships and guns and training
young men to die? It's a terrible responsibility."

It was, of course. That was why I could not understand her
behavior. Franklin had plenty of people to argue with him.
When he came home, he needed someone to encourage him.
Instead of always saying, Franklin, do you think that's a good

idea, why couldn't she just, now and then, say, Why, Franklin, what a grand idea!

I heard the repeated cricket-chirping of a lighter being struck several times, then Mr. Howe's racking cough. "Did McCarthy tell you about that newsreel he saw the other night?" he went on when he stopped coughing. Mr. McCarthy was Franklin's secretary.

"The one where they laughed at TR?" Franklin asked.

I knew the newsreel they were talking about. Eleanor had been so distressed by Mr. McCarthy's report she hadn't been able to help repeating it. Mr. McCarthy had gone to the motion pictures, and when the newsreel had started and her uncle had come strutting across the screen, the audience had burst into laughter. They'd chuckled and tittered and guffawed as if the greatest president of recent times were a vaudeville clown.

I understood Eleanor's feelings, but I could see the audience's point of view. At least, I can with hindsight. The only time I met President Theodore Roosevelt, I, like everyone else in the room, was overwhelmed by him. His big head turned this way and that, his blue eyes—one piercing, the other blind from a White House boxing accident—glared, his brush of mustache twitched, his teeth flashed. He never stopped talking. His high shrill voice went on and on. "Aieee believe," he told us. "Aieee know . . ." "Aieee am convinced . . ."

The newsreel would not have captured his voice, of course, but it would have made his bantam strut seem even more awkward and jerky. And people would remember what he'd been saying lately. "Aieee am afraid we are passing through a thick streak of yellow in our national life. The people have forgotten that a just war is in the long run far better for a man's soul than the most prosperous peace."

"They laughed at TR," Mr. Howe said, "but they cheered the secretary."

"J.D.?" Franklin asked, and I could hear the incredulity in his tone.

"None other." Mr. Howe's voice came from the front hall now. "All the same, boss, the imitation's killing. Absolutely killing."

I heard the door open and close, then the house went quiet. The garden beyond the window was in darkness. I'd finished sorting the checks and even answered two letters I'd decided to take care of before leaving. I ought to have gone home. I went on sitting at Eleanor's desk.

A moment later Franklin appeared in the doorway. I hadn't been waiting for him. He'd said he was going upstairs to tuck in the chicks. He certainly hadn't expected to find me still there. I knew that from the look of surprise on his face. Intent did not figure into it. What happened was an accident.

He recovered from his surprise and slipped into his smile. "Have you no pity, Miss Mercer, no ruth for your poor mother sitting in the window waiting for your return?"

"I was just leaving, Mr. Roosevelt, and as for my mother, you know perfectly well her name is Minnie, not Ruth."

The pun was silly, but I knew he liked wordplay, and foolish jokes, and humor that could only be called corny. Sometimes I looked at the photographs of the stern assistant secretary of the navy which I clipped, and read the weighty things he had to say, and thought, if only people knew what he was really like. Recently I'd gone to the Raleigh Hotel to hear him speak to the women's council of the D.A.R. on preparedness. A room full of colored feathers and artificial flowers and wooden fruit had bobbed in eager agreement with the dire warnings of this preternaturally wise young man, and I'd sat among them, my own flower-trimmed hat stock-still with staring, and thought, they haven't an inkling.

He crossed the room to a gas lamp on the far wall which had been smoking and began fiddling with it. "You should have called one of the servants. We can't have the lovely Miss Mercer expiring from carbon monoxide inhalation." The stream of smoke stopped. He took a handkerchief from his pocket and wiped his hands. "Impossible things. They consume oxygen, which is unhealthy for the chicks, and you can't move them around to read a book or get a better look at a print. If Aunt Bye doesn't electrify the house soon, I'll have to do it myself. If only out of concern for your poor eyes, Miss Mercer. I don't see how you can work in this gloom."

"I don't mind. Sometimes I prefer it to electric light."

He tossed his head back and looked at me through his pince-nez. "I'll tell you a secret. I do too, sometimes."

"It isn't a secret, Mr. Roosevelt." I bent my head over the desk and went on tidying the piles of papers.

"It's not?"

I looked up again. "Anyone can see that the more progressive you become in your public life, the more you cling to old-fashioned ways in private."

There was a moment's silence, then that grin that had more wattage than the electricity he was threatening to install beamed at me.

"Fortunately, *anyone* can't, but since you can, Miss Mercer, I'd appreciate it if you would refrain from telling my friends in the Democratic Party, or, more important, my enemies in the Republican."

I thought of the figures he'd given Mr. Gardner. "Perhaps these days it's the other way around."

He went on looking at me, and I knew he was surprised,

but I didn't think he was displeased. He crossed the room to the desk and perched on the edge of it, one leg braced to hold his weight, the other swinging easily.

"I didn't know you were interested in politics, Miss Mercer."

I had to tip my head back to look up at him. "I heard you speak at the Raleigh."

"And what did you think?"

"I thought you sounded more like a Republican than a member of the administration."

"Unfortunately, so do Secretary Daniels and several other Democrats. But did you agree with me, Miss Mercer? About preparedness, I mean."

"I'm still hoping we won't get into the war, although my sister writes that we absolutely must. She's with the Red Cross in France."

"That's right, I'd forgotten. What do you hear from your sister?"

I thought of Vio's letters. Lately someone called Dr. Marbury had been crowding out the war news. His name left a deep imprint in the thin sheets of paper. His handsome profile, his Maryland ancestors, his fascinating tales of the year he'd spent sailing the world as personal physician to the rich Mr. Joseph Leiter, crowded the margins. Even when Vio did not write of him, I could sense his presence between the lines. Mama was delighted. I wanted to be, but something held me back. Dr. Marbury was perfect, Vio wrote, except for his dark moods. But who in a military hospital could help succumbing to moments of despair. And in the wake of the war, with the love of a good woman, which Vio unmistakably was, wouldn't they vanish?

In any event, Franklin didn't want to hear about Dr. Marbury. He wanted to know about the war. I told him what Vio wrote about the air raids, and the cold and the rain, and the endless stream of wounded young men. I watched him as I spoke. I was holding his interest, or Vio was.

When I finished, he took his pince-nez between his thumb and forefinger and removed it. The intensity of his gaze pinned me in place.

"That's the dope, Miss Mercer."

He relished slang, perhaps because his mother and wife didn't. It was a little like his evening cocktails. He didn't intend it as an offense against them, merely a defense of himself. That was another secret I knew about Franklin that the D.A.R. ladies didn't.

"I only wish we could pass your sister's letters on to the secretary." He wasn't flirting now. This was the war, and he was serious. "I finally got him to support the naval bill, but that's only the beginning. We've got to push this national defense board through. And we need a fleet of small boats to patrol our coast. What I call a mosquito fleet. Made up of private yachts the government buys from their owners at a fair price."

"What a grand idea!"

He beamed down at me. "Yes, isn't it? The only problem is that some of the owners aren't willing to sell at a fair price. One fellow was demanding a hundred and twelve thousand dollars for a boat that was appraised at thirty. In cases like that, we'll simply have to seize the vessel."

"But, Mr. Roosevelt, that's socialism!"

"That, Miss Mercer, is coastal defense."

His leg went back and forth, back and forth as he spoke, steady as a metronome, and just as mesmerizing.

"Of course," I said, "I hadn't thought of it that way." And until then I hadn't.

There was a moment of silence. He was still sitting on the edge of my desk, Eleanor's desk, and I was still looking up at him, and something strange happened. His hand, the one with the small bandage, which had been lying palm up on his leg, flexed. I felt it as surely as if he'd touched my cheek. I dropped my eyes.

He cleared his throat. "But the biggest problem," he went on quickly, "is U-boats. If we don't stop them from sinking our ships soon, we won't have any bottoms to transport our troops once we get into the war. Now some people think they can't be stopped."

It was safe to look at him now. "But you believe they can?"

"I know they can. All we need is a mine barrage of the North Sea passage between Scotland and Norway."

"A mine barrage?" The word made me feel as if I were purring. His hand flexed again. I felt it on my cheek again.

"To bottle up the U-boats," he hurried on, "and keep them from breaking through to the Atlantic. Until recently I wasn't sure exactly how it would work, but the other day a fellow came strolling into my office. He was quite a sight, long beard, inventor's black bag. He looked like a typical crank. My first instinct was to send him down to the crank department. We have one, you know." He hesitated, as if he were waiting for me to contradict him. I said nothing. He went on. "But he insisted on showing me his model, and the moment I saw this antenna firing device, I knew it was what we were looking for. The secretary thinks it's wide-eyed, but I've had some tests run, and it works. I tell you, Miss Mercer, this mine barrage will win the Battle of the Atlantic."

I was trying to concentrate on the Battle of the Atlantic, but sitting there looking up at him, all I could think of was the depth and vastness of those ocean-blue eyes. I would have drowned in them, if he weren't married.

I swam up for air. "Isn't it lucky, Mr. Roosevelt, that the crank came to you and not someone with less vision?"

"Isn't it," he agreed, then cocked his head, as if he were listening to something. "Do you hear that, Miss Mercer?"

I tilted my head in a mirror image of his, trying to hear what he did, but there was only silence. No footsteps approached down the hall, no servants rustled outside the room, no voices echoed from upstairs.

"Listen," he said.

Then I heard it. The sound wasn't coming from the house. It was in the garden.

"It's a thrush. Trying to attract a lady thrush to set up housekeeping." The smile he gave me was one I'd never seen before. It looked as if he'd borrowed it from the devil. He whistled the notes of the birdsong. It sounded real to me.

Then I heard the footsteps. I looked away from Franklin in time to see Eleanor appear in the doorway. She was wearing the silver evening dress that rippled like water in the light from the gas lamps and a wide diamond dog collar that lifted her chin so that now she was the one who seemed to be looking down her nose.

"There you are, Franklin." No bird beat its wings against a cage. Her voice was a hum of indulgence.

He slid off the desk with the easy grace of a man of clear conscience. "There's a thrush in the garden. I was demonstrating the call for Miss Mercer."

"I couldn't tell the difference." My own voice sounded breathless and insincere.

Eleanor stepped into the room. Her dress shimmered and

her collar glittered and she towered over me, a dull thing of black and white, serge and cotton, hunched over a desk.

"He is good, isn't he?" she said. "Only a practiced ear can distinguish between Mr. Roosevelt and the real thing."

∾ Eleanor's words followed me down N Street. No matter how fast I walked, I couldn't get away from them. They dogged my steps like a couple of disreputable strangers, trying to catch my eye.

Years ago a group of rowdy boys had surrounded me once on the way home from school, winking and smirking and calling me vulgar terms of endearment. I'd tried not to look at them, I'd refused to answer them, but the faster I'd hurried, the closer they'd circled. Suddenly one of them had called me Lucy. I don't know how he'd known my name. Maybe he'd frequented the neighborhood. But my face must have given away the fact that he'd found me out, because all the boys had taken it up. "Lucy," they'd called. "Sweet Lucy," they'd said. "Can I walk with you, Lucy?"

I'd begun to cry. I hadn't when they'd danced around me, and jumped in and out of my path, and called me kewpie doll and sweetie pie, but I had when they'd called me Lucy, because suddenly it had been as if they knew me.

I'd finally got away from them by running into a church, and now I turned and started back toward Seventeenth Street. Even before I reached Rhode Island Avenue, I could see the green dome of St. Matthew's looming against the sky. I hurried up the broad flight of steps and pushed open one of the wide bronze doors. Eleanor's words would not follow me here.

But they did. They jostled my arm as I dipped my fingers in the holy water. They nudged me as I hesitated at the head of the aisle to cross myself. They rustled into the pew beside me. I knew what they were whispering. It was a sibilant hiss in the silence. Shame.

My knees found the soft comfort of the prie-dieu. My hands knotted on the backrest in front of me. I let my head rest on them. I began to pray.

When I lifted my head, the whispering shadows were gone. I was alone in the church. The light from the candles flickered in the gloom that hung from the great domed ceiling. The saints looked down on me as I made my way up the aisle. I pushed open the heavy door. A breeze caught my skirt and made it dance around my ankles. I felt suddenly happy and vaguely foolish. Mr. Roosevelt had talked about the war and thrushes, and Mrs. Roosevelt had teased him, which she didn't do often but she did do occasionally, and standing in the clearing night outside the solid stone church, I could not imagine what I'd gotten so upset about.

~ Four

"A woman's moods are sent her, just as a man's temptations."
    ∽ Eleanor Roosevelt in a letter to Franklin D. Roosevelt

"I said [to Alice] . . . that I did not believe in knowing things which your husband did not wish you to know, so I think I will be spared any further mysterious secrets."
    ∽ Eleanor Roosevelt in a letter to Franklin D. Roosevelt

Years later I would sit in the audience during his inaugurations, watching him make his way across the stage step by agonizing step, and hate myself for having found such easy solace that night. I would see him leaning on Jimmy's or Elliott's or a Secret Service officer's arm for support, dragging several pounds of braces on his legs, heaving his weight from one useless leg to the other in a parody of movement that, by sheer will, convinced an entire nation he could walk, and tell myself we cannot know the ways of God. I would stare at his knuckles turning white with the effort of gripping the podium to hold himself upright, and try to believe it wasn't the will of God, merely a case of being in the wrong place at the wrong time. But as I looked up at him towering over the audience, and dependent as a baby for life's simplest needs,

I would remember another night and know we had earned this affliction.

I blamed myself. That was all right. That was only just. What I couldn't stand was his blaming me. He never said a word. He was all blinding optimism and heartbreaking courage. But I knew. Later Miss LeHand would say that, though he was an early riser, he sometimes could not get out of bed until noon. It took him that long to claw his way up from damnation and slip into his big winning grin. Surely someone must be held accountable for that.

But the wheelchair and the braces and damnation were still in the future that June night when he came toward me across the dance floor of the Chevy Chase Club. My breath caught in my chest, but I told myself it was the tightly laced stays, the last steel ones I owned, thanks to the war effort. My pulse throbbed against Mama's pearls, which circled my throat and wrist, but I ascribed that to the heat of the ballroom. The hair on the back of my freshly powdered neck stood on end. I couldn't imagine the reason for that.

"The lovely Miss Mercer," he said, and as if the words were an invitation, his gloved hand went around my waist, and mine came to rest on his shoulder. As we moved onto the dance floor, his palm burned through the cotton of his glove and the silk of my dress to the small of my back. But it was his legs scissoring in and out of the folds of my skirt that I would remember.

The music ended, and the other dancers, who'd faded into the background, became familiar people. Alice Roosevelt Longworth was watching us. The notoriously gossipy Misses Patten—don't telephone, don't telegraph, tell a Patten, the joke went—were staring. Over Franklin's shoulder, I saw Eleanor.

The orchestra started up again in a ragtime beat. Franklin's arm went around my waist. I looked at Eleanor. Her eyes held mine.

"I'm sorry, Mr. Roosevelt," I said, "I don't know how to do the Grizzly Bear."

But he knew it was a ruse. And he had faith in himself. "Just follow me, Miss Mercer, and you can't go wrong."

I did. His smile flashed, and his legs went in and out of the folds of my dress, and my shoulders went up and down to the foolish music, and the room revolved around us faster and faster until Mrs. Longworth and the Misses Patten and Eleanor were no more than a blur.

ॐ I didn't learn what happened after the dance until later. By then Eleanor's cousins had told a few close friends, and they'd told other friends, and the story got back to me. I was ashamed of myself. But I was ashamed for her too.

Eleanor left the dance early, or at least earlier than Franklin. She didn't usually do that, but her cousins, Mr. and Mrs. Warren Robbins, were houseguests, and she must have thought they would bring Franklin home safely.

I saw her saying good night to him. I even heard a snatch of the conversation as I danced by with Nigel Law. Nigel was the third secretary of the British Embassy, and *Town Topics* was always linking us romantically. *Town Topics* wasn't the only one, but that came later.

"You stay here, honey," Eleanor said, "and enjoy yourself. I'll take a taxi home."

Honey, she called him. It wasn't the first time I'd overheard her use the term of endearment. In the past I'd always envied the sweetness between them, but the way she said it now, or the way I heard it as I danced by in the wrong pair of arms, gave rise to a more mean-spirited feeling. For the first time I didn't envy them. For the first time I was jealous of her.

Eleanor went out into the spring night. Franklin asked me to dance again. And again after that. The fourth time he approached, I looked over his shoulder and noticed the Misses Patten. They were in a huddle.

"People will talk, Mr. Roosevelt," I said, though I should have known the protest was futile. Criticism only made him more determined.

"Have we done anything wrong, Miss Mercer?"

I admitted we hadn't.

His arm went around my waist. His smile spread over my bare shoulders. "And if we did have something to hide, what better way to do it than in plain sight?"

When Franklin and his cousins returned home the next morning, the sky was blushing dawn, and Eleanor was sitting on the floor of the portico waiting for them. I can see her now, her back straight and sore against the hard white pillar, her pale blue gown lapping around her like water on the damp stone, her face and heart hard with misery. I can imagine what she was thinking too. It was outrageous. It was immoral. In Europe men were dying and women and children were starving, and here in Washington her husband, the man on whom she'd pinned all her hopes, was dancing the night away.

Franklin stopped. For once Eleanor had stopped him. He walked away from her tears, and fled her conflicts with his mother, but even he couldn't ignore martyrdom on his doorstep.

He asked what on earth she was doing there. She explained she'd forgotten her key. Why didn't you ring the bell? he said. She told him she hadn't wanted to disturb the servants. Why

didn't you take a taxi back to the club and get my key? he
wanted to know.

"You were all having such a glorious time," she answered.
"I couldn't bear the idea of ruining your evening."

At least that was what Mrs. Robbins said Eleanor said.

⮞ Five

The papers were black with more than war news that summer.

PARALYSIS KILLS

22 MORE BABIES

162 NEW ILL IN CITY

A poliomyelitis epidemic had started in New York and was spreading throughout the East. Cities were the worst centers of contagion, but no place was safe. Nonetheless, a small Canadian island across the Bay of Fundy from Maine was likely to be less dangerous. We began making preparations for Eleanor and the chicks' annual move to Campobello. Franklin

60

would join them for an occasional weekend or holiday when he could.

We made lists, packed boxes and trunks and suitcases, and reserved tickets to transport Eleanor, five children—by then the second Franklin, Jr., whom she'd been carrying the day we met, and John had arrived—several servants, a governess, and a tutor by train and steamer and carriage and motorboat.

Eleanor didn't mind the ordeal of arranging it all. She loved Campo, as they all called it. It was the only place, she'd told me as we were packing the summer before, where she was in her own home. Springwood in Hyde Park, which Franklin and the chicks called the Place, as if there were no other in the world, belonged to her mother-in-law. Even Franklin couldn't plant so much as a tree without Mrs. James's permission. The townhouse on East Sixty-fifth Street in New York, which Mrs. James had built for them as a wedding gift, was nominally Eleanor's, but it was connected to Mrs. James's own townhouse by several interior sliding doors. I could imagine what it must be like to live in constant fear of the sudden scrape of casters announcing Mrs. James's arrival with advice on how to raise children and manage servants and care for Franklin. This house in Washington and the previous rentals in Albany were merely way stations. But in Campo Eleanor was mistress of her own home, and she reveled in it. That was why I couldn't understand her reluctance to leave that summer. I blamed it on the war. German U-boats had been spotted close to shore in the Northeast. And as a part of the British Empire, Canada was a belligerent. Even Franklin worried about the U-boat threat to Campo. But he worried more about the polio epidemic.

∾ Once Eleanor and the chicks were gone, the rugs in the house came up, the draperies down, and the slipcovers turned the heavy furniture into dusty ghosts. Mrs. Cowles's servants, Millie and Francis, stayed on to care for Franklin when he returned late at night from the State, War, and Navy Building, or early in the morning from a dinner party or dance. He stayed only long enough for a cool bath or a cold meal and a few hours of sleep. Then he was off again.

Mrs. James thought he was working too hard. Eleanor didn't see the need, after a long day at the office, for him to go driving around the countryside, stopping at various clubs and houses, drinking and dancing and playing poker till all hours, especially when he was with his friend Livingston Davis. She thought Livy was a bad influence. He drank incessantly and chased women indiscriminately and was, she was certain, unfaithful to his wife. Eleanor said even his name reminded her of a Roman orgy. Both Franklin's mother and his wife nagged him to take better care of himself. He laughed and flexed his muscles, played eighteen holes of golf in the morning heat and another eighteen in the afternoon sun, and danced away the night.

I continued to come in once or twice a week to tie up loose ends. The work was less demanding during the summer, but that didn't make it more pleasant. I hated the echo of my footsteps in the abandoned rooms, and the look of the sepulchre slipcovers, and the way papers stuck to my fingers and ink smudged my hands.

Mrs. Roosevelt wrote frequently to ask me to see to some matter. She always said "please" and "if you would not mind," and included news about the weather and the children and various guests. I hated those letters too. Mrs. Roosevelt had a habit of covering a page, then turning it sideways to write perpendicularly across what was already there. The result was called lacework, and she'd learned it from Mrs. James, who traced the frugality back to the eighteenth century, when paper was expensive and postage prohibitive, but it was impossible to read.

The only advantage I could find in my position that summer was that the shuttered house on N Street was cooler than the Decatur. The apartment, crowded with family heirlooms that only made it seem smaller and more shabby, simmered in the midday heat. At night I tossed miserably on hot sheets beneath windows open to the stifling darkness. One evening a bat flew in. Mama screamed and hid under the sheets, and I spent the better part of the night tossing pillows at the ceiling to chase it out.

I arrived at the house on N Street the next morning just as the door opened and Franklin stepped onto the portico. The day's heat was already beginning to close in, but he looked fresh as sunrise. Under the brim of my straw hat, I had to squint against the sight of him.

He came down the steps, removed his own straw hat, and asked if I was feeling all right. I wondered just how tired I looked, cursed the bat, and told him I was feeling fine.

He went on staring at me. "Are you sure?"

His concern surprised me, until I remembered that these days every cough or chill or fever was cause for alarm, though I was scarcely at an age for childhood diseases.

I told him about the bat. He threw back his head and opened his mouth to let out the laughter. The light bathed his freshly shaven face and splintered off his pince-nez. I could easily have gone blind with the reflected brilliance.

"You wouldn't have found it so funny, Mr. Roosevelt, if you had been there."

"But I was—there, I mean, in a manner of speaking. I had two bats last night. What we have here, Miss Mercer, is an infestation of bats. Except that's not what it's called."

He cocked his head to one side to indicate he was thinking. A faint mustache of perspiration had come out on his upper lip. I couldn't take my eyes from it. Beneath my long-sleeved linen jacket and shirtwaist, I felt a similar dampness under my arms and in the small of my back and between my breasts. I prayed that it would not show. Perspiration was all right for him. He was a man. But I was supposed to be a lady.

"It's an exaltation of larks," he said, "and a parliament of owls, and an unkindness of ravens." He was grinning broadly, and I couldn't help smiling back at him. Franklin did that to people. "There's also—now, you're not going to like these, Lucy—a rage of maidens, and an impatience of wives, and a superfluity of nuns."

He was right. Normally I would not have liked the last. I loved his teasing, but not about the books I couldn't read and the hymns he thought I couldn't sing because of my religion, though his jokes didn't bother me as much as Eleanor's pained politeness when she forgot I was there and made an unkind comment about Catholics. Then she'd remember me, and her smile would stiffen and her voice climb, as she'd reassure me she could distinguish between the respectable religion of the early Maryland settlers and the superstitious faith of her uneducated Irish servants and the corrupt Tammany bosses who plagued her husband, until finally I felt more sorry than angry. But as I stood in the circle of sunlight with Franklin that morning, nuns were the last thing on my mind. He'd called me Lucy. I knew he had a tendency to use people's Christian names, but he had never used mine, and the way he rolled it around on his tongue made me think he was tasting it.

"They're called collectives, Lucy."

He liked the flavor. I could tell.

"Or multitudes, or multitudinous nouns. Also venereal nouns, after Venus, not Venus the goddess of love"—he winked—"but Venus the goddess of the hunt. Only there doesn't seem to be a collective for our bats. We have our work cut out for us, Lucy. *Tout de suite.*" *Tootie sweetie,* he pronounced the words. "I'm leaving it in your capable hands." He started to turn away, then hesitated, and turned back. The smile was gone. The creases on either side of his frown were dark as crayon marks.

"One thing more, Lucy. When you write Mrs. Roosevelt today, please remind her to be sure to kill any flies I might have left. They collect in that window overlooking the water. Hundreds of them."

At first I didn't understand what he meant. Then I realized he was speaking of the house in Campo. He'd just returned from a long weekend.

"I don't know if there's any truth to this theory that they carry the infantile paralysis," he went on. "Some experts say it's flies, others that it's the damp spring we had. But I have no intention of taking any chances."

I told him I would be sure to remind Mrs. Roosevelt. He thanked me, turned again, and started down the street. I climbed the steps and was about to open the door when I heard the sound again.

"Lucy!" It floated on the morning air.

I turned back.

"That's another one we have to get to work on." I stood looking at him, waiting. "An annoyance of flies?"

"A sting, Mr. Roosevelt. A sting of flies."

He nodded, turned, and started down N Street. I stood,

feeling the sun beating on my back, and watched him go. His head turned this way and that to take in the morning, and his arms swung easily, and his legs ate up the distance.

ᔐ The medical authorities were calling it the worst infantile paralysis epidemic in memory. New York was hardest hit, though all of the East festered with contagion. Everyone knew someone who was ill. Mrs. James wrote that her coachman's three-year-old daughter had been stricken. Mr. Spenlow, who lived on the same floor as Mama and I at the Decatur, told us his nephew, not a frail child, but a great strapping man in his thirties, lay in a hospital bed. The worst part of it was there was nothing anyone could do. No one knew what caused the disease or how it spread, though, as Franklin had pointed out, there was no shortage of theories. So we took whatever futile precautions we could, and went about pretending not to think about it, and sometimes managed, through the pretense, to forget for a few hours or even a day. Each morning I put on layers of clothing—stays, stockings, a high-collared shirt-waist, yards and yards of skirt—and went out to roll bandages and knit sweaters and smile across a well-set table at the same faces I'd smiled at the day or week before.

One afternoon I had tea with Cousin Elizabeth Cotton, who said she'd had a letter from another, more distant cousin, Marguerita Pennington. Marguerita had been at the convent school in Melk with Violetta and me, but instead of returning home, she'd married a German officer and stayed on in Austria. It was strange to think of her and Vio on opposite sides of the war. They'd been good friends at school. We all had, ever since that first day when Sister Agnes-Marie had come up to supervise our unpacking.

Mama had sent Vio and me off to stay with Papa's aunt,

the Countess Heussenstamm, with trunks full of dresses, and hats, and shoes. She'd wanted us to be able to hold our heads up in Austrian society. She also loved to buy things. That was before the money evaporated and our mysterious American relative began sending checks through a Boston attorney, and the countess assumed our expenses at the convent. When Vio and I reached the lingerie drawers of our trunks that day, Sister Agnes-Marie let out a shocked lament for the state of our souls. Our lingerie, she'd whispered in horror, was fit for *une putain*.

"*Qu'es-ce que c'est qu'une putain, Mademoiselle?*" I'd asked, and Marguerita had held her hand over her mouth to stifle the giggles.

"What a wicked little convent girl you are, Lucy Mercer," she'd said when the sister left the room, but Marguerita had been wrong. I hadn't been wicked. I'd merely been an obliging girl trying to stay out of trouble. I still was.

When Elizabeth and I said good-bye, she told me to be sure to send her regards to Violetta and I told her to give mine to Marguerita, and for a moment, standing there in Lafayette Square, the war, which was unbelievable in the vastness of its horror, became real in the shards of a splintered friendship.

I was still thinking about Vio and Marguerita as I started up Connecticut Avenue. That was when I caught sight of him. Despite the heat, despite the war, despite the epidemic, he was loping down the sidewalk as if he didn't have a care in the world. I forgot about Vio and Marguerita and even the heat. It was hard to look at Franklin in motion without feeling happy.

He hadn't seen me, and as I stood watching him coming toward me, I remembered something I'd overheard his aunt Bye's husband, Admiral Cowles, say to him. "Bye calls you her debonair young cousin, but the girls will spoil you soon enough, Franklin, and I leave you to them."

He caught sight of me and lengthened his stride. We were face-to-face in a few seconds. He took off his straw hat with the striped ribbon around the crown.

"The lovely Miss Mercer," he said. Since that morning when we'd discussed venereal nouns, he'd called me Lucy occasionally but not invariably.

"Good evening, Mr. Roosevelt."

"Isn't it!" he cried, as if the heat weren't steaming up from the streets and hanging from the sky like damp laundry.

I had to laugh. "You must be the only one in the entire District of Columbia who thinks so."

"You're right," he said. He was still grinning, and I was smiling back at him, and a passerby would have thought we were either mad or feebleminded. "It's hotter 'n hinges. What you need, Lucy, what we both need, is a drive in the country."

I hesitated for a moment, but only a moment. I could not see the harm of a drive in the country.

We walked to the garage and waited while the attendant brought out the Stutz. Then, as Franklin helped me up to the running board, a strange thing happened. Though the sun still hung above the horizon, I had a sudden impression of gloom, as if I'd passed into the shadowy confines of a confessional. I shook my head and stared into the sun. He strode around to the other side of the car and climbed in behind the wheel. His closeness came at me in waves of heat. I smelled the melting wax of candles and the wintergreen breath of the priest wafting from the other side of the screen. I decided it must be the heat. Remember, it was a time when ladies fainted easily and stronger women than I carried smelling salts.

He started the engine and pulled away from the curb. I

watched him out of the corner of my eye. He drove with the large, easy movements of a man who prided himself on the quickness of his reflexes and the dependability of his body.

The city fell away and the countryside opened before us. The sun spooled a ribbon of scarlet along the horizon, then slipped behind it. Stars burned holes in the hot sky, and a warm breeze insinuated itself into the pleats of my shirtwaist. I imagined myself lifting my hands and removing my hat. The wind whipped the pins from my hair, and it sailed loose in the darkness. I reached up to make sure my hat was secure on my head. Franklin didn't take his eyes from the road, but he must have noticed the gesture, because he laughed.

"Don't worry, Lucy. I won't let you come undone."

We drove in silence. We stopped to talk. He told me about the war and the navy and the coming election. Only once did he say anything that could be construed as even faintly personal.

He'd stopped to turn the Stutz around to start back to town, and he hesitated for a moment before putting it in gear. When he turned to face me, his features disappeared into the darkness.

"Do you know what I like about you, Lucy?"

I held my breath. A moth fluttered against the windscreen. Katydids sawed the night. What if what he liked was not really me? What if I were an imposter or simply a mistake?

"With you I can be me."

The words walked down my spine, one after the other, as if they were his fingers.

∾ A few days later the Stutz ended up in a ditch a few hundred yards from where he'd told me what he liked about me. At least it sounded like the same spot to me.

I was at Eleanor's desk in the back parlor working on her correspondence, and Franklin was standing at a table rifling through the mail, when Mr. Howe came by to walk to the State, War, and Navy Building, which, as Mr. Howe never tired of pointing out, was just across from the White House. That gorgeous hunk of real estate, he called it.

"Morning, boss," he said. "And the lovely Miss Mercer." He took a chair, turned a little so that his back was to me, reached into his pocket, and pulled out a crushed pack of Sweet Caporals. "I got the dope, boss, and you're not going to like it." He shook his head as he broke into a fit of coughing. "It just goes to show there's no limit to the sheer stupidity of the average adult male. Especially where the average adult female is concerned."

The statement was crude and a little risqué, not the kind of thing Mr. Howe would ordinarily have said in front of me. At the time I thought he'd forgotten I was there. Now I wonder if it wasn't intentional. There wasn't much that Mr. Howe missed, especially if it concerned Franklin.

He stubbed out the old cigarette he'd used to light the new one. "Your esteemed chauffeur, Mr. Albert Golden, was so broken up over his wife's deteriorating health that he borrowed the Stutz and went looking for a soft shoulder—and I don't mean the kind on the side of the road—to cry on. Along comes this skirt, and she gets her claws into him, and before you know it, she wants to go joyriding, with the usual highballs for fuel. Next thing, our friend Golden's in the hospital and the car's in the shop. And if that ain't enough, it turns out he's been pocketing money on gasoline and tires and the garage all along."

"Are you sure?" Franklin asked.

"He practically admitted it. I went to see him in the hospital. Now that he's been caught with his hand in the cookie jar, he's got a bad case of contrition. Kept begging me not to let on to the missus that there was anyone else in the car. The question is, what do we do about it? Besides fix the Stutz."

"Pay the hospital bills."

Mr. Howe nodded.

"Then fire him."

"Me?"

"You know I can't do it. I'm just an old softy."

Franklin put down the mail he'd been glancing through and started for the door, and Mr. Howe stood and followed him.

"The way I see it, boss," I heard Mr. Howe say as he trotted along trying to keep up with Franklin, "the anxiety's a good thing. No man is beyond redemption as long as he don't want his wife to find out."

∽ A few days later I saw the letter. It lay open on Eleanor's desk. The handwriting was obviously hers, though this time it went in only one direction. It occurs to me now that she wanted to make sure she was understood. The salutation said, "Dearest Honey." Perhaps I shouldn't have read it, but it was on her desk, and I thought there might be something in it that she wanted me to take care of. Why else would Franklin have left it on his wife's desk where he knew I worked?

There was a paragraph about the naval bill and how pleased she was that his count of noses had been correct and it had gone through. The next few sentences were less clear, though the handwriting was perfectly legible. I stood looking down at the words:

"Isn't it horrid to be disappointed in someone? It makes one so suspicious!"

At first I didn't understand. Then it came to me. She was talking about the chauffeur.

꙳ Eleanor wrote from Campo that she was eager to return home, but even if she were willing to risk bringing the chicks back to Washington or Hyde Park, there was no way to transport them. Angry villagers were turning away motorists with children in the car. Terrified parents were meeting trains at stations with signs: NEW YORKERS KEEP OUT. WE SYMPATHIZE BUT WE HAVE CHILDREN.

Franklin and I went for another drive, and one after that. The Stutz had been repaired, though it still lacked a windshield and searchlight. We streaked into the night, the hot wind in our faces, the darkness giving cover. The third night we drove out, I took off my hat. I couldn't risk having it blow away. The wind tore the pins from my hair. I felt it fly loose behind me. This time Franklin didn't joke about it.

꙳ It was early October by the time Eleanor returned to Washington. Two weeks earlier Franklin had borrowed the secretary's official yacht, the *Dolphin*, and sailed it up to Campo to bring his family home, though, to be on the safe side, he and Eleanor had left the chicks with Mrs. James in Hyde Park before continuing on to Washington.

The air was shot with gold as I made my way down N Street that morning. Dead leaves crunched under my shoes, but the sound was invigorating rather than elegiac. The heat wave had broken. The newspapers said the epidemic was over.

The door to 1733 swung open just as I reached the bottom of the steps. Franklin was suddenly there. Nothing had prepared me for the sight of him. I reached out to steady myself, but there was nothing to grab on to.

He saw me. His face opened in a smile, and his voice wrapped itself around my name. He took the steps two at a time. He was only inches from me, so close I could smell his shaving soap and sense the heat he gave off, despite the coolness of the morning. I felt myself tilting toward him.

"Lucy," he said again.

I couldn't answer him. An ordinary greeting would have been too mundane, his name, even with Mr. in front of it, too intimate.

We went on standing there, the happiness so palpable it seemed to be another weather condition. Then beyond his shoulder a movement blurred the bright morning. I turned toward it. Eleanor stood in the doorway.

"Franklin," she called.

I felt him list toward me.

"You forgot this," she said.

I sensed him pull away. He turned toward her. She was holding a large official-looking envelope. He climbed the steps and took it from her.

"Thank you, Babs," he said as he came back down. "Isn't it a grand morning, Miss Mercer?" he added as he went past.

I turned in his wake. Behind me I could feel Eleanor still in the doorway. We went on standing that way as we watched Franklin moving away from us, his head thrown back, his optically-corrected myopic gaze focused on the horizon, his long legs chewing up the distance to his office just across from the White House.

❧ Six

It was always a jarring experience to walk into the apartment at the Decatur after leaving the house on N Street. Both places had a worn and faded air, but the drab upholstery and paling chintz of the Roosevelt household looked as if it had aged not only gracefully but eagerly, as if newness would have been an embarrassment. The tarnished gold brocade on which Mama sat gave off a powerful whiff of regret.

"*Pauvre* Lucy," Mama said. "They've kept you late again."

I turned to the mirror to take off my hat. My elbow jostled a lamp. I caught it before it went over. We lived among too much furniture scaled to grander spaces.

"We can only be glad that it won't go on for much longer," she continued. "Despite this foolish statement from Mr. Roosevelt."

The sound of his name stopped me. I was always looking for opportunities to insert it into the conversation. I was just as eager to hoard the sound of it for myself. Perhaps if Violetta had been there I would have confided in her, though I can't imagine what I would have said. Could I tell her that sometimes when he looked at me, I wanted to get up and strut around the room? A few days earlier, when I was on the floor sorting correspondence, he came and stood beside me, and in a surge of pure joy I almost reached out and circled his ankle with my fingers. Even Vio would be shocked.

Mama picked up a newspaper from the table and held it out to me. It was folded open to a political story rather than the society page. I was surprised. Like most Washington cave dwellers, as the group called themselves, Mama viewed politics as a passing, slightly disreputable parade. Papa agreed. He thought politics was beneath the dignity of a gentleman, the profession he'd listed on my birth certificate, and probably on Vio's as well, though no one could be sure, because the original of that along with the marriage license had disappeared in their travels, and we had to rely on Mama's memory for the dates of the various events.

I took the paper from her. Franklin stared up at me. I knew the blue of those eyes even in black and white. I forced myself to look away from them to the column of words. The assistant secretary of the navy had just returned from a campaign trip. He was, he said, optimistic. "A large number of men whom I talked with—factory hands, mechanics, and store-keepers—were regular Republicans who had never voted for a Democrat. These men did not wish to announce publicly that they would vote for Wilson, but told me that this was their present intention."

"According to this," I said, "the president will be reelected, and Mr. Roosevelt won't be leaving Washington after all."

Mama shook her head. "Mere whistling in the dark. Everyone knows Mr. Wilson does not stand a chance."

I couldn't imagine where Mama had acquired her information, but I knew she wasn't wrong. Not only did I follow the political news, I heard Franklin and Mr. Howe talk. The country was still solidly Republican. And though the president was running on the slogan "He kept us out of war," Franklin said even the president didn't believe it. " 'Any little German lieutenant can put us into war at any time by some calculated outrage,' " Mr. Wilson was supposed to have said. "I wish any little German lieutenant would," Franklin had added.

"And it will be a good thing too," Mama went on. "It's about time someone reminded Edith Galt of her place."

Now I understood Mama's sudden interest in politics. She'd always pitied her old friend Edith Bolling, who'd had the bad judgment to marry Mr. Galt, who was in trade, but Mr. Galt had died, and Mrs. Galt had become Mrs. Woodrow Wilson, and now Edith presided over the White House, while Mama retrenched at the Decatur. Poor Mama just couldn't understand how the world could be such a heartless place.

"Who would have thought," Mama continued, "that plump little Edith Bolling was so cunning?"

"Perhaps she isn't cunning," I said. "Perhaps she's in love with Mr. Wilson."

Mama shook her head, as if there were no end to my naïveté. "Of course she's in love with him. It's no great achievement to be in love with the right gentleman."

I found the statement perplexing, in view of Mama's separation from Papa, and her first marriage to an Englishman, whom she'd divorced for a variety of unspeakable but occasionally hinted-at cruelties. But I believed Mrs. Galt loved Mr. Wilson. I knew for a fact the president loved Mrs. Galt. Franklin had told me so. That was one of the things we'd talked about during those drives in the country. Not love, but politics.

Franklin said Mr. Wilson had been so crazy for Mrs. Galt he'd ignored his advisers' warnings that the American people would not reelect a man so susceptible to romance that he would take a second wife a scant year and a half after the death of his first. He'd even refused to postpone the wedding until after the election, which I'd heard Mr. Howe say any ward heeler would have the brains to do. I liked the fact that the president had lost his sense as well as his heart.

There was another incident Franklin had related about the president and Mrs. Galt. The night of their wedding a railroad porter had come upon Mr. Wilson outside the presidential compartment singing happily to himself. Telling me the story, Franklin had thrown back his head and imitated the new groom. "Oh, you beautiful doll, you great big beautiful doll."

In all the photos I'd seen of Mr. Wilson, he looked like an austere saint in a medieval painting, or the schoolteacher he'd once been. His eyes were cold, his jaw long and stubborn, his expression unforgiving. I was tickled pink by the idea that love could strip such a man, the president of the United States, of his dignity so completely that he'd wander the corridors of a railroad car in the dead of night singing silly popular tunes.

"You'll have to look for a new position," Mama said.

"There's plenty of time for that," I told her, though I knew there wasn't. That was something else Franklin had told me. The president had informed his advisers that the times were too dire to leave the country in a four-month interregnum. If he lost the election, as he was likely to, he would not remain in office until the inauguration next March, but resign immediately and move out of the White House so Mr. Hughes could move in. I was glad Mr. Wilson had risked all for love, but I regretted that he'd lost the gamble, and now he and his entire administration would be leaving Washington. My life would go on. I would find a position with someone else who needed help with her letters and lists. I would continue to lunch and talk of engagements and marriages and births and war. I would knit for Allied soldiers and Bulgarian women and Russian children. And several nights a week I would sit beside an eligible gentleman at dinner, and draw him out, and buff him up. It was not a difficult or unenjoyable task. Until recently I hadn't thought of it as a task at all, merely an instinct. After I had sat beside the same gentleman often enough, and he had enjoyed being drawn out and buffed up, he and I and the world would become accustomed to the arrangement. Perhaps the gentleman would turn out to be Franklin's friend, Nigel Law, the third secretary of the British Embassy. Just the other day, *Town Topics* had called attention to the number of times Nigel and I had danced at a ball for Greek relief. I saw my future life as if it were one of those new moving pictures, a murkily lit drama of a gesturing, grimacing woman racing at inhuman speed toward an unconvincing end.

⌐ These days we have become accustomed to hearing news on the radio, even a portable or automobile radio. We sit in our living rooms and wonder where Pearl Harbor is. We go to the beach and find the Japanese have surrendered. We speed through the dusk, getting farther and farther away, and discover the unthinkable has happened, the president is dead. But that autumn when everyone was predicting Mr. Wilson's defeat, radios were still rare, and frivolous, objects. It would be years before Franklin turned them into weapons. Pull up a chair, he'd say in that voice that was as solid as Fort Knox and as jolly as Santa Claus and as reassuring as a father, right here in front of the fire, and let's have a chat about banks, or farms, or lending a hose to put out your neighbor's fire. But that election night, news still traveled slowly. There was nothing we could do but wait for it.

I tried to read. I tried to write to Violetta. Finally I told Mama I was going to sleep, but I couldn't sleep. I lay in bed staring at the mottled ceiling trying to get used to this unhappiness that had sneaked up on me. I didn't understand how I hadn't seen it coming.

Later Franklin told me he'd lain awake that night too. "Uncle" Henry Morganthau, as Franklin called him, had given a party at Democratic Headquarters in the Biltmore Hotel in New York, though most of the guests were fairly sure there was nothing to celebrate. Afterward, Franklin had come out of the hotel into a city that glowed a deathly white. The pall streamed down from the Woolworth Tower, bleached the silvery skyscrapers, and drained the streets of color. He knew what that meant. "From the Tower of the Woolworth Building tonight," the advertisement had said, "The *Tribune*'s powerful searchlights, reinforced by a new Edison storage battery searchlight, will announce the next President of the United States. Should the *Tribune* searchlight throw a straight steady beam, Hughes will have been elected. Should the searchlight flash in a zigzag direction, Wilson will be in the White House for four years more." The white light beat down as relentless and unblinking as the moon.

Franklin was disappointed, but not despondent. He'd lived through worse defeats. On the midnight train back to Washington, he told Franklin Lane, the secretary of the interior, that he was going to start a law practice with Franklin Polk, and added that Mr. Lane should join them. "We could call it Franklin, Franklin, and Franklin," he joked. He always said that no situation was so dire it couldn't be leavened by a little humor.

His first sign that something was wrong came after the porter had made up the berths. He tipped the porter and said thank you, George, though his name might be Harry or John or even Franklin, but George was what you called every porter, and good night, Frank, and climbed into his berth. He expected to be asleep by Princeton Junction. Franklin had no trouble sleeping on trains. He had no trouble sleeping anywhere. He hadn't lost a wink after his defeat in the Senate primary two years earlier. Even in the blackest days of the war, the second one, when everything rested on his shoulders, he would be able to sleep, or so he would insist. There was only one other time he'd lain awake through the night, and he didn't tell me about that until later. The story about not sleeping on the train election night was an affirmation of love. The account of the other time he hadn't been able to sleep was an admission of weakness. That took longer.

On election night he'd stretched out diagonally in the berth, and closed his eyes, and listened to the rhythm of the wheels as he waited for sleep. But the wheels kept clacking down the track, and the roadbed turned rough and then smooth again, and the train pulled into Trenton and out of it, and he was still awake. He said he couldn't understand it. Introspection was not his game. Crying over spilled milk was not his style. If he lost an election, or failed to get a bill through, or backed the wrong side in a political skirmish, he picked up the pieces and started over. As long as he did his best, as long as he did something, he could, he insisted, sleep the sleep of the innocent, or at least the just. But he could not sleep that night, and he didn't figure out why until the train crossed the state line into Maryland. Both the Carrolls and the Mercers had settled Maryland. That was when it came to him. He saw me sitting in the Stutz the night I'd taken off my hat and the hot wind had whipped the pins from my hair.

"I didn't know you'd noticed," I lied when he told me about it.

"I'm myopic, Lucy, not blind," he answered.

When he stepped off the train in Union Station the next morning, the papers were reporting the election was, after all, still too close to call. By the time the afternoon editions reached the stands, returns from the Midwest had begun to roll in. Things were looking brighter for Mr. Wilson, but I refused to hope. It would be tempting fate.

I'd been right not to hope. On Thursday morning banner headlines proclaimed Mr. Hughes's "sweeping victory." According to one article, when a reporter called for a statement, Mr. Hughes's son replied the "President cannot be disturbed." As Mama had warned, I would have to begin looking for a new position.

By midday Thursday the tide had begun to turn again. The afternoon papers reported that returns from the western as well as the midwestern states were erasing Mr. Hughes's lead. This time I couldn't help but hope.

I went to bed early again that night. I knew I wouldn't be able to sleep, but I wanted to hurry the morning editions of the papers. Everything hung on California. My life was being determined a continent away.

I have no idea what time the cry of "Extry, extry" rose from the street below. Without stopping to look at the clock, I leapt out of bed, threw open the window, and called down to the newsboy to wait. It was the most unladylike thing I had ever done. What I did next was even worse. I pulled on my shoes without stockings, threw my coat over my nightdress, and, buttoning as I went, raced down the stairs and through the lobby into the fading night.

I stuck two pennies in the boy's hand and grabbed a paper. Even in the dark the headlines jumped out at me. WILSON and VICTORY and FOUR MORE YEARS. At twenty-five, four years is a lifetime.

∾ What happened next was forgivable, or at least understandable. We'd come so close to losing each other before we'd realized we'd found each other that it was only natural we should let down our guard in the rush of relief.

We tried not to stare at each other. We couldn't look anywhere else. We were scrupulous not to touch, but clumsiness made our hands brush or shoulders collide. As I sat on the floor surrounded by Eleanor's papers, or behind her desk scribbling lists and letters, I felt his eyes on me hot as a tropical sun, and I stretched and strutted and strained toward them as no nice woman should. When he returned home from eighteen holes of golf in the morning and another eighteen in the afternoon, his body humming like a tuning fork, I trembled to the vibrations he gave off. Once, when he was romping with the chicks, I saw him toss Franklin, Jr., into the air, and my heart flexed with the swell of his biceps beneath his proper dark wool jacket. The peal of Franklin, Jr.'s laughter should have reproached me. It merely duped me. How could there be sin in the presence of such innocence?

On a January morning after he and Eleanor and the chicks had returned from spending Christmas at the Place, I wore a new shirtwaist Violetta had managed to send me from Paris. It was the height of fashion and had a small oval cutout beneath the mother-of-pearl button at the throat. The opening was decorative and decorous. I had evening dresses that revealed more flesh. But months later Franklin teased me about that shirtwaist. He said he'd gone off to his office to keep an eye on the trouble in Mexico, and oversee the Marine occupation of Haiti, and reassign a hospital steward from Brooklyn so the steward's parents would vote for Congressman Fitzgerald in the next election and Tammany would know what a friend they had in Franklin D. Roosevelt. He said he'd spent the day juggling half a dozen problems here and abroad, but that small oval cutout in my shirtwaist kept distracting him. That cutout, he said, was his window on the world.

Seven

"A great man cannot be a good man."
 ᔕ Thomas G. Corcoran to Arthur M. Schlesinger, Jr.,
in an interview about Franklin D. Roosevelt

"There was a sense of impending disaster hanging over all of us."
 ᔕ Eleanor Roosevelt

Perhaps it would not have happened if America hadn't gone to war. Violetta said people do crazy things in wartime, though she was thinking of a different war when she said it. I disagree. I think people do as they like, then blame it on war.

The weather was inclement the day America went to the Great War, as we used to call it before another war turned it into the First War. The rain had been light in the morning, little more than a mist, really, and the newspapers reported that President and Mrs. Wilson played a round of golf. By afternoon a chilly drizzle had begun to fall. It did nothing to dampen the excitement simmering in the city. The president had asked Congress to convene in an extraordinary session. Everyone knew that meant war. Unless it meant something else.

The next morning I would read the news reports of what happened that day, and though by then I would tell myself my problems were small and foolish in a nation suddenly plunged into war, I didn't believe it for a moment. I grieved for all the men who would be lost and the women and children who would lose them. I worried about Violetta, and though I didn't know it at the time, I had good reason to. She had contracted a highly communicable disease, which the war-weary doctors either couldn't or didn't have the time to diagnose, and been given up for dead. Later she would tell me how it felt to have a doctor pull a hospital sheet over her face in a premature last rite of mercy. Later still, she would say she would have been better off if she had died in that hospital in France. But that was in the future the day the president convened Congress in an extraordinary session.

The trains began arriving at Union Station early that morning. By midday thousands of Pilgrims of Patriotism waving American flags and shouting themselves hoarse, and other thousands of pacifists wearing white armbands and carrying white tulips, were fanning out to the White House, and the Capitol, and the State, War, and Navy. One pacifist forced himself into Senator Lodge's office and called the senator a damned—the papers didn't print that, but Franklin told me later—coward for wanting to go to war, and the distinguished senator called the pacifist a damned liar and hit him. I suppose even a pacifist has his limits, because he hit the senator in return. The police moved in then and subdued and jailed the pacifist.

It was not one of my mornings to go to N Street, and I was sorry, because I wanted to hear what Franklin made of the situation. He would not be home, but Eleanor would report. Mr.

Roosevelt says. Does Mr. Roosevelt think? Even now, when he'd come between us, he still held us together.

The Decatur Apartments, like every other building in Washington that housed more than one person, was a hotbed of gossip and speculation masquerading as news. Neighbors gathered in the halls, and knocked on one another's doors, and ambushed each other in the lobby. When a cry of "Extry" sounded from the street early that evening, dapper Mr. Spenlow dashed out and returned with a damp paper to a lobby filled with Decatur residents in various states of dress. War cast our neighbors in a new light. Mrs. Dawkins was dining out. Mr. and Mrs. Brenner were staying home and did not dress for dinner. Even Mama had ventured out of the apartment, though she was not a woman given to mixing promiscuously with her neighbors.

As it turned out, the edition should not have been an "Extry" at all. It carried no new information, merely more speculation on what the president was going to say to the extraordinary session.

"It's war for certain," Mr. Spenlow announced.

Old Mrs. Vance let out a cry and collapsed in her chair with her hand over her heart.

"We are utterly unprepared, and we will be annihilated," Colonel Dawkins's wife announced.

"How on earth could the Germans annihilate us?" Miss Vance asked.

"Why, they'll just come over in their ships and submarines and do it!" Mrs. Dawkins shrieked.

That was when I went up to the apartment, buttoned myself into a mackintosh, took an umbrella, and slipped out of the building. I had no destination. I simply had to get out of there, and not merely because of the foolish speculation about the war. Lately I found myself eager to leave someplace I'd just arrived or longing to be someplace I'd just left. I could not sit still.

Outside, I stood for a moment debating which way to turn. Rain rattled the leaves. Florida Avenue was a dark water-slicked mirror. I remembered it was Holy Week and started East toward St. Matthew's. I'd pray for peace, my own as well as the world's.

By the time I reached Rhode Island Avenue, my laced calf-skin boots were soaked. The soggy hem of my skirt hung heavily around my ankles. I longed for the dry incense-fragrant refuge inside.

I started up the broad steps. They were treacherous with wet leaves the wind had torn from the trees. I stopped and looked up at the church. The red brick facade was streaked black by the rain. The bronze doors looked too heavy to open. I turned and made my way down with careful mincing steps. I did not want to fall. As I reached the bottom, a line of lightning sizzled over my head. I was mad to be out in this. I couldn't think of anywhere else to be.

In the east the sky was turning pale, though night was just coming on. Even nature had become unreliable. As I drew closer, I realized the effect was man-made. The Capitol shimmered into focus through the mist. Light steamed up from the ground and hung like a halo over the dome. I had never seen the Capitol lit up. Later Franklin told me it never had been before that night.

I kept walking toward it. I knew I couldn't get inside. The day before, Eleanor had told me Franklin had had difficulty getting her a seat in the gallery. Senators and congressmen were fighting for tickets. Speculators were reselling them for ten or twenty or fifty dollars. The war hadn't even started, but

the profiteers were making money. Eleanor said it was unconscionable. I agreed with her, but I kept going.

I was in the midst of a crowd now. It ebbed and flowed
along the sidewalks and between the traffic-stalled automo-
biles, cheering that we were finally in it, shouting that we had
to stay out of it. I have read that a single opinion can turn a
group of ordinary individuals into a monster. Two beliefs
make it even more dangerously mindless. The umbrellas
didn't help. Surely someone would lose an eye before the night
was out.

I reached the edge of the Capitol grounds. Soldiers and
policemen and Secret Service officers lined the perimeter and
stood like gargoyles on the roof. There were rumors of pacifist threats against the president's life, though assassination
seemed a strange way to avoid bloodshed.

A woman crashed into me and knocked my umbrella from
my hand. As I bent to pick it up, she stuck a miniature American flag in my hand. I fumbled for my purse, but the woman
was already gone. She wasn't selling patriotism, she was giving it away. A group of boys danced by, quick rain-slippery
devils, singing and shouting and celebrating their hatred of
the kaiser. A man opened his mouth and shouted he'd be
damned if he'd lay down his life for the House of Morgan. All
around him men and women lifted their heads and bayed
"Coward" at the cloud-shrouded moon.

On the steps of the Capitol a crowd stood shoulder to
shoulder, jostling, pushing, ebbing this way, flowing that. A
line of guards was fighting to keep a path open for the people
who had tickets.

Congressmen and cabinet members and diplomats fought
their way up. I recognized many, I knew more than a few, but
tonight they were not husbands and fathers and friends, but

public men, stewards of the country's, of the world's, fate. Their faces were serious, but even in the crowd, even from this distance, I saw something else. They were like children trying to behave, but incapable of suppressing their excitement. This was their party, their piece of history, their moment of greatness.

Suddenly, above the mass of wet heads and churning umbrellas, Franklin's profile jumped out at me. He was shouldering his way up the narrow path between the guards, his face lifted to the sky in that characteristic gesture of optimism and myopia that masqueraded as arrogance. Eleanor was a step behind him, her head bent, obviously watching her step, her expression grim. I stood in the screaming, pushing crowd as the Roosevelts disappeared behind the pillars.

"He's coming! He's coming!" The cry leapt from mouth to mouth. It turned heads and stretched necks.

I heard the sound of hooves. "The cavalry!" someone shouted, and as the mass of people flowed toward it, I was carried along until I could smell the horses and see the steam rising from their nostrils. Then the soldiers were marching past, their boots beating a terrifying tattoo on the wet pavement. After them, slow and majestic and faintly menacing, came the long black auto.

The crowd went mad at the sight. Patriots cheered. Pacifists hissed. Beside me, a woman with the round soft face of a doll opened her mouth and screamed, "I have two sons, Mr. President! Take them!"

The mob pushed me to within a few feet of the long black auto, which resembled nothing so much as a hearse. It stopped. A guard sprang forward to open the door. The Secret Service swarmed around, but before they closed ranks, I caught a glimpse, quick as a snapshot, of a tall gaunt figure, slowed by the event that had charged everyone else with such energy. The medieval saint came back to mind. It was hard to believe he had ever sung a popular song or fallen in love once, let alone twice.

The guards did not have to fight the crowd back as he made his way up the steps. It parted before him, then closed behind him, every face turned in his direction. They had seen the president. That was their piece of history.

He disappeared into the blaze of light at the top of the steps, and the shoving and shouting started again. People jockeyed for position, and fought their way into the rotunda, and loomed out of it with sudden airs of importance, shouting snippets of news that the crowd picked up and passed from mouth to mouth.

"They're cheering him!"

"They're still cheering!"

"He's beginning to speak."

Snatches of oratory rolled down the steps. I don't remember if they were accurate. I read the words in the paper the next day. We all know them from the history books. But that night no one had ever heard them before.

". . . it is a fearful thing to lead this great peaceful people into war . . .

". . . but the right is more precious than peace . . .

"The world must be made safe for democracy."

War! War! War!

The single syllable came twisting out of the chamber, across the hall, down the steps, and through the crowd like a tornado. People cheered and wept, waved flags and shook fists, threw children into the air and slapped one another on the back, hugged loved ones and kissed total strangers. Boys who would be soldiers before they knew it grabbed government girls they'd never met, and wives and mothers embraced the husbands and sons they might lose. It was an orgy of recklessness and revenge—revenge against German atrocities and U-boat sinkings, we thought at the time; against the human condition, I know now. The crowd seethed and surged with it, pressing against the lines of soldiers and police and Secret Service, spilling into the street, carrying me along with it into the path of speeding life.

I was several blocks from the Capitol when I caught sight of him again. The president had come back down the steps and disappeared into his hearselike auto. The Supreme Court justices and diplomats and congressmen had dispersed. The viewers were trickling out of the gallery. But the crowd continued to celebrate, though of course no one admitted that was what they were doing. And Franklin was suddenly among them. This time he wasn't moving away from me, but coming toward me. He had no umbrella or hat, and the rain plastered his hair to his skull. He was using his body as a wedge to pry his way through the crowd. People bumped into him and jostled me and darted between us, but he kept coming, getting bigger with each step. When he reached me, he took the umbrella from my hand and held it over us.

"I saw you from the car," he said. "It's not safe," he added. "We'll drive you—" He stopped and stood staring down at me. His deep-set eyes were narrowed against the rain, and his mouth was a thin line of determination. A man crashed into him, and he cantilevered toward me. I reached out to steady him. My hand came to rest against his heart. We stood that way for a moment. He opened his mouth again.

"I love you," he said.

That was what war did to people, Violetta would say. It had nothing to do with war, I would insist.

❧ Eight

Four days later, on Good Friday, President Wilson took a
gold pen, which he'd given his wife, that beautiful doll, as a
gift, and signed his name to a joint congressional declaration
of war. Then Ike Hoover, who would still be chief usher of the
White House when Franklin moved in, pressed a button that
alerted an aide, who ran out onto the White House lawn and
waved both arms to signal an officer in the State, War, and

Navy Building across the way. Within minutes a message flashed to every navy shore installation and ship at sea that the country was officially at war with Germany.

I learned all that from the papers. When I finally saw Franklin, we didn't speak of the navy or even the war, though Mr. Wilson had signed the declaration only a few hours earlier. We were in the back parlor of 1733. It was the first time we had been alone since he'd blurted out those impossible, inevitable words, though I'd been looking for a moment of privacy and he had too. The furtiveness had already begun.

This time he didn't blurt out the words. The man whom I'd never seen at a loss for the right phrase, who in later years would explain complicated issues of economics and social policy and war in terms any child could understand, had trouble finding the right words for this. I was glad. Love should never trip off the tongue easily.

He managed to get the words out, and then the world went quiet. We were standing on opposite sides of Eleanor's desk, and the light filtering in from the garden lit half his face and left the other in shadow. It was as if someone had drawn a line down his features, separating light from dark, but the expression on both sides was the same. His ocean-blue eyes had turned black with bad weather. His mouth was sharp as the edge of a knife. When he told me he'd meant what he'd said that night, his voice was so solemn that if he had been speaking another language, one I didn't understand, I would have thought he was talking of death. So he knew what he was saying, and asking.

I would live a shadow life. *When he had a moment. If he could get away.* I would not even have the solace of church. The memory of the last time I'd taken Communion came over me like homesickness.

The silence went on. I was trying to make sense of the situation, as if there were sense to such a thing. In two weeks I would be twenty-six. Beyond that, the future was a dream that would never happen. Worse than that, it was a lie. From where I stood the day America went to war, *when he had a moment, if he could get away* was enough.

Later he told me he knew what he was asking too. He thought of his friend Livy Davis, and his cousin Alice's husband Nick Longworth, and his half-nephew Taddy, whom he'd never forgiven for disgracing the family, and hated himself for being like them, even while he stood there half crazy with glee. That was why what happened next turned out as it did.

The parquet in the hall creaked under footsteps. Eleanor's voice came winging toward us. "Franklin." It flew into the room and darted this way and that. "Franklin."

"I'm sorry," he murmured. "I never should have," he said. "It's not fair to—"

The words were meant to push me away. They tugged me closer. A man might lie about love, but he could not fake honor. At that moment I would have done anything he asked. But Eleanor appeared in the doorway, and we took a step away from each other and turned to her, and I knew what that meant. All he was asking, all I was agreeing to, was that we behave well.

～ I went out of my way to avoid him, then lurked in the parlor listening for his step and straining for his laughter and praying he would come looking for me. The possibility of him made me move through the house like a thief. Things—his gloves, his bowler hat, a book he'd just put aside—sprang into my hands. I lived in fear that someone would come in and find me touching them. It was fortunate Mr. Howe had not yet given him the cigarette holder that became his hallmark. I could not have kept it from my lips. I began leaving the Decatur later in the morning in hope that he'd be gone when I reached 1733, then found myself racing around DuPont Circle and down N Street to hear a snatch of his conversation or catch a glimpse of his back swaggering toward Connecticut Avenue. One minute I wanted him to be happy, the next I hoped he was suffering as much as I was.

The war should have helped. I was busy. He was seldom around. When he did come home for lunch, he brought people with him. I would hear Eleanor making the arrangements. There would be four or six or ten, admirals and administrators and businessmen and labor leaders. The servants were to take the platters of food from the dumbwaiter which carried them up from the kitchen, serve them, and depart, closing the doors behind them. It was the only way, she explained to me, that Mr. Roosevelt could keep his secrets.

One afternoon, when he arrived home with guests while I was still at work, I waited until I heard the sliding doors to the dining room roll closed. Then I hurried down the hall toward the front door. As I lifted my hat off the hall stand, I heard his voice.

"Congress will appropriate the money eventually, so I'm just getting a head start by authorizing the expenditures."

"You're lucky you're not behind bars," another voice said.

"I may still be, if anyone finds out about it before Congress gets around to the appropriations."

His laughter came barreling down the hall like a steamroller. It wasn't forced or false like my own laughter with Eleanor and Mama and the gentlemen I turned my face to at dinner night after night, but the genuine article.

In the years since, I have heard people speak of Franklin's cruelty. Some of his closest advisers have said he never minded making others uncomfortable. One or two so-called admirers have even used the word *sadistic*. I never agreed with them. And I'm sure he didn't intend to make me unhappy then. He didn't even know I was in the house. But standing in the hall, staring into the bleached mask that had become my reflection, I did not understand how he could laugh when I was so miserable.

✍ Then something happened that changed everything. It's odd to think now that Eleanor's conscience absolved Franklin's and mine.

The family was still at breakfast when I arrived that morning. Once again, I'd dawdled at the apartment, then hurried to get to 1733 before he left. As I made my way past the open sliding doors to the dining room, he called out.

"Come and have a cup of coffee with us, Miss Mercer."

The words stopped me. I didn't know if he was giving in to temptation or had passed beyond its reach.

"While we still have coffee," he added. "My missus is on a rationing crusade."

It had become a continuing joke. While Eleanor was constantly trying to conserve food for the war effort, Mrs. James was still sending milk and eggs and asparagus and chickens by train from the Place every week. She'd been sending Franklin home-raised food since he'd gone away to Groton. She'd still be sending it when the chicks went off to boarding school and college. Perhaps that was one reason for Franklin's powerful connection to the Hudson River Valley. Its soil and sun and air were the stuff of his blood and bones and flesh. The family was grateful for her shipments. Even guests were grateful. Springwood strawberries were heavenly. The cream was thick as sin.

"Yes, do come in, Miss Mercer." Eleanor's voice fluttered the way it did when she was trying to be gracious to Mr. Howe.

I stepped into the room. I had no choice. Eleanor sat at one end of the table, presiding over the coffee urn and small silver bell that summoned the maid, Franklin at the other. Anna and James were on one side, Elliott and Mr. Howe were across from them. Mr. Howe was lighting one Sweet Caporal from another. As he inhaled, the ashes dribbled into his coffee. He didn't call me the lovely Miss Mercer. He didn't even glance in my direction. I should have guessed then what he was capable of.

"We've even saved a place for you." Franklin nodded toward the empty chair between Anna and James. A linen place mat was set with silver and china and a napkin tucked neatly into a ring.

I moved toward it. As I said, I had no choice. I pulled out the chair. The chicks began to giggle.

Franklin lifted his head and peered down at them through his pince-nez. "May I ask what is so funny?" His voice was stern, but they knew he was teasing.

"Miss Mercer can't sit there," Anna said.

"Why not?"

"Because that's for Mr. Hoover," James explained.

"Mr. Hoover is joining us for breakfast?" Franklin asked.

The children turned toward Eleanor. The rest of us followed.

"Please sit down, Miss Mercer." For a while she'd called me Lucy when we were alone, but lately she'd reverted to Miss Mercer.

I slid into the chair.

"Miss Mercer is sitting in Mr. Hoover's seat," Elliott said with a giggle.

"I wish someone would let me in on the joke," Franklin said.

Eleanor looked down the table at him, good intentions lighting her eyes, earnestness straining her shirtwaist. "The idea came to me as I was passing the White House yesterday afternoon. When I noticed the sheep on the lawn, the ones that were brought in to free the gardeners for war work. That and the victory garden."

"We already have a victory garden," Franklin said, "not to mention an abysmal absence of bacon and abundance of cornbread. It's lucky Anna's too young to be a bride." He winked at his daughter. Anna beamed. "I played golf with Mr. Hoover the other day, and he let slip that his Food Administration is thinking of banning rice at weddings."

"It's more than what we do," Eleanor went on. "It's how we feel. The empty place is to remind the children, to remind all of us, that while we think we're making sacrifices by eating meat only once a day or giving up teatime, thousands of Europeans are starving. It's to remind us not only of our good fortune but of others' misery." She smiled the beautiful smile that revealed not only her unfortunate teeth but her huge heart.

Since that morning I have met other women like Eleanor, women who are unable to give themselves over to pleasure, who are always on the *qui vive* for moral lapses in themselves and those they love. The breed is not rare. But I have never known anyone who turned her personal unhappiness to so much public good. That is Eleanor's true greatness, and even then I was beginning to sense it.

"If you think it's foolish, Franklin, I won't continue to do it."

"I think it's a grand idea," he said. "Absolutely grand."

He smiled at her. She relaxed a little, but only a little. Eleanor's shoulders rarely came in contact with the back of a chair. And I took the seat intended to remind us of all the suffering in the world and knew I was not wrong for Franklin.

∾ I had made my decision. Franklin had too, though I wasn't sure of that at the time. He'd silenced the echoes in his head, not only the enticements of the reprobates like his friend Livy, and his cousin Nick Longworth, and poor Taddy, for whom he now felt a new sympathy, but the censure of the men at the other end of the spectrum, like his father and his cousin Ted and old Peabo, as the boys called the Reverend Endicott Peabody.

Franklin hadn't had an easy time at Groton. He'd come two years later than the other boys in his form because his father was elderly and ill and his mother couldn't bear to part with him. As a result, he was always trying to measure up and catch up, though it seems to me all anyone had to do to see his superiority was look. But he was happy there too. More than that, he was formed. Years later Franklin told me that at odd moments throughout his life, old Peabo would loom up before him, just as he used to stand above the boys in chapel, and Franklin would hear the words *duty* and *honor* and *God* and *country* as only the rector could pronounce them, and see the world spread out before him as sharp and clear and simple as a medieval map.

It hadn't been easy to silence the Reverend Peabody, who believed in chastity as well as duty and honor and God and country, but Franklin finally had. His problem then was what to do about it. He wasn't as experienced as he pretended. How shabby it would have been if he were.

Secretary Daniels was the one who showed the way. Later Franklin would laugh at the irony. Mr. Daniels was so determined to stamp out sin he'd not only banned alcohol in the officers' mess, but he'd also stopped the navy from passing out certain preventive packets for shore leave. Franklin told me about the secretary's puritanical streak, but there was one thing he didn't mention. When Mr. Daniels's brother-in-law, who had bailed him out of financial problems several times in the past, confided he wanted to divorce his wife and marry another woman, the secretary fired him from the family newspaper and drove him from the state of North Carolina. I imagine Franklin didn't want me to worry about his position.

The secretary's memo was the first thing Franklin saw when he walked into his office that morning.

From: SECNAV
To: ASTNAV

Is there any law that says a yeoman must be a man?

Franklin didn't dictate an answer. He went straight down the hall to the secretary's office and told him there wasn't a reason in the world. In view of the manpower shortage, he added, they ought to start enrolling women immediately. Ten days later I reported to the Navy Yard.

I'd expected Mama to disapprove, but by then the society pages were studded with announcements of ladies joining one auxiliary corps or another. A certain patriotic matron boasted that she already had three different uniforms in her closet. One would be more than enough for me. I had never seen anything as ugly as that lady yeoman's suit. The skirt was too short to be fashionable and too long to be flattering. The baggy jacket with a loose belt made a halfhearted and unsuccessful attempt at a Norfolk look. The hats were flat blue sailor models that sat on the top of the head like dinner plates. I dreaded having Franklin see me in the uniform.

At seven o'clock on a sun-buttered June morning, I reported for my physical examination. No well-bred young lady would have subjected herself to the process except for patriotism, or love. They stripped us of our stockings, stays, everything. I hugged the regulation gown around me, but there was no way to cover my bare legs. The woman in front of me was close to tears from embarrassment.

"If you think this is bad, dearie," the matron snapped at her, "try a trench in Flanders."

I must have filled out a dozen forms. Now I understood Franklin's complaints about red tape. It was after eleven by the time I reached the small alcove where one of the doctors sat. A few wisps of white hair lay plastered to the shiny dome of his head. Dead eyes lurked under heavy lids. I was glad. I would have hated going through this in the hands of a young doctor with good looks and a silken bedside manner.

The thought reminded me of Dr. Marbury. Bill, as Violetta now referred to him. I'd gotten a letter from her a few days earlier. Bill had asked for her hand in marriage. "I know you have had reservations about him," she wrote, though I'd never expressed any. "But any flaws you suspect are the result of the war, not the reflection of his character. If you have not lived through war, Lucy, you cannot understand the despair of it. But he says I have saved him from that, which is another reason I love him."

It was an old story, a troubled man saved by the love of a good woman, but I didn't realize that at the time, any more than I guessed that my own situation, a young girl risking all for love, was just as much of a cliché. I'm glad I didn't. I'm glad neither of us did, despite what happened later, to me, and to Vio. Cynicism is the coward's armor.

I had sat reading Vio's letter and wondering what she would think if she knew. She was older by two years, and the difference made for a small but lingering habit of protection. She might warn me or pity me, but she would never blame me. That was one thing I knew for certain.

"Next." The word came out of the dead-eyed navy doctor's mouth as a massive yawn. The cold metal of the stethoscope raised goosebumps on my flesh. The wooden depressor scraped my tongue. The doctor's breath, as he peered into my eyes, was sour. I welcomed the small indignities as if they were penance for the sin I knew I was going to commit.

✍ Nine

"There came to light during this time a register from a motel in Virginia Beach showing that father and Lucy had checked in as man and wife and spent the night."

✍ James Roosevelt, *My Parents: A Differing View*

A week later I received my orders. Mama got to the mail first, brought me the envelope, and stood there as I tore it open.

Yeoman (F) Lucy Page Mercer, Serial No. 1160, will report to the office of the assistant secretary of the navy at eight hundred hours on the morning of June 24, 1917.

"It seems you are destined," Mama said, "to spend your life with the Roosevelts. We can only hope there will be other gentlemen, eligible gentlemen, on the premises."

✍ I had never been in Franklin's office. I had seen his bedroom, his and Eleanor's. I had glimpsed his silver-backed hairbrush, and his leather cufflink box, and the old-fashioned straight razor he used to the end of his life. I had noticed piles of his stiff white shirts and even his underwear on the way from laundry to armoire. But his office was another side of him, perhaps even closer to his core, and the intimacy of it thrilled me.

I had an impression of walls covered with nautical prints and maps, and ship models on every surface, and a carved mantel cresting a flower-filled fireplace, but it was only an impression, because no matter where I tried to look, my eyes went back to Franklin. He was sitting behind a large cluttered desk in his shirtsleeves. My fingers imagined the fabric. I was not a lady.

He stood, reached for his jacket, and slipped into it. "Thank you, McCarthy," he said, and his secretary turned, left the room, and closed the door behind him.

Neither of us moved. Later I realized he was giving me a last chance. I could tell him he had misunderstood. I wanted to serve, not surrender. Or I could try to negotiate terms. But he hadn't misunderstood, and I was incapable of negotiating with him. I would not haggle about love.

He said he'd heard of a place in Virginia Beach. There was not a chance in the world of our running into anyone we knew. I didn't doubt him. I had never been to a roadside cabin. I don't think I knew anyone who had.

I almost lost my courage on the drive. I tried to look at the scenery. I even tried to make out the billboards in the darkness. All I saw was an image of Eleanor and me as we stood shoulder to shoulder at her desk. All I heard above the wind was the shriek of the chicks as Franklin bounded from bed to bed shouting are you snug as a bug in a rug.

I gave up on the scenery and the billboards. I turned to Franklin. His face carved a white profile out of the night. The image of Eleanor faded. The squeals of the chicks died.

At one point he looked over at me and opened his mouth, then closed it again without speaking. Franklin speechless was someone I did not know. A moment later, he glanced over again. This time he spoke.

"Are you sure?" he asked, and I loved him even more for the question.

A little while later he spoke again. "I'll leave, Lucy. Really I will. We'll be married."

The wind snatched the words away before I could grab on to them.

I waited in the Stutz while he went in to register. I wondered what name he was using. Not his own, certainly. Odd, to think that I was taking the most momentous step of my life, that I was, possibly, throwing away my life, under an alias I did not even know. I had put myself in his hands.

He came back, helped me out of the Stutz, and reached back for the small overnight bags. I caught a glimpse of his face in the lights of a passing automobile. His mouth was a sliver of determination. His eyes were hooded. This was what he must look like when he was alone. The thought thrilled me.

He took my elbow with his free hand, and we started down the path. We reached number thirteen. I was surprised. He'd forgotten his superstitiousness. He put down the bags, took a key from his pocket, and opened the door. A light from another passing auto rolled through the room. In the moment before it went dark again, I saw a cave of tawdriness.

I stepped into it. He followed and closed the door behind us. We were in darkness. He switched on a lamp. The room was even uglier than I'd thought. A cheap dresser lurked against one wall. A chair, greasy with other people's lives, reproached us. In the center of the room a double bed, sagging under a balding chenille spread, dared us to look at it, or away.

We were on opposite sides of the room now. I could feel him watching me.

"Do you want to leave?" he asked, as if a chair or a lamp or the rest of the world could undo us.

I shook my head no, though I still couldn't look at him. My eyes were on the floor. A black crack ran like a fault line across the worn linoleum. He took a step across it. I met him halfway, as he knew I would.

1917–1918

ɝ Ten

Daylight saving time was still almost a year away—President Wilson would not sign the bill putting it into effect until the spring of 1918—but the afternoons lingered longer that summer, and when evening finally came, the sunsets blushed violet with shame for blotting out the astonished blue sky. On the streets automobile horns played Bach and Vivaldi, and startled horses danced to a ragtime beat.

I was an infant opening my eyes to the world. I had never seen colors before. Even white was new. I remember the snowy glare of Franklin's shirt as he sat, jacketless, behind his big desk, and the gleaming slice of smile in his sun-browned face when he looked up and realized it was my fingers that had

knocked on the open door to his office. I no longer worried
about his seeing me in my dowdy yeoman's uniform. His eyes,
as astonished as the sky that summer, looked through it and
made me shiver.

I walked to work each morning as if I were marching down
an aisle, but more rapidly. When I turned the corner and
caught sight of that big granite wedding cake of a building
that was the State, War, and Navy, I could barely keep from
breaking into a run. Franklin was inside.

We saw each other constantly. If there was a message for the
ASTNAV, I managed to be in line to deliver it. If he needed an
extra clerk in his office—I was sorry now I hadn't taken that
course and become a typewriter—he told Mr. McCarthy to
request Yeoman Mercer. If Mr. McCarthy suspected anything,
he was too good a secretary to give any sign. When Franklin
and I passed in the wide marble halls, our bodies strained
toward each other, and we had to lean in the other direction,
like sailors on the deck of a ship, to keep our balance.

"Miss Mercer," he'd pronounce as we came abreast of each
other, his voice grave, his smile secret.

"Sir," I'd answer slyly.

And all the while officers and officials and clerks, whose
ordinary loveless state almost broke my heart, walked right
on by. The building churned with excitement, and sometimes
I had to remind myself that all those busy bodies were waging a war, not celebrating our happiness. No one had a right
to be as happy as we were.

We met socially as well. Alice Longworth invited her
cousins and me to dinner on the same evening. Even then I
knew she did not do it out of kindness. Senator Borah was
there too, his dinner clothes rumpled, his cleft chin making
him look as if the devil had taken a piece out of his fleshy all-

American face. He gave Alice his arm to go in to dinner with an air of perfect hypocrisy, and she took it with a wicked grin that made me think of another of her dinners. I hadn't been invited to that one, but Eleanor had told me about it. "One of the ladies had a cocktail, two glasses of whiskey and soda, several liqueurs, and fifteen cigarettes, all before I left at ten-fifteen," she'd said the next morning. "I'm glad I'm not so fashionable."

At the time I'd found her comment overly fastidious. Mama smoked cigarettes. And I was not a prude. Now, improbable as it seems, I found myself on Eleanor's side. And it wasn't only the sight of Alice swanning in to dinner on the arm of her lover that offended me. Her friend Cissy Patterson was among the guests. The gossip about Mrs. Patterson and Nicholas Longworth caught *in flagrante* at another of Alice's dinners had just begun to die. The same rumor mill said Mrs. Patterson had also had an affair with Senator Borah, but while Alice had yielded her husband, she had fought for, and held, the senator. Until that night I hadn't paid much attention to the stories. They were a little too juicy to be reliable, and in any event, they had nothing to do with me. But standing in the silk and damask drawing room of the Longworth house, I knew they did have something to do with me. I was one of them. That was why Alice had invited me.

Alice started toward the dining room set with family crystal and silver and china. I was worse than they were, from a practical if not a moral standpoint. Unlike Alice, I did not have a husband. Unlike Mrs. Patterson, I was not heir to a newspaper empire or protected by a former husband's European title. I was an unmarried young lady who went out to earn her living. The rules about that were clear. I would pay.

I saw Franklin approaching. Alice had seated us beside each

other, of course. I felt a moment of panic. He reached my side
and gave me his arm. I took it, and the world fell into place.
Alice and Senator Borah and Nick Longworth and Mrs. Patterson were having affairs. Franklin and I were in love.

What of Eleanor during all this? If I thought Alice's going
in to dinner on her lover's arm under her husband's and his
mistress's noses was indecent, how did I manage to meet
Eleanor's level gaze over her cousin's centerpiece that night?
How had I stood beside her at the meeting of the Patriotic
Economy League as we signed pledges to dress simply, and
save food, and curtail unnecessary spending, while I was asking her to give up more than luxuries? How did I go on sitting
next to her on Saturday mornings as we passed out wool to
the ladies of the Navy League and took in the scarves and
socks and sweaters they'd knitted the previous week? Had I
no shame? Obviously not. Had I no sympathy? Too much.
Every time I looked at her I wanted to weep. Not because her
husband was in love with another woman, or the social secretary she'd treated with kindness was repaying her with
betrayal, but because she was not part of the exquisite equa-
tion that was Franklin and me.

Did she know? Did she even suspect? She has written that
the bottom dropped out of her particular world. She has confided in friends who confessed to the world that she could forgive but not forget. But that was *after*. What were her
thoughts that summer when auto horns played baroque music
and horses danced in the street? What was she thinking when
she spoke to me cordially and smiled self-consciously and
treated me with the same unfailing kindness? If she was suspicious or angry, why did she invite me for dinner one evening
a week after Alice's party when she was short a lady? She
seated me beside Livy Davis, but if anything that was a vote

of confidence. She believed Livy needed handling. She wasn't entirely wrong, but I will not speak ill of Livy, not after what happened. It's easy to condemn human weakness, until you feel the brush of its broken wing against your own skin. The only sign Eleanor gave of knowing, or at least fearing, was the first weekend cruise aboard the *Sylph*. It was not like Eleanor to be late. It was even less like her to make a dramatic entrance.

Franklin had requisitioned the motor yacht that had once served Presidents McKinley and Taft and "Uncle Ted" for the weekend and invited a few friends, including my "beau" Nigel Law, for a cruise on the Chesapeake. He must have asked Eleanor to come along, though he and I never spoke of her. It was delicacy, but it was more than that. When we were together, she ceased to exist. But Eleanor must have refused to go. How could she spend a weekend cruising a clement bay when on the other side of the ocean war raged, and men died, and women and children starved?

On Saturday morning we set out from the Navy Yard without her. The air was sticky and the sky bleached a pearly gray, but the sun was already burning holes in the fog, and a light breeze, which is the most one can expect on the Chesapeake at that time of year, made cats' paws on the water. Franklin was ebullient. Water was his element. Later it would become his curse, and his salvation. But the morning we set out on the *Sylph*, his spirits were high, and since Franklin's joy was infectious, everyone else in the party was delighted too.

An hour or so after the crew had cast off the lines and we'd motored out of the harbor, Franklin appeared on the afterdeck and announced that his missus had decided to join us after all. The *Sylph* would stop at Indian Head, and she'd come out in a launch.

I was disappointed for myself, but I felt sorry for Eleanor. I knew how much she hated being on the water. She was always afraid she'd get seasick and disgrace herself in front of Franklin. And she'd never gotten over being handed off a sinking ocean liner when she was a child. But half an hour later there she was in the motor launch, her back, as she bounced over the waves, arrow straight, her hand clamped on her straw hat to keep the wind from whisking it away, her unhappy determination growing steadily clearer as the launch drew closer to the boat and the land fell away behind her. So perhaps she suspected something after all. Why else would she waste a weekend being uncomfortable among people having fun when she could have been happy doing good for people who knew nothing but misery?

꩜ She kept postponing her departure for Campo. By the first week in July, I began to think she would remain in town all summer. She was devoted to her war work, and there were U-boat scares off the coast of Maine again. Even Franklin said that though it was five hundred to one against the possibility, there was still the chance the Boche would do the fool thing and try to shell Eastport. Then, halfway through July, when the sun seared the rest of the city and thunderstorms brought rain but no relief to people who were not in love, in a procession of three dozen trunks and boxes and barrels, Eleanor and the chicks left for Campo.

I was glad for her. She'd be happier in the only house she called her own. I could imagine her there thanks to the family photographs. I envisioned her perched on the wooden railing of the long porch or sitting on the wide steps leading down to the grass. I saw her at the water's edge with her aunt Maud, their long white skirts lifted to their knees, their feet leaving

imprints in the cool sand; and with a group of friends pic-
nicking on the beach; and with Mrs. James and Anna on
Franklin's boat, the *Half Moon*. He sold it later that summer,
though it broke his heart because he loved that sailboat—he
told me this the night he signed the papers turning it over to
the navy to use in its campaign against German U-boats—as
much as he'd ever loved anything. Then he stopped and
turned to me and added, "Almost."

There was another photograph from Campo that came to
mind when I imagined Eleanor there that summer. In it she
and Franklin are on a blanket spread on a rocky beach just
below a dune. Behind them picnic hampers and a straw hat
and a couple of books lay scattered. Half sitting, half reclin-
ing with her back propped against his, she is turned away
from the camera so her face can be seen only in profile, but
the smile playing around her mouth is unmistakable. He is
lying on his side, his back to hers, his eyes closed, his body
curled like a contented comma. She's wearing a white dress,
and he's in a white shirt and trousers, and it is almost impossible to tell where one of them stops and the other begins. The
photograph, like the thought of Eleanor herself, made me
want to weep.

With Eleanor and the chicks gone, Franklin stayed even
later at his office. On the nights he did, I did too. I was no
longer shy in the big high-ceilinged room with Mr. Wilson's
commission and charts of ocean routes hanging on the walls,
and models of ships and a bust of John Paul Jones on the mantel over the fireplace. A bouquet of fresh flowers always filled
the hearth that summer, and in front of it lay a thick Turkish
carpet. One night we both looked up and found Admiral
Jones looking down on us with his impassive bronze gaze.

"I feel," Franklin said, "like the *Bon Homme Richard*." He

rolled the *r* in the French way, and the sound in his chest rumbled in my ear like an earthquake.

"The *Bon Homme Richard*?" I asked.

"Afire."

I lifted my head and looked at him. "Didn't the *Bon
Homme* sink?"

"Only after Jones—his real name was John Paul; he added
Jones after he killed a mutinous sailor in self-defense—
boarded the *Serapis* and made the enemy ship his own." His
smile glinted in the faint light of one electric lamp.

Sometimes we went to the Raleigh roof to dine. I was wary
of being seen together in public, but he insisted, as he had the
first night we'd danced, that there was no better way to hide
than in plain sight. So we sat in the soft summer darkness
while a baby's breath of breeze skipped over my hot cheeks
and ruffled the fine hair on the back of his beautiful hands.
The orchestra played the songs that were new that year,
"Whose Little Heart Are You Breaking Now?" and "Send Me
Away with a Smile" and "Love Will Find A Way," and though
it was too hot to dance, Franklin pushed back his chair and
came around the table and pulled mine out for me, and we
moved onto the floor. One hand came home to the small of
my back, and the fingers of the other tangled with mine, and
his legs singed the rough fabric of the uniform I'd thought
he'd hate.

We believed we were a secret, but people must have known
or suspected or even approved, because they kept inviting us
to the same dinners and luncheons and weekends. There were
more invitations from Alice Longworth, and though I didn't
like her air of conspiracy, I suffered it to spend the evening
with Franklin. Other hostesses were more subtle. When Edith
Eustis invited us to dinner, no illicit undercurrents seeped

through the rooms of her beautiful Corcoran House. She always seated me next to Franklin, but I remember one night when she put her brother-in-law, Mr. Winthrop Rutherfurd, on my other side. It was, she told me, the first time he'd dined out since his wife's death, and as I turned from Franklin to him and back to Franklin with each changing course, I felt criminal for our happiness in the face of poor Mr. Rutherfurd's loss of it.

Mr. Howe was furious. At the time I thought he disapproved for all the conventional reasons. Now I know his objection was more personal. He saw his dream of putting Franklin in the White House foundering on mine. He tried to stop us. He dogged Franklin's steps more closely than ever. Though he rarely looked at me, I could sense that he never stopped watching me. But he was no match for Franklin. "Go home, Ludwig," he'd say, "before your missus forgets what you look like."

"She remembers, boss. That's why she ain't eager to have me around."

But Franklin would find something for him to do, and it would not be a trumped-up task either. There was always a labor leader who had to be sweet-talked, as they called it, or a contract that had to be negotiated, or someone who had to be dressed down, which Franklin couldn't do because, he always insisted, he was too much of a softy, and poor Mr. Howe would go off leaving his lifelong dream in the notoriously careless hands of two people in love.

✐ A week after Eleanor left, Franklin requisitioned the *Sylph* again. This time he invited the Munns—Mary Munn and I ran Eleanor's wool Saturdays for the Navy League in her absence—and the Graysons—Dr. Grayson was the president's physician; his wife Altrude was Mrs. Wilson's ward—and of course my "beau," Nigel Law.

There was no fog to burn off that Saturday morning. A warm wind herded cumulus clouds, docile as sheep, across a clear blue sky. The *Sylph,* a blaze of blinding white hull and gleaming teak decks, bobbed lazily in the water while the crew made ready to cast off. The current was with us, and land fell away swiftly.

We dropped anchor to swim four times that afternoon, and the air that had grown still over the Chesapeake rang with squeals of delight.

On Sunday Franklin inspected the fleet, and lunched with Admiral Rodgers on the *Arkansas,* and was all spit and polish and solemnity. He worried about preparedness and complained about "old lady" officers, and if I hadn't known better, I would have thought he'd forgotten I was along. I didn't mind. I loved this Franklin too, his dedication, and his brilliance, and the way other men shrank an inch or two merely by standing at his side.

In the afternoon we made our way up the James to Richmond and went ashore to see some of the old houses. As we were going through one of them, the sky split with lightning, and thunder rumbled overhead, and a torrent of rain trapped us inside. The wrath of God, someone in the group joked, and Franklin caught my eye. We knew joy like ours could not displease God.

At dinner on the afterdeck Sunday night, Mrs. Grayson teased Franklin about the sumptuous meal. "Obviously the assistant secretary of the navy hasn't heard of meatless and wheatless days," she said.

No one spoke for a moment. The only sounds were of water slapping against the hull and wood groaning. Mary

Munn shifted in her deck chair. Even the unflappable Nigel
Law looked uncomfortable. We had all read or heard about
Eleanor's interview, which had run in the *New York Times* the
week before. Since the war, she'd told a lady reporter, the family of Assistant Secretary of the Navy Franklin D. Roosevelt
ate meat only once a day. Luncheon was a mere two courses,
dinner a meager three. And the servants were encouraged to
keep a watchful eye on the wasteful habits of one another.
"Making the ten servants help me do my saving has not only
been possible but highly profitable," she had said, or so the
reporter had written. Heaven only knows where the number
ten came from.

"Haven't heard of meatless and wheatless days?" Franklin
boomed, and the tension shattered. "I'm the leading exponent
of the New Household Economy for Millionaires. I get
telegrams of congratulation and requests for further details
from Pittsburgh, New Orleans, San Francisco, and other
neighboring cities. Don't you love it! Don't you just love it!"

But he didn't. He hated it. In her naïveté about the ways of
the world, and of newspaper reporters, and her determination
to do good, Eleanor had made a fool of herself, and of
Franklin. That was another reason I pitied her. It was like the
empty chair for Mr. Hoover. Her intentions were admirable,
but her hand was heavy, and if there was one thing Franklin
admired, if there was one thing Franklin needed, it was a light
touch.

∽ He didn't try to keep the weekend cruise a secret. He
wrote Eleanor about it. I know because I have read the letter
in the collection of his correspondence which Eleanor and
Elliott have just published. He called it a "bully" trip. "Such
a funny party," he wrote, "but it worked out *wonderfully*.

The Charlie Munns, the Cary Graysons, Lucy Mercer and Nigel Law, and they got on splendidly."

I picture Franklin sitting at his big desk under the unwavering gaze of John Paul Jones, his shirt white against his weekend-browned face, the fabric clinging to his hot back. I see him fold the letter and put it in the envelope. And I imagine his thoughts. He is no longer hiding in plain sight. He needs to declare me, as I do him. And I know our future is determined.

But then, sitting in my garden all these years later, I read the next entry in his published letters.

Dearest Babs,

Yesterday I wrote you all about our trip but posted the letter in our corner box which was marked "Paint" and it occurs to me too late that perhaps the postman will hesitate to open it.

And now after all these years I recognize that a different future was bearing down on us.

ꝫ Eleven

"Remember I *count* on seeing you on the 26th. My threat was
no idle one."   ꝫ Eleanor Roosevelt in a letter to Franklin D.
Roosevelt, August 1917

"*You* are entirely disconnected and Lucy Mercer and Mrs.
Munn are closing up the loose ends."

ꝫ Franklin D. Roosevelt in a letter to Eleanor
Roosevelt, September 9, 1917

I knew as soon as Mr. Howe walked into the office that
morning that something was wrong. I can't remember how I
knew. Beneath his straw hat, so battered it looked as if some
animal had been gnawing on the brim, he wore his usual dour
expression. He took a lighter from his pocket, snapped it
open, and held it against a limp cigarette. His eyes pierced the
smoke and settled on me for a fraction of a second. Perhaps
that was how I knew something was wrong.

"The boss is in the hospital." His glance veered to me
again, then away.

I bent my head over the papers I was filing, while my mind
careened through a horror house of possibilities. There had

121

been no reports of an infantile paralysis epidemic so far this summer. It couldn't be his appendix; he'd had that out two years earlier. I remembered the gun he'd carried for several days a few months ago when navy intelligence had reported a German plot on his life. The threat had terrified me. The gun, not a gentleman's hunting rifle but a menacing snub-nosed little piece of machinery, had been even more chilling.

"A throat infection," Mr. Howe said, and began to cough.

"Does he want visitors?" Mr. McCarthy asked.

There was a moment's pause. This time Mr. Howe looked directly at me. "Mrs. Roosevelt arrived from Campo this morning. The rest of us are, as the French say, *de trop*."

For the first time that summer, I stopped pitying Eleanor.

⌒ Mr. Howe had exaggerated. All of us were not *de trop*. He was in and out of Franklin's hospital room half a dozen times a day. He carried papers from the office there, and decisions and signatures and medical reports back.

"It seems like if there's a germ in the room, it just naturally makes a beeline for the boss. One of the docs has the crackpot idea that it's because the boss wasn't exposed to enough germs when he was a boy. Living alone in that big house, not going to school with other kids, not building up what he calls immunities. Can you beat that?"

I hoped Franklin would find a way to get word to me from the hospital, but he never managed to. At the time I was disappointed, but it occurs to me now that if neither of us had ever put pen to paper, if we'd done without the *Dearests* and the *All-my-loves* and the words between, Eleanor would have reached into his suitcase that night and come up empty-handed, and my life, and Franklin's, might have turned out differently. But then so might the history of America, and the entire world, in the twentieth century.

∽ The trouble started with another letter. I recognized the familiar Campo address when Mama handed me the envelope across the breakfast table that morning. We were living in a small apartment at the Toronto by then, another outpost of genteel poverty that wasn't appreciably different from the Decatur, only now we were paying thirty-five dollars a month. Washington was swollen with war workers, and living space was at a premium, but Mama had wanted to move. She still associated the fresh paint of a new apartment with a fresh start.

Mama was using the silver letter knife, so I tore the envelope open with my finger. As I took out the single sheet of stationery, another piece of paper fluttered to the floor. I bent to pick it up. It was a check.

At first I didn't understand. I still helped Eleanor with her social obligations on occasion, but I hadn't done anything recently. The only task I'd taken on since she'd left was the wool Saturdays. Once a week Mary Munn and I handed out yarn to the ladies and took in the pieces they'd knitted the previous week. It was charity work, my contribution to the war effort, as Eleanor knew perfectly well, and even that was likely to end soon in view of the struggle going on between Secretary Daniels and the head of the Navy League, which the secretary implied was nothing more than a bunch of shipbuilding war profiteers. Two grown, supposedly intelligent men had gotten into a spat about who would be allowed to collect sweaters and socks and scarves for the soon-to-be-freezing American doughboys and foreign soldiers and helpless women and children.

I sat looking at the check. That was when it struck me.

Eleanor was saying that I was the kind of woman who took money for acts other women performed for purer motives. There was a word for women like that. I hadn't known it when the nun had scolded me about my lingerie at the convent school in Austria, but I knew it now.

Mama looked up from her mail. "What's that?"

"Just another letter about the Navy League Comforts Committee," I said and stuffed the letter and the check back in the envelope.

I didn't tell Franklin about the check. I was too ashamed. And I knew he would not want to hear. I'd seen him when Eleanor and his mother turned to him to settle a disagreement between them. Harry Houdini could not have extricated himself more skillfully.

The check sat in the top drawer of my dresser, nestled among my handkerchiefs, all week. I had no intention of keeping it, but I didn't want to send it back in anger. I would not give Eleanor that satisfaction. I preferred to let her think I had missed the point.

I waited till Mama was asleep to write the letter. I did not want her coming in and glancing over my shoulder. I thought she wouldn't understand why I could not accept the check. I was sure I could not tell her. I know now that I underestimated Mama. Because she said nothing, I thought she knew nothing. It never occurred to me that she'd guessed everything and still remained silent, because years ago she had been married to one man and in love with another, and, despite everything that had happened since, could still remember what that had felt like. I never dreamed that though she was worried about my future, she was a little in love with my present.

"My dear Mrs. Roosevelt," I began. The pen scratched noisily against the paper. I imagined the sound radiating out from the small circle of light cast by the desk lamp through the dark apartment and into the summer night. I pictured Franklin sleeping a few blocks away in the moonglow that spilled through his open window and turned his beautiful body silver. I could be gracious in my letter. I could be generous.

"It is shocking to think your letter has been on my desk a week—and unanswered."

In the privacy of my imagination, Franklin stretched and turned. His elegant foot tangled in the sheet he'd kicked off.

"Of course, you are mistress of the situation and I must abide by your wishes! I am only too sorry to have been unbusinesslike for I know that is annoying.

"I regret too that I must return the cheque for subtraction and give you more trouble as the two last wooley parties were not held . . ."

Franklin reached out in his sleep. He was dreaming of me.

". . . according to the Assistant Secretary's instructions—and on the 21st of July I was not there! I have not written you about it all as I knew you would hear at first hand. I went for a little while last Saturday to answer questions and list what came in—and to tell the dear ladies the distribution would in all probability be resumed.(?) Poor dears, they are so distressed!"

I sat deliberating how to sign it. Franklin's sigh floated through the open window and wrapped itself around me.

"Affectionately,

Lucy Page Mercer"

The next morning when I arrived at the State, War, and Navy, Franklin was already sitting behind his big desk, stripped down to his shirtsleeves. Poor Eleanor.

∾ It is always dangerous to think we have had the last word. Two mornings later Mama handed me another envelope postmarked Campobello. I felt the air hissing out of the day ahead.

"I know you have done far more work than I could pay for," Eleanor wrote. The stationery was crisp, but the check was limp and wrinkled. What appeared to be a fingerprint stained one corner. For some reason the sight of it reminded me of that night at Alice Longworth's when Senator Borah had taken her in to dinner.

This time I did not wait to return the check. I fired it off with another letter that morning, though I was fairly sure Eleanor would send it back a third time. Like the conflict dragging on across the ocean, this was a war of attrition.

Then Eleanor surprised me, Eleanor and Franklin both, though I should have anticipated their actions. I'd spent a great deal of time with her. I was betting my life on him.

Eleanor turned to Franklin, as she had so many times in disagreements with his mother. She should have known by that time that he did not take sides. At least he never had in the past.

We were sitting in his office. I was taking down some information about the new knitting organization, which Mrs. Stotesbury, who was a friend of Secretary Daniels's wife, was forming under the auspices of the Red Cross. The door was open, and there were several people in the outer office. That was why Franklin felt he could mention Eleanor. This was official business.

"Incidentally," he said without looking up from some papers on his desk, "I told my missus she's entirely disconnected from the old Comforts Committee and that you and Mrs. Munn will close up the loose ends. I also told her you had volunteered for the war effort and did not wish to be paid for your work."

He had taken sides. He had taken my side.

❧ Twelve

"I . . . continue to feel that *home* is the best and happiest place and that *my* son and daughter and their children will live in peace and happiness and keep from the tarnish which seems to affect so many." ❧ Sara Delano Roosevelt (Mrs. James) in a letter to her son Franklin Roosevelt, October 14, 1917

Four days later Papa died. The immediate cause was cardiac decompensation and exhaustion. The primary cause was chronic nephritis and valvular disease of the heart. I know all that now from the certificate of death. At the time all I learned was that he'd been taken to Sibley Hospital two days earlier. I hadn't visited him. I hadn't even known he was in the hospital. I didn't go to the funeral at Arlington either. Mama asked me to stay home with her. I would have preferred to pay my last respects to Papa, but I had always deferred to Mama in family matters. This did not seem the time to stop. Nonetheless, I couldn't help thinking she was being vindictive. She was punishing Papa for sinking into drink and debt and stained linen, and for taking her down with him. Now I think it was more complicated than that. She was punishing Papa, but she was grieving for herself. As long as Papa had breathed, there was a chance he might reform, and love.

127

I consoled myself with the thought that the end hadn't been difficult. I cheered myself by imagining that he hadn't known it was the end at all, but had spent his last brandy-laced months, his body dozing in his favorite club chair, his mind smartly buttoned into his old officer's uniform, pursuing the beautiful young woman who had been Mama, beaming over the winning little girls who had been Vio and me.

Franklin could not have been kinder. He repeated the stories about Papa he heard in the clubs. Suddenly everyone was remembering that Carroll Mercer had helped found the Metropolitan and the Chevy Chase. Some of the stories were so flattering I accused Franklin of embellishing. He swore every word was God's own truth.

Of course Eleanor wrote. It was a beautiful letter about fathers and daughters and the special love they share. Years later, when I wrote to Anna, I found her mother's letter to me, and reread it, and cried because of all the wonderful things Eleanor said about her father and mine, which didn't apply to them and us, but did to Franklin and Anna.

It was hard to believe that Papa was gone. I had been living with the memory of him for so long. Secretary Daniels brought the fact home. He pretended he wanted to protect Franklin, and me, but what he really wanted was to punish us. A man who drives his own brother-in-law from the state for contemplating divorce clearly believes vengeance is at least partly his.

I knew something was wrong as soon as I walked into Franklin's office that evening. I'd been working elsewhere in the building all day, but late in the afternoon I'd received orders to report to the office of the ASTNAV at nineteen hundred hours. At first I thought it was a joke. Once or twice during the summer Franklin had summoned me officially because, he said when I arrived, the blue of my eyes was good for morale and the timbre of my voice pierced a man's heart so deeply it ought to be classified as a secret weapon. But when I knocked on the open door at precisely nineteen hundred hours and Franklin looked up and saw me, he barely managed an anemic smile. I almost asked if he was feeling all right, but caught myself in time. Eleanor and Mrs. James were always nagging him about respiratory infections and stomach ailments and other minor illnesses he preferred to ignore. Only later, when Franklin was seriously ill, would Eleanor stop worrying about his health, but that was partly my fault.

Mr. Howe was the only one left in the outer office. Franklin stood and went to the door, but instead of sending him off on some piece of urgent business or telling him it was time to go home to his wife, he simply closed the door. Then he came back to his desk and stood behind it for a moment. It was all so odd, so terrifyingly formal, that I went on standing at attention. Perhaps it was the absurdity of my standing there in that dowdy uniform with my shoulders squared and my chin up that cut the tension.

"Parade rest, Yeoman Mercer," he said, and we both laughed.

He pulled one of the visitors' chairs close to his, waited until I'd taken it, then turned his own chair toward me. We sat, smooth-serge knee to rough-government-issue knee. He took my hand in both of his. I knew there was something he had to tell me and didn't want to, but I couldn't imagine what it was. It never occurred to me he might have fallen out of love with me. I loved enough for two.

"I had an order from the secretary this morning, Lucy. About you."

I could not imagine why the secretary would write to

Franklin about me. Eleanor might suspect. Alice Longworth might scheme. The Misses Patten might gossip. But no one knew about us for certain. Surely not the dour secretary of the navy.

"He has discharged you. With an outstanding record for good conduct," he added quickly, as if my military record were the point, as if I were one of his admirals.

"I don't understand. I was just promoted from yeoman third class to yeoman second," I answered, as if my military record really were the issue.

"Here it is," he said and handed me the official order. Like the check that had flown between Eleanor and me, it looked well thumbed. Franklin must have been picking it up and putting it down all day.

I took it from him. "By special order of the Secretary of the Navy," it said. "With an outstanding record for good conduct," it added. And there was one more phrase. ". . . for reasons of hardship."

I looked up from the order. "What are the 'reasons of hardship'?"

"Your father's death," Franklin answered, and that was when I understood. Papa's death meant no new hardship. Mama and I had been living without him for some time now. The dismissal wasn't to help me; it was to save Franklin. That was all right. I wanted to save Franklin too.

We went on sitting there, knee to knee. Gradually the small stone of silence began to send ripples of fear through the room. For the first time I realized loving enough for two is a dangerous act.

The windows were open to the October evening. A breeze wandered into the office carrying the smell of burning leaves. I shivered. Suddenly we were on our feet, clinging to each other like two people who have narrowly escaped a speeding automobile or falling boulder or careening madman. We were giddy with relief. We were dizzy from the closeness of our call. We held each other and swore, mouth against mouth, that it would take more than the United States Navy to separate us.

∾ I was indomitable. The secretary couldn't stop me. Eleanor couldn't get Franklin to take her side against mine. She was no longer even trying to. Perhaps she'd convinced herself there was nothing between Franklin and me. Perhaps she'd merely decided to behave as if there were nothing. I suspect she lived somewhere between the two. I imagine her lying awake at three o'clock in the morning, when the faint cough of a child sounds like tuberculosis and a single unpaid bill heralds bankruptcy. She watches Franklin sleep, and adds up the injustices she has collected from him, and knows that he is in love with me. The next morning she opens her eyes to the square of newborn sunlight on the bedroom carpet and recognizes the clear lines of the familiar furniture and smiles with relief. But then, before she can grow accustomed to the safety, the sound of Franklin's big straight razor on the strop and the strains of him humming a popular song we'd danced to the night before or singing one of the Methodist hymns he loved floats like a shadow across the square of sunlight, and she is in doubt again. Knowing is agony. Indecision is worse. But Eleanor believed in confronting her fear. It was, she always insisted, the only way to conquer it. So when she returned from Campo, she went on asking me to help out now and then with her social duties, and even to fill in at luncheons and dinners.

My own fear that fall and winter was that Franklin would resign his position and enlist for active service. My heart hammered against my rib cage every time he talked about it, though I never let him see how frightened I was. I knew Eleanor worried too, and I was grateful to her. Sending him off to war would have gotten him away from me, but she loved him too much for that.

She and I were in the back parlor of the new house on R Street, which she'd rented from her aunt Bye because 1733 N had grown too small for the family, when we heard the door open that evening, but no voice came rolling down the hall. She hurried toward the foyer. I pretended to go on working while I listened shamelessly. The house was larger, but no more private, especially if the eavesdropper was determined.

"What did the president say?" She was breathless, and not from the dash to the front door.

Franklin cleared his throat the way he did when he was about to launch into one of his imitations. " 'Neither the Secretary nor you nor I, Roosevelt,' " he began in a stentorian tone, but his heart wasn't in it, and he slipped out of the president's voice and back into his own, " 'has a right to select his place of service. Stay where you are. That is where you can do the most good.' "

I determined then and there that if women could vote in the next election, which people were saying they would be able to do, I would cast my ballot for President Wilson, though it was unlikely I'd have the opportunity to. This was his second term, and no president had ever run for a third.

"The president is right," Eleanor said. "It's just as you're always saying. You're the one who runs the department. Still, I can imagine how awful you must feel."

I wished she wouldn't chirp.

"I feel grand," he said, and I knew how miserable he was. He might have been back at Groton, weighing in too light for football, and losing the boxing match, and managing the baseball team rather than playing on it. He might have been back in his rooms in Cambridge the night he learned he had not made Porcellian. He had lain awake in the darkness thinking of his father, and Uncle Ted, and the Reverend Peabody, and all the men he admired, and some he did not, who had made it. He had not tossed and turned, but lay staring at the ceiling, apologizing to his father, explaining to Uncle Ted, recalling Dr. Peabody's sermons about courage and honor, and railing against the injustice. What had gone wrong? Who had betrayed him? No matter how many times he went over it in his mind, he could not figure it out. He saw the sixteen men sitting around the table, watched the small wooden ballot box go from hand to hand, envisioned the white balls dropping in one after another. He was sure all the others had been white. Then he saw it. A single black ball. It slid secretly, silently into the box. It clattered for all the world to hear. And he would never know whose fingers had dropped it. That old wound had never healed. Now the president's refusal added one more blow to the injuries of his youth, the long-ago breaks in his heart that he brought to me in the darkness to make whole.

"But after all, Franklin, you are in good company," Eleanor went on, and I wanted to run down the hall and clamp a hand over her mouth. I knew what was coming, and it was not what he needed to hear. "The president turned down Uncle Ted too, when he wanted to raise a division of volunteers."

Franklin hated the comparison. This was modern mechanized warfare, he'd explained to me after, in a sweet seesaw of power, he'd managed to get TR an appointment with President Wilson. There was no place in it for a reunion of old Rough Riders. But Franklin was in his prime, and as for understanding modern warfare, he was the one who'd seen the promise of a mine barrage of the North Sea. He'd finally gotten in to see the president about it last June, and now plans were under way.

As I lingered in the back parlor listening to Eleanor trying to console Franklin, I knew there was one more reason she should not have mentioned her uncle. All TR's sons were in uniform. He crowed about their bravery and neglected to mention, Franklin had told me with wicked glee, the fact that his own father, Eleanor's grandfather, Theodore, Sr., had paid a German immigrant to fight for him in the Civil War.

"It was a common practice at the time, but it still tickles me pink when Cousin Ted begins to talk about"—Franklin had raised his voice to an imitation of TR's squeak—" 'the thick streak of yellow in our national life.' "

He'd laughed, and I had too, but I knew he was brooding about how it would look after the war when all the Roosevelts were running for public office and he was the only one with-out a war record.

"He outsmarted me," Franklin said later when he told me about his meeting with the president. "Hoisted me on my own petard. I began by telling him there was a need for men with a knowledge of modern warfare, but he cut me off. 'I am well aware of what there is need of, Roosevelt,' Franklin said in the president's voice, because by then he'd gotten over the first flush of disappointment. And he was with me. " 'You have been hammering preparedness at us for some time. Your fore-sight is admirable. That is the point. The Department of the Navy cannot do without your foresight and your expertise.' "

I imagined Franklin standing in the big oval office as the president spoke. A breeze from the windows open to the wide lawn rippled the flags behind the desk. From where Franklin stood, the undulating red and white stripes of one flag must have seemed to be waving good-bye as the presidential seal disappeared into the folds of the other. He saw his dream receding. Everything Franklin did, he did for the dream. I was the only exception.

⌒ A few weeks later Franklin had an argument with Mrs. James. Franklin did not argue with his mother. He teased her. He managed her. He treated her with that peculiar blend of affection, pride, and dismissiveness which doted-upon sons reserve for the mothers who have spoiled them. But he did not argue with her. Even when he'd gotten engaged to Eleanor against her wishes, he'd done it by stealth. But he argued with his mother about me.

No one mentioned my name or even referred to me obliquely, but I was in the big library of the Place as surely as if I'd been invited for the weekend. The four of us were gathered in front of one of the two stone fireplaces at either end of the room, Franklin and his mother in their twin thrones on either side of the hearth, Eleanor in a lesser chair a little distance away, and I hovering, as insubstantial and inescapable as the air they breathed.

Mrs. James must have gotten wind of something, though I doubt she could admit to herself what it might be, despite the fact that the family history was not lacking in that sort of thing. Her stepson, James Roosevelt Roosevelt, known as Rosie, had enjoyed a long affair with a British shop girl, though he was a terrible snob, and had made an honest woman of her only after an attack of gallstones put the fear of God in him. Rosie's son Taddy had run off from Harvard with a woman from the Tenderloin called Dutch Sadie, and two nights after reporters had confronted his grandfather with the news, Mr. James had suffered a serious heart attack

from which he'd never fully recovered. After the death of
Eleanor's father, who had been Franklin's godfather, a woman
called Katy Mann had turned up with a child she'd named
Elliott Roosevelt Mann in honor, she said, of his father, which
made him a half-brother to Eleanor. There was plenty of scandal to go around in the Roosevelt family, as there usually is in
large clans, but Mrs. James's husband had been above
reproach, and she was determined that her son would be too.
Yet she sensed something was wrong. Franklin was touchy
and snappish. He admitted as much to me. Eleanor, on the
other hand, had become strangely affectionate. She wrote her
mother-in-law almost daily. "I wish you were always here," I
heard her say as Mrs. James was leaving after one visit.
"There are always so many things I want to talk over and ask
you about." Mrs. James could not have helped sensing something was in the air.

She didn't confront it head-on. Instead she brought up the
subject of Algonac, her childhood home, which had burned to
the ground the previous winter. The family had rebuilt it, but
the fragility of monuments to Delanos and Roosevelts was
much on her mind. She asked Franklin to swear to her that no
matter what happened, he would always keep the Place in the
family. What she really wanted him to promise was that he
would always keep things exactly as they were. Franklin, who
would have liked nothing better than to hold on to Springwood but was less certain about the family, demurred. The
more Mrs. James insisted, the more obstinate he became. By
the end of the evening, he would not have agreed to do the
thing he still hoped desperately to be able to do, even if he
could have. Franklin never had a sadistic streak, no matter
what some people who were subjected to his teasing said, but
he did have a stubborn one.

It must have been an icy leave-taking. I picture the three of them standing on the dark station platform. Gusts of Hudson-chilled wind buffeted them. Dead leaves swirled around their feet. The desultory conversation provided no insulation. When the train puffed to a stop, Franklin kissed his mother hastily, handed Eleanor up the stairs, and bounded after her.

He told me about the argument and about the letter that arrived from his mother the following day. Once again, she did not spell things out. To name things would be to admit they existed. Instead she talked of home and family and *noblesse oblige*. How much finer the old feudal call to duty sounded than the scandalous whisper of divorce. But the meaning behind them was the same. She was pleading with Franklin not to do anything foolish. She was warning him of the consequences of fleeing family responsibility and following the call of unsanctioned love.

Franklin agreed with his mother, though he never wrote to tell her so. He believed in home and family and *noblesse oblige*. And the Hudson River land was in his blood. But so was I. No wonder I felt indomitable.

❧ Thirteen

"If I feel depressed, I go to work. Work is always an antidote to depression." ∽ Eleanor Roosevelt

"I am a juggler. I never let my right hand know what my left hand does." ∽ Franklin D. Roosevelt

I was in the canteen the morning the accident occurred. Eleanor and I frequently worked the same shifts. She spent so many hours there that most of the ladies who volunteered worked with her at one time or another. But I was there the morning of the accident.

The war had come home to us that winter. Not the way it had to Violetta, whose continued references to Bill Marbury could not blot out the images of bed after bed of limbless torsos and lungless chests and noseless faces, of maimed boyish bodies inhabited by old men's souls. Our sacrifices were paltry by comparison. The Food Administration urged two wheatless and meatless days a week. The Fuel Administration ordered electric advertising signs darkened every Sunday and Thursday. Women said no to enough steel stays to build two battleships. The president even appointed a commission of

138

advertising executives to "sell" Americans the war, as if it were a soap or a cereal. I was scandalized at the idea, it seemed so unpatriotic, so commercial, but Franklin explained that the country was full of isolationists, and it was necessary to convince them the war was worth fighting. He called it molding public opinion. He also predicted that after the war advertising would be a respectable profession. I would not have believed it, if it hadn't come from his mouth.

It had been months since the first American boys had arrived in France, inadequately trained, overly confident, and startled to find themselves fighting for people who didn't speak English and kept mountains of manure in their front yards. And still the men kept going. Some days as many as ten troop trains came through the yards where the Red Cross had set up the canteen. That meant three or four thousand men. Other days, it was quiet, and the ladies grew bored waiting for a chance to do good.

The morning of the accident I'd been assigned to make sandwiches. There was a small army kitchen in one of the tin shacks where we brewed great cauldrons of coffee and put together hundreds upon hundreds of sandwiches. That morning my hands were so cold I could barely hold the knife to spread the jam. As the day wore on, the cauldrons of coffee heated things up a bit, but not much.

On my way in, I'd noticed Eleanor in the small room where we sold cigars and cigarettes and chewing tobacco, as well as candy and postcards at cost. She drew that duty frequently. She was the only one of us who never made a mistake giving change, no matter how long the line or how impatient the men who had only minutes before the train whistle blew. Eleanor was good at that job, and all the others in the canteen, for another reason as well. She cared about the men coming through. She looked them in the eye, and asked where they were from, and worried about where they were going. I saw them file past, taking a sandwich, thanking me, ma'am, for the coffee, and couldn't meet their gazes, because I was so shamefully relieved that they were getting back on the train that would take them to the ship that would take them to war, and Franklin was not. I preferred scouring cauldrons and mopping floors to facing those men I cared so little about. Eleanor scoured cauldrons and mopped floors too. There wasn't a job she didn't take up eagerly and do superbly. Everyone marveled at her. I think she marveled at herself. She was discovering abilities and strengths she'd never dreamed she possessed. She was becoming the woman other women admired and emulated. Only her cousin Alice remained unimpressed. Eleanor, she told people, had taken her virtue public.

Alice came down to the canteen one afternoon. Perhaps she envied the attention her cousin was getting for her work there. Miss Patten handed her a mop and pail. Alice replied that she had come to help the war effort, not wash floors. Miss Patten said that at the moment what the war required was a clean floor. I happened to glance at Eleanor as the exchange was going on. I had never seen such a wicked grin on her face. Alice didn't come back. She told people she had developed canteen elbow. I don't think Eleanor was sorry her cousin didn't return. The canteen was her territory.

Franklin spent an afternoon there too. I was on sandwich-making duty that day as well. He'd come to collect Eleanor, but when he saw how busy we were, he took off his seersucker jacket, rolled up his sleeves, and picked up a knife in one hand and the jam jar in the other.

"You're wasting motions, Miss Mercer. I'll show you the

scientifically correct way to spread jam." He was teasing me, but he also managed to set a record for the greatest number of sandwiches turned out in the shortest period of time. He said he expected a plaque to be put up.

On the morning of the accident, two trains had come through early, but they'd pulled out by a little after ten, and the canteen grew quiet again. I went on making sandwiches because we were expecting three more trains that afternoon. After Eleanor tallied up her receipts and made her entries in the ledger, she came into the kitchen and asked if there was anything she could do to help. I was standing at the table spreading jam on the slices of bread I'd laid out. Someone, I don't remember who, suggested that Eleanor ought to rest for a while. Eleanor insisted she wasn't in the least tired. I'd finished spreading jam and was covering each piece of bread with another. She came over to the table and began wrapping the finished sandwiches in paper and putting them in the big baskets we carried out to the arriving trains. We went on that way for a while. I'd begin laying out the new slices of bread while she was still wrapping the sandwiches from the last batch, then she'd catch up as I spread the jam. We worked well together, but it was a contest too. We were racing to keep up with each other.

We'd made eighty or a hundred sandwiches when Miss Patten came into the shed and said she'd just heard there would be four trains that afternoon rather than three. There were the usual yelps of alarm and cries that we'd never do it, but Eleanor said of course we would do it, and everyone got down to work. Miss Patten put one of the younger volunteers on sandwich-wrapping duty and sent Eleanor to cut more bread. Slicing bread was one of the worst jobs, more awful than mopping the floor or washing down the walls. The bread-cutting machine was a steel demon that was as likely to mangle as slice. Most of the ladies were terrified of it. Eleanor, of course, had tamed it.

She took one of the loaves from the large bag of them on the floor, ran it through the machine, and passed it on to me. I began lining up the slices on the table. Eleanor picked up another loaf. I was spreading jam on the last piece of bread when she handed me the freshly cut loaf to cover the finished slices. The girl who was wrapping couldn't keep up with us.

Eleanor was on her fifth or sixth or maybe seventh loaf— I'd lost track—when we heard the train whistle.

"We haven't nearly enough sandwiches," Miss Patten said.

"Hurry," someone else cried.

My knife flew over the slices. Beside me the girl's hands fluttered as she wrapped. Eleanor took another loaf of bread from the bag and began to insert it in the cutter. There are two things I remember vividly. One was the spurt of red liquid, like a geyser, that rose from the machine. The other was that she did not make a sound.

"Mrs. Roosevelt!" Miss Patten cried. "Your hand!"

"It's nothing," Eleanor said, though the bread was soaked red, and when I glanced at her face, I saw it was white.

A circle was pressing in around her, and Miss Patten was insisting that someone call a doctor, and someone else was asking if there was a first-aid kit, and another lady was calling for smelling salts, though I couldn't say whether she wanted them for Eleanor or herself.

"It's nothing," Eleanor said again, and this time her voice silenced everyone. She took a handkerchief from her pocket. She turned to Miss Patten, hesitated, then swiveled to me. "Miss Mercer, your sister is a nurse. You must be able to tie a tourniquet."

I said I could try.

She handed me the handkerchief and held out her hand. The blood was still gushing, which was probably fortunate, because I found out later the cut went clear to the bone, and if I'd seen that, my knees would surely have gone weak beneath me.

I wound the handkerchief around her finger, pulled it tight, and began to tie a knot.

"Tighter, Miss Mercer," she said.

"I don't want to hurt you."

"I can stand the pain, as long as we stanch the flow."

I pulled it as tight as I could and knotted it. Then we tied several more handkerchiefs around it. We could hear the hiss and squeak of brakes on the tracks in the yard. She picked up another loaf of bread.

"You can't," Miss Patten cried.

"Those young men are hungry," Eleanor said.

We all went back to work.

The next day she was at the canteen again, though now she had a proper bandage on her finger. I asked if she'd had a doctor look at it.

"Mr. Roosevelt sent for a doctor when I got home last evening," she answered. "But he said it would probably be too painful to sew it up so long after the fact, so he simply bandaged it again."

She worked a full shift again that day. She even used the bread cutter.

"Mrs. Roosevelt," Miss Patten said, "you are indomitable."

∾ "He cut his finger," Franklin said. "He was so excited when he heard the news that he drove a screwdriver straight through to the bone."

Should I have seen a pattern here? Of course not. People cut their fingers all the time, especially active people, though I'm not sure *active* is a word I'd apply to Livy Davis, however energetic he was in his pursuit of pleasure. But as I said, I will not be unkind to Livy. He was hard enough on himself, though none of us could have guessed it.

Franklin had brought Livy to Washington as his special assistant after I'd left the Navy Department. Eleanor didn't like Livy, though she'd helped arrange for the appointment as a favor to his wife, but I was glad. Franklin needed someone on the premises who knew how to wear a smile, and laugh at a joke, and see the ludicrous side of things. Livy's greatest contribution to the war effort, aside from providing light relief for Franklin, was his Eyes for the Navy Campaign. He succeeded in convincing several thousand yachtsmen, bird-watchers, and music-lovers to give up their binoculars, telescopes, and opera glasses for the duration of the war.

The news that made Livy cut his finger was more serious, at least to me. Franklin had finally gotten the secretary to send him overseas on an inspection of all naval forces in European waters.

"I went next door to his office to tell him to pack up his old kit bag," Franklin said, "because I was taking him with me. He was trying to change the combination on his office safe—heaven only knows what he keeps in there—and he was so excited when he heard the news that his hand slipped and he drove the screwdriver straight through his finger.

"You mustn't tell a soul," he went on. "About the trip, I mean. I haven't even told Mama."

I didn't ask if he'd told Eleanor. He would, of course. I just wondered if he already had.

I asked when he would be going. He said soon. There was a moment's silence.

"It's top secret. No one is supposed to know when I'm sailing. Of course, there's no chance of seeing me off."

Sometimes war solves problems as well as creates them.

∾ A week later we said good-bye. He was taking the train for New York the following day and sailing the day after that. We spent our last evening together as we had some of our first, on a quiet country road under a dark sky. A sliver of moon swung over our heads. Franklin said it looked like the sickle on the flag that flew over Russia, which wasn't Russia anymore but, since last November, something called the Union of Socialist Soviet Republics. Franklin couldn't forgive it for signing a peace treaty with Germany. But except for joking about the flag, he didn't talk about the war or government affairs that night. He didn't say much at all. We sat, his arm around my shoulders, my head on his chest, looking at that slim promise of moon and storing each other up for the long separation ahead. The night was silent too. No owls, no frogs, not even katydids. The world was holding its breath.

I don't know how long we remained that way, memorizing each other, but the silvery sickle moon had moved from one side of the auto to the other when he said there was something he had to tell me before he left. I stiffened. He must have sensed it, because he didn't continue. The silence pressed in on us, heavy and ominous as weather. Finally he started again, but badly, something about not being able to go on this way.

I *can* go on this way, I wanted to scream.

It wasn't fair to me, he said, and I wanted to tell him I had stopped looking for justice a long time ago.

"I'll tell Eleanor," he said, "as soon as I get back."

The words jolted me upright. I turned to face him. I must have been as white as the moon, because he said, "What's wrong, Lucy? Don't you want to marry me?"

Two days later at seventeen hundred hours on July ninth, he sailed from New York on the U.S.S. *Dyer*. We had promised to write.

ᴇ Fourteen

"Yes, of course, everything is *naturally* 'off the record'—It never occurred to me that needed to be said."

ᴗ Lucy Mercer in a letter to Margaret Suckley,
FDR's distant cousin, December 11, 1944

U.S.S. *Dyer*
July 11th

Dearest Lucy,

The weather has turned filthy. Moving about is difficult, and the rule is one hand for the ship at all times. Several officers are ill, and there has been much feeding of the fishes, but I have not missed a meal. I roam the ship in my "destroyer costume" of khaki riding trousers, golf stockings, flannel shirt, and leather coat. Very warm and comfy. Having a grand time, though I find myself questioning my long-held conviction that women do not belong aboard ship. I miss you desperately.

All my love,
Franklin

Washington
July 11th

Dearest Franklin,

The heat wave continues. Yesterday a girl fainted in the canteen. Perhaps we ought to buy one of those new "refrigerators" that maintain a consistent temperature without the use of ice. The ladies could take turns stepping inside for a moment of cool, though I have little need of it. My heart has been frozen since you sailed. It seems to me all Washington is in mourning for your departure. Auto horns play dirges. Flags fly at half mast. Mr. Wilson has ordered the White House painted black until your return. I feel as if half of me, the best half, is gone.

All my love,
Lucy

U.S.S. *Dyer*
July 13th

Dearest Lucy,

We had a bit of a dust-up yesterday. I was standing on the port wing of the bridge, when a green youngster, not realizing the port gun was trained as far forward as it would go, pulled the lanyard. A four-inch shell went by only a few feet outboard. Though I was sure my next landfall would be St. Peter's gate, my life did not flash before my eyes, only your face.

All my love,
Franklin

Washington
July 18th

Dearest Franklin,

Last Sunday at the Church of the Covenant Mr. Wood urged the young ladies of the congregation to go to the camps and "make it pleasant" for the boys whether they knew them or not. Apparently the girls followed his suggestion so enthusiastically that now the boys' mothers are complaining that they don't want their sons cheered up after all.

Has it been only eleven days since we sat in the auto beneath that old Russian moon? I was a squirrel that night, storing bits and pieces of you away for the long lonely summer. Now I take out the memories slowly. I am determined to make them last.

All my love,
Lucy

Cliveden
July 30th

Dearest Lucy,

Yesterday I came in from Cliveden for an audience with the king. We had forty minutes of conversation *à deux*, though interviews of this sort are supposed to last only fifteen. He is very open and cordial, and not as short as I expected. His face is stronger than it appears in photographs, and when we got to talking about German atrocities in Belgium, his expression became fierce.

Lunched with my old friend Ned Bell at the St. James Club, then went to the army and navy stores and purchased a pair of silk pajamas for the extraordinary price of sixty-one shillings. They are blue, not the blue of a robin's egg or a jay or the Bay of Fundy, but the exact blue of your eyes.

All my love,
Franklin

Washington
July 30th

Dearest Franklin,

I just received yours of July 13th. I think the green youngster should be keel-hauled. Take care of yourself, my darling. I will permit no accidents.

All my love,
Lucy

Cliveden
July 31st

Dearest Lucy,

I went on so about the King and my pajamas (an unseemly juxtaposition, I admit) I did not have time to tell you about my dinner that evening with the war ministers at Gray's Inn. Mr. Winston Churchill, the Minister of Munitions, was exceedingly rude to me. In fact, he behaved like a real stinker, lording it over all of us. I wanted to say to him, "My good man, you may insult the Assistant Secretary of the United States Navy. You may snub the scion of the Hyde Park Roosevelts. But how dare you visit your bad manners on the man who has the extreme good fortune to be loved by Miss Lucy Page Mercer."

All my love,
Franklin

Washington
August 1st

Dearest Franklin,

The scandal in the camps continues. While visiting her son, Senator Bailey's wife saw a khaki-clad young woman come out of a tent. She is now clamoring for a Senate investigation. Personally I think the Senate should investigate Mrs. Bailey for conspiring against love. I would like the whole world to be as happy as I am, though I know that is impossible. After all, there is only one you. All the more reason to take care of yourself, my darling.

All my love,
Lucy

Paris
August 3rd

Dearest Lucy,

In addition to seeing Marshal Joffre, Premier Clemenceau, and President and Mme. Poincaré, to whom I had to explain who I was, I had tea with my Oyster Bay cousins. Ted Jr. and Archie are recovering from wounds. We talked about their brother Quentin, who died a hero's death flying behind the enemy's lines. His father, Cousin Ted, is extremely proud of him.

The afternoon gave me much food for thought. I am too young to spend the war behind a desk. As soon as I return, I am going to resign my post and get assigned to active duty. I must get into this before it's too late.

All my love,
Franklin

Washington
August 7th

Dearest Franklin,

My recommendation to Mr. Churchill is that he give up public life immediately. Such an inferior judge of character has no future in government. Your observation, however, is true. You are indeed loved by Miss Lucy Page Mercer, deeply, truly, eternally.

All my love,
Lucy

Somewhere in France
August 7th

Dearest Lucy,

Captain Jackson, my naval attaché who considers himself responsible for my safety, kept ignoring my requests to get to the front and continued to arrange days touring villages around Chateau-Thierry, where the fighting has ended, and nights in comfortable hotels. As a result, I am now running the show. Tomorrow Lieutenant de Tessan will take us up the line to within a stone's throw of the actual fighting. But do not worry. The lieutenant is prudent, and I have every intention of returning to you in one undamaged piece. We have a future together.

All my love,
Franklin

Washington
August 20th

Dearest Franklin,

How thrilling for you to be finally at the front, though I do feel sorry for poor Captain Jackson, who was only doing his duty. Of course, I worry. How can I not? But I want my love to give wings, my darling, not clip them.

All my love,
Lucy

Scotland
August 31st

Dearest Lucy,

Yesterday we inspected the North Sea mine barrage. Do you remember when I first told you my idea for it that night on N Street? There was a thrush singing in the garden. I told you he was looking for a lady thrush to set up housekeeping. I started to write "little did I know," but I think I did, even then.

All my love,
Franklin

Washington
September 7th

Dearest Franklin,

There is talk of a new illness along the Atlantic Seaboard. It is called Spanish Influenza, from the Italian for influence, a mysterious and malignant force. Some say the germs have been spread intentionally by the Germans, but I think that is simply war hysteria. There is no doubt, however, that it has arrived from Europe. I, as you know, am disgracefully healthy, but take care of yourself, my darling. I have stopped counting the weeks till I see you and begun counting the days.

All my love,
Lucy

Scotland
September 8th

Dearest Lucy,

I have picked up a bit of the flu, and Livy and everyone else have come down with it too. We medicate with frequent doses of the national beverage, and do not let illness interfere with the fishing, which is grand.

We sail on the 12th. I expect my respiratory system to be strictly according to Hoyle by then, but even if the fever should linger, I know there is a miraculous cure waiting for me at home.

All my love,
Franklin

CABLEGRAM

BREST FRANCE
SEPTEMBER 11 1918

MISS LUCY MERCER
THE TORONTO
WASHINGTON D C
ARRIVE NEW YORK ON OR ABOUT SEPTEMBER 19TH WILL TELEPHONE OR CABLE AS SOON AS HUMANLY POSSIBLE ALL MY LOVE FRANKLIN

❧ Fifteen

"That marriage would have taken place, but as Lucy said to us, 'Eleanor was not willing to step aside.' "

❧ Mrs. Lyman Cotton, Lucy Mercer's cousin

"I remember one day I was having fun with Auntie Corinne. I was doing imitations of Eleanor, and Auntie Corinne looked at me and said, 'Never forget, Alice, Eleanor offered Franklin his freedom.' " ❧ Alice Roosevelt Longworth

There is a young war widow who is a friend of my daughter. Her husband died on D-Day in the first assault on Omaha Beach, but the telegram from the war department did not arrive until early August. For two months she went on waiting for his letters and writing her own, confiding the large dreams and small verities of everyday life, the deep love and loneliness, the movie she saw the night before and the flowers that were blooming in the garden. For another six weeks her envelopes kept coming back to her, each one stamped with a single word of reproach: DECEASED. I almost mentioned the cruelty of it to Franklin. It was unconscionable that the War Department could be so derelict in its duty. But just as I was about to speak, I noticed the dark circles beneath his eyes and remembered that Eleanor was always nagging him to do this or fix that—everyone knew about the basket by his bedside which she filled with letters and requests and directives—and I could not bear to burden him with one more problem. But I know a little of what that young war widow endured. I went on waiting for Franklin to telephone or wire long after Eleanor read my letters of love and loneliness, of gossip about the canteen and the camps and news of where I'd dined and whom I'd seen. My sister Violetta talks of the ravages of time passing. We are old. We are gray. We are no longer the girls our husbands fell in love with, she says. But to me the pain of time passing is nothing compared to the agony of time stopped.

September nineteenth was a Friday. Security had prevented Franklin from wiring what ship he was arriving on or what time it docked, but even if he landed in New York early in the day, he would not be able to slip away from his wife and mother and perhaps even some official duties immediately. I went to my Red Cross meeting. I knew he would want me to. He hated indolence. The meeting didn't take my mind off Franklin, but it was better than languishing in the apartment, jumping at every sound that faintly resembled a ringing telephone or a Western Union knock at the door.

When I arrived home around noon, I was not surprised there had been no call or wireless. It never occurred to me that while I was taking off my hat and smoothing my hair, orderlies were carrying his stretcher gently, I hope they were being gentle, down the gangplank of the *Leviathan* and sliding it into the waiting ambulance. I didn't dream that as Mama and I sat down to lunch, Eleanor was climbing into the ambulance after him, or did the doctor go with Franklin in the ambulance, leaving Eleanor and Mrs. James to follow in their auto?

And as I sat chatting happily with Mama because in no time at all I was going hear his voice, the orderlies were carrying Franklin, his face drenched in perspiration, his fever so high he was almost delirious, up the steps of Mrs. James's townhouse on East Sixty-fifth Street. I was giddy with anticipation because my future was about to start, but as they put him to bed in a room at the back of the house where it would be quieter, Eleanor was sick with fear. The Spanish influenza had raced through the ship, and several officers and men had died and been buried at sea. Later she would say that Franklin had not seemed to her as sick as some of the other men aboard ship, but that was after she found the letters. At the time she must have been wild with worry.

I was still confident at teatime, but by dinner I was becoming impatient. Would Eleanor and Mrs. James never give him a moment? I imagined the two women at table with Franklin, hanging on his words, reveling in his voice, drinking in his face. They were sitting at his bedside, listening to his breathing, tracking his fever, competing to care for him. Maybe that was why Eleanor decided to unpack his bags herself. She needed a moment's respite from her mother-in-law. She wanted to stake her claim to his possessions, and therefore to him. Or perhaps she was just being Eleanor. She and Franklin had rented their own side of the Siamese twin townhouses and were staying in Mrs. James's half. Eleanor would not have wanted to inconvenience one of her mother-in-law's maids. Whatever the reason, she decided to unpack her husband's bag that evening.

I see her undoing the straps, hear the smart snap of the locks as she springs them, feel the grainy finish of the worn leather as she opens the bag. She is all efficiency now, sorting this for the laundress, that to be polished, that to be arranged neatly on a desk until Franklin feels well enough to deal with it. I see her running her fingers over the rough fabric of his uniform and inhaling the scent of his shaving soap, or was she too purposeful for that? I think not. Eleanor was a romantic. Only a romantic can carry disillusion a lifetime.

She is making swift progress. The piles on the floor and desk are growing. The contents of the bag are dwindling. She reaches in again. Her hand finds the packet of letters and draws them out. She is not surprised at the water-waffled, dirt-stained envelopes. She and Mrs. James and the chicks have been bombarding him with mail. It's the velvet ribbon holding them together that she can't place. She stands there knowing what it is, not wanting to know, refusing to know. Her mind swerves from one thing to another. The man she married is better than that. The man she married is like all men, like everyone she has ever loved. He has let her down.

She looks at her husband's name on the front of the envelope. The writing is familiar. It takes her only a few seconds to place it. I have been sending out her words in my hand for years. But these, she knows, are not her words.

Does she debate for a moment? I will not open these letters. They are not addressed to me. Even Eleanor is not that virtuous. Does she have another thought? If I have not seen these letters, if I put them in a pile with other papers and tell Franklin that the maid unpacked his bag, they do not exist. At least, I do not have to acknowledge them. But she is incapable of doing that. She cannot live with a man who falls short of the perfection she strives for.

She carries the letters to her room, closes and locks the door, pulls the straight-backed chair out from the desk, and gets down to her task. A few hundred miles south I sit in the living room of the apartment. Mama is playing solitaire. I am trying to read. *The Marne,* if I remember correctly, by Mrs. Wharton. The ormolu clock on the mantel ticks noisily, and I have trouble keeping my mind on the book. Eleanor, however, has no trouble concentrating.

Dearest Franklin,
    I feel as if half of me, the best half of me, is gone.

> All my love,
> Lucy

Dearest Franklin,
    I want my love to give wings, not clip them.

> All my love,
> Lucy

Dearest Franklin,
    You are indeed loved by Miss Lucy Page Mercer, deeply, truly, eternally.

> All my love,
> Lucy

It came to me in the middle of the night. While Eleanor lay wide-eyed, holding her grief like a lover, I awakened with a start. ARRIVE NEW YORK ON OR ABOUT SEPTEMBER NINE-TEENTH, Franklin had cabled with supreme confidence, as if there were no such things as U-boats and torpedoes and war. On the eastbound crossing they'd had two nighttime alarms, despite their zigzag course, and each time, he'd written, he'd raced to the bridge, barefoot in his silk pajamas, to scan the dark sea. He'd made it sound like a lark. At three o'clock in the morning, holding my fear as close as Eleanor held her grief, I did not find it amusing.

The terror did not fade in the sunlight. I went down to the street, bought several papers, and carried them back to the apartment. FOE IS SLAUGHTERED IN COUNTERATTACK one headline screamed. HAIG HAS 10,000 PRISONERS another exulted. I searched the inner pages. German crowds were demanding peace, and a toothbrush company was touting the efficacy of regular brushing in the fight against influenza, but there was no word of a German U-boat attack or a ship going down. I was only slightly reassured. I knew that war news traveled slowly. I had no idea how long President Wilson or Secretary Daniels would wait to announce the loss of a public official. And I was not next of kin to be notified. There was not even anyone I could call. Livy had gone abroad with Franklin. Mr. Howe would think Franklin's well-being was none of my business.

I stayed in the apartment all that weekend. The ormolu clock on the mantel ticked, and the minutes dragged. Saturday crept. Sunday was immovable.

Though I was scheduled to work at the canteen on Monday afternoon, I arrived in the middle of the morning shift. I pretended I'd come to help, but I could barely pour coffee or spread jam on bread. My mind raced, but my hands were paralyzed. I drifted from group to group in the hope of hearing something, anything, of Franklin. They were all so fond of Eleanor. But no one mentioned her that morning. Clouds of steam rose from the coffee urns, and the September heat baked the tin shed, and I knew I was in hell.

When the shifts changed, someone asked if Mrs. Roosevelt would be coming in.

One of the Misses Patten said she'd gone up to New York. "Mr. Roosevelt has returned from his fact-finding tour."

The perspiration ran down my sides like tiny insects. The heat singed my cheeks. "Has he?" I asked.

"I assume so," Miss Patten said. "Mrs. Roosevelt told me

that was the reason she was going to New York and would not be able to work at the canteen this week."

∞ Alice Longworth gave me the news. A letter came from her on Tuesday morning. I don't think she was being malicious, at least not to me.

Dear Miss Mercer,

My cousin Franklin arrived home with double pneumonia. He was carried off the *Leviathan* on a stretcher and taken to Sixty-fifth Street by ambulance. My father is very proud of the work he did overseas.

Sincerely,
Alice Roosevelt Longworth

I wrote back thanking her for her kindness and begging her to tell me the moment she heard anything more. Instead of posting the letter, I gave the porter a nickel to deliver it by hand to Mrs. Longworth's house.

There was no word from Franklin or his cousin the following day or the day after that. I stayed in the apartment, claiming a cold, flinging myself from chair to chair, room to room, acting, Mama said, like someone who was not me. I was not being melodramatic. You must remember this was before the last war, the second one. No one had heard of penicillin. I was sure I was losing Franklin.

Finally I telephoned Mr. Howe. I was afraid he would not take my call, but he did.

"Mr. Roosevelt is improving," he said. I was too relieved to notice that he didn't say "the boss."

"Does that mean he's out of danger?"

There was a silence. Even Mr. Howe had a heart. Once it had beat so passionately that he had convinced a young girl to defy her mother and elope to another state with him. I sometimes wondered whether she regretted it, but I was not thinking of Mrs. Howe that day.

"Just about," he said finally. "And I have that straight from the doc. I don't call the house. I don't want to disturb him. Mrs. Roosevelt says the phone is ringing off the hook all day and night."

I knew it was a warning. He'd heard the desperation in my voice. He knew I would call even Eleanor for news of Franklin.

I did not have to call Eleanor or even Mr. Howe again. Word of Franklin's convalescence began to circulate. I could even ask after him. Everyone knew I worked for Mrs. Roosevelt. I heard he was out of danger. I heard he was gaining strength. But I did not hear from him.

⁓ The morning the wire finally came, I was working at the canteen again. Mama directed the Western Union boy to deliver it to me there. It arrived during a lull between trains. It would have been better if it had come while we were busy. Then no one would have noticed.

Every eye in the shed turned to me. They all knew I had no husband to lose, though a few remembered I had a sister in a Red Cross hospital.

"I hope it is not bad news," one of the Misses Patten said.

I pretended I hadn't heard her and slipped out of the shed. I could not wait another minute.

The light outside was blinding, the sky so blue it seemed to be vibrating. Even the grit and cinders of the railroad yard shone like jet. The world was all sharp edges and stinging clarity. I found a quiet place in the lee of an empty boxcar. My fingers tore open the envelope. The wireless rattled in the October breeze. I had to grip it with both hands to read the words.

THIS IS AS SOON AS WAS HUMANLY POSSIBLE WILL BE UP
AND ABOUT IN NO TIME I MISS YOU DESPERATELY LOVE
                                              FRANKLIN

I fairly skipped back into the shed.

"Not bad news, I hope," Miss Patten said again.

"Not bad at all," I sang and began wrapping sandwiches.

I worked like a demon that afternoon. The more sandwiches I made, the more boys I fed, the sooner Franklin would
come back to me.

A few hundred miles north, Eleanor carried a tea tray into
Franklin's room in the house on East Sixty-fifth Street. As I
stacked the sandwiches in the big wicker baskets, Eleanor put
the tray on Franklin's lap and sat in a chair a little distance
away. As I carried the basket out to the yard because there was
a train due in seven minutes, Eleanor told Franklin that she
had given the matter a great deal of thought. She had been
thinking of nothing else since the day he'd returned.

The train arrived. I began passing out sandwiches. I even
managed to meet the boys' eyes and smile into their faces.

Eleanor sat with an inch of afternoon light between the
chair and her back. "I will give you your freedom, Franklin,
if you want it."

"Thank you, ma'am," the boys said.

"I ask only that before you do anything, you think of the
children," Eleanor added.

Two days later a letter arrived. The tone was sober, but how
could it not be under the circumstances? He had told Eleanor,
he said. He had asked for a divorce. We would be together
soon. He signed it with all his love.

That day I worked in the little store that sold cigarettes and
chewing tobacco and candy. I was sure I would not be able to

add two purchases together or make change for one. My head
was reeling with plans for the future. We would find a small
house in Washington. He would show me the Place. I saw us
sailing in summer and ice boating in winter. Franklin had told
me about Christmas there. I saw the big tree lit with candles
because Franklin's father always lit the tree with candles, and
the chicks, and more children whose features I couldn't quite
make out, but whose beauty shone as bright as the flames on
the tree, gathering around Franklin, chattering, squealing,
vying to climb into his lap as he took his old Groton copy of
A Christmas Carol down from the shelf and began to read.
But in fact I had no trouble adding up purchases or making
change that afternoon. I was a financial wizard. There was
nothing I could not do.

There was money at issue in the house on East Sixty-fifth
Street that day too. Franklin and Eleanor and Mrs. James sat
in the front parlor. There was a tea tray again, this time the
big silver service. It was a family council.

Mrs. James handed a cup to her daughter-in-law. "It's all
very well for you, Eleanor, to speak of being willing to give
Franklin his freedom."

She poured another cup and handed it to Franklin. "And if
you are determined to leave your wife and five children for
another woman and bring scandal upon the family, Franklin,
I cannot stop you."

Franklin took the cup from her somberly. He had expected
this. He deserved this for what he was doing to both of them.
Franklin's faith was simple, straightforward, unshakable. He
believed in punishment for transgression. He also believed in
redemption.

"But you must understand, Franklin," Mrs. James went on,

"that if you do this disgraceful thing, I will not give you another dollar. And Springwood will go directly to the children."

He had not expected this, and it shook him for a moment, but he stood his ground. In his next letter, he told me about Mrs. James's decision, and asked if I would be able to get along on an assistant secretary's salary, and made jokes about living on love, and I knew from the tone of the letter that he did not believe any of it. His mother was a formidable woman, and he loved and admired her for it, but she had a single weakness. Him. It would break her heart to make him unhappy.

Our future was getting closer. I could feel it bearing down on me. That is a sensation I will never forget, the feeling of being in happiness's path.

 Sixteen

"I don't think one can have any idea of how horrendous even the *idea* of divorce was in those days. I remember telling my family in 1912 that I wanted one and, although they didn't quite lock me up, they exercised considerable pressure to get me to reconsider."

                         ∾ Alice Roosevelt Longworth

"Everybody behaved well and exactly as one would expect each of the protagonists . . . to behave."

                    ∾ Corinne Robinson Alsop, a
                           first cousin of Eleanor Roosevelt

I spotted Mr. Howe before he noticed me that afternoon. He was hurrying along Massachusetts Avenue in the direction of the new Union Depot, carrying a gladstone bag, and looking as if he were spoiling for a fight. I knew immediately that he was headed for New York. That was what made me stop to greet him. He was on his way to Franklin.

I said good afternoon. He looked up and recognized me, and something in his face changed. I remember thinking, he knows for certain. It is no longer a suspicion or a fear, it is a fact of his life. It seems impossible to me now that I felt triumphant.

∾ I did not hear from Franklin for three days. I like to think he put up a fight. I see him going round after round with Mr.

Howe, swinging wildly, hitting below the belt, trying every trick to knock himself unconscious of Mr. Howe's truths.

This was 1918, Franklin argued, not the Dark Ages.

If the year 1918 was so advanced, Mr. Howe wanted to know, why were men living and dying like animals in trenches?

People got divorced all the time, Franklin insisted. Look at his old Harvard friend Ned Bell.

Yeah, Mr. Howe admitted, but Bell's only ambition was to spend the rest of his life in the State Department fooling around with codes, and now he'd be lucky if he could do even that, because no one wanted a divorced man, whose former wife was living in Paris with a bunch of Sapphists, handling top-secret information.

Louis was behind the times, Franklin repeated. Soon women would have the vote.

Mine gawd, Mr. Howe howled his favorite term of frustration. You think the women of America are going to cast their brand-new votes for a man who left his wife to marry her social secretary?

That was what they said about Wilson. Franklin was getting angry now. All the political handicappers had predicted that the president would not be reelected if he married Mrs. Galt, and look who was sitting in the White House.

The president had been a widower, Mr. Howe reminded him, not a divorced man, and even Wilson, the man misguided enough to confess to his second wife that he'd cheated on his first, because he didn't want to start the marriage off on the wrong foot, hadn't been dumb enough to let the great American public in on his secret.

By now Franklin was on the ropes, bloodied, punch drunk, in pain. That was when Mr. Howe moved in for the knockout. I know that from what Franklin wrote in his letter. Passionate as he was about American history, it was not something he would bring up in a letter like this.

"Okay, boss, give it to me straight. Do you or do you not want to be president?"

"I do," Franklin answered.

"So let's assume you divorce your missus and leave the chicks and marry Miss Mercer. I figure if you love her enough to risk throwing away the presidency for her, you better marry her. You know what St. Paul said. It's better to marry than to burn. But you know your history as well as your Bible, boss."

Franklin was too smart not to sense that something was coming, but I don't think he knew what. There was no history of divorce in the White House. That was the point.

"I'm talking about Andy Jackson. Or rather Mrs. Jackson, because Old Hickory could take it, but his wife wasn't so tough. They accused her of every sin in the book. She'd been married before. She hadn't been married before, which made her a woman of easy virtue. They screamed adultery, living together without benefit of clergy, and bigamy, though it beats me how she could have pulled off the last two at the same time. And don't tell me this is 1918. I told you before. I could pick a better year out of a hat. They'll smear you, and her, with every half-truth and outright lie in the book. Now, I know you're like Old Hickory. You can take anything they dish out. Like the time you were just starting out and showed up at that political club in those fine English boots and riding britches, and one gent told you if you wanted to run for office, you better get yourself some pants. And you just laughed it off. But what about Miss Mercer? It killed Rachel Jackson. She read one of the news articles. It wasn't even one of the slanders. This was a defense saying she hadn't committed adultery or bigamy or any of the sins they were trying to pin on her. Next thing anyone knew—less than a month later, in fact—she was dead. The shame and scandal killed her. Now, I know Miss Mercer's not that fragile. I also know she'd go through anything for you, boss. But are you sure you want to make her go through all that for the White House? Or," he added, "for a near miss at it?"

∽ The letter came on the first Monday in October. Sun poured from a cloudless sky. The air was soft. Rumors of peace were everywhere. I have never been so full of hope, not even on the day they put my newborn daughter in my arms.

The letter was waiting for me when I arrived home. I cannot remember where I was returning from that morning. I understand shell-shocked soldiers often have the same problem. They either forget everything or cannot stop remembering. I had both responses. I can't recall where I'd been that morning, but I could not stop going over and over odd moments of the past few years. I saw Franklin perched on Eleanor's desk, teaching me about war while he was really talking about love, as a thrush sang in the garden; and standing in the rain with his hair slicked to his head the night war broke out; and beaming down the breakfast table at me the morning I took the seat reserved for Mr. Hoover, and we both gave up the fight. Perhaps it would have been easier if I could have mustered some anger at him, although Violetta's rage turned out to be no help to her. But I could not get angry at Franklin. I knew all the talk about Andrew Jackson and his wife and my happiness was only window dressing, though he didn't believe that. I knew he was doing this for himself. He

could leave Eleanor and the children. He might even be able
to get along without his mother's money. But he could not give
up his dream. If I were going to get angry at him for that, I
should never have fallen in love with him in the first place. I'm
not suggesting that Franklin was perfect. I believe he was
great, but that is another matter. I'm saying that if you cannot
tolerate imperfection, you cannot love. So the letter telling me
that though he would always love me he could not marry me
did not make me think less of him. I had always known
Franklin was hugely, gloriously human.

      We met once more that autumn, at the Raleigh, not on
the roof close to the stars, but on the ground floor in a well-
lit corner of the tea salon. As I made my way toward him
through the sound of tinkling china and hushed conversation,
I had to mask my surprise at his appearance. Though I didn't
know it at the time, my ability to hide my shock at physical
changes in Franklin would stand me in good stead in the
future. That afternoon in 1918, his face was gaunt, his color
pale, his skin drawn tight over his beautiful bones. Only the
smile that broke out when he saw me approaching was familiar. Then it dimmed too, because that afternoon even hello
held the seeds of good-bye.

He said he was glad I had agreed to see him, and I answered
how could I not. He said he hoped I didn't hate him, and I told
him the truth. No matter what he did I would never stop loving him. But I did tell one lie that afternoon. I had to because
of the way he sat across the tea table looking at me. His eyes
burned with a febrile intensity, though his fever had subsided
weeks before. It was not a terrible lie. In fact, if I'd loved him
less, it would have been the truth. I told him that the more I

thought about it, the more certain I was. I could not have married him. My faith did not permit it. And he believed me.

∾ Three weeks later, on November eleventh, peace broke
out in Marshal Foch's railroad car in the Forest of Compiègne
and reverberated around the world. Bells rang, and horns
blew, and children marched in the streets banging pots and
pans. Soldiers bellowed with relief, and wives and mothers
wept with joy, and strangers kissed one another in celebration. It was not unlike the spree that had met the outbreak of
war, but in the interval ten million young men had died and
other millions of men, women, and children were too weak-
ened by the Spanish influenza to rise from their sickbeds. Sitting on the wide wooden porch of my cousins' house,
shrouded in the soft smoky twilight that comes to North Carolina in November, I mourned with them. Not for my love. It
still lived within me. That was the heartbreak of it.

~ March 4, 1933

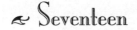 Seventeen

"I'm not going to be conquered by a childish disease."

⌁ Franklin D. Roosevelt

The crowd stood eerily quiet in the shadow of the Capitol, shoulders hunched against the March wind, faces bleached by the gray afternoon, and the times. President Hoover said no one was starving, but I'd read of twenty thousand malnourished children in the New York City schools, and once, as I was going from auto to apartment, I'd glimpsed a man and a woman scavenging through garbage cans like alley cats. Breadlines snaked around blocks, and perfectly nice people averted their eyes as they passed for fear of seeing, and embarrassing, someone they knew. The headlines grew worse every day. The numbers were numbing. Five thousand banks had failed. Thirteen million people were out of work. The suicide rate had tripled. What else could a man, crushed by the shame of not being able to feed and clothe his family, do?

The violence was not only to self, or so a gentleman I'd sat beside at dinner recently had told me. It was madness to go near a city these days, he'd warned. He confined himself to his plantation in South Carolina and his house on Long Island, both of which he'd stocked with food, water, his best wines, and an arsenal of weapons. "Mark my words. We'll have a revolution before the year is out."

We didn't have a revolution. We had Franklin. It was the nation's triumph, and his. He had saved himself, and now he would save us. Standing in the Franklin-hungry crowd, I was still an innocent.

A hush muffled the Capitol grounds this morning, but throughout the rest of the city the festive spirit hung like bunting. People had been pouring in for days. The Pennsylvania Railroad and the Baltimore & Ohio had put on dozens of low-rate excursions. Eastern Air Transport had scheduled a record number of planes. For the first time a traveler could buy a through ticket to fly to Washington from almost anywhere in the country. I'd come up from Aiken the day before, and there hadn't been an empty compartment, bedroom, or seat on the train, though I hadn't run into anyone I knew. The people I lived among were not eager to celebrate Franklin's inauguration.

He and Eleanor had come down with family and friends on a special train. I'd read about it in the paper, along with reports of what Eleanor would be wearing to the inaugural ball. She'd chosen a gown of silver lamé in her favorite shade of periwinkle blue, which overnight had become Eleanor Blue. I wondered how her cousin Alice Longworth, whose Alice Blue had been all the rage when her father was in the White House, felt about that. According to the papers, Eleanor's original choice had been white satin Chinese brocade, but at the final fitting she'd been so pleased with the silver lamé she'd changed her mind. Both dresses had been designed by Mrs. Sally Milgrim of H. Milgrim and Brothers, and made, Eleanor assured the interviewer, by union labor.

The days were long gone when a mischievous reporter could get her to talk about scaling back from four meals a day to three and encouraging her ten servants to turn one another in for wasting food.

I'd bought something new for the inauguration too, though it had been an absurd thing to do. Franklin wouldn't be able to see me in the crowd, and even if he could, he would not know my new coat and dress from things that had been hanging in my closets for years.

People were still crowding into the viewing area below the south portico, but with each new wave the hush grew only deeper. The feeling of expectancy was as insistent as the March chill. Every face was turned toward the platform hung with garlands of laurel and draped with medallions of the Great Seal of the United States. I had a perfect view of it all. Franklin had made sure of that. Or rather Miss LeHand had. He'd called to invite me to the inauguration. He said I might enjoy the hoopla. He meant he wanted me to share his triumph. But Miss LeHand had made the arrangements.

"I will send a car for you," she had said, and known the number of Violetta and Bill's house on Q Street without my telling her. "The driver will have your ticket. If there is anything I can do, please don't hesitate to call me." Her voice was polite and crisp, set to a perfect secretarial pitch, but there was an undercurrent in it I couldn't place. It wasn't a chill. She could not have been more accommodating. It was, it occurred to me as I hung up the phone, graciousness. Miss LeHand sounded like a hostess welcoming me to her party.

I pulled my furs closer around my neck. Even the raw weather couldn't discourage the crowds. When I'd driven up Pennsylvania Avenue in the car Miss LeHand had sent, a dark discreet Packard that would attract no undue attention, the parade route had already been packed ten deep and a mile long with women bundled against the cold, and men balancing children on their shoulders, and boys hanging from the iced branches of trees like out-of-season fruit. The roofs of the office buildings flanking the Capitol grounds were black with dark overcoats standing shoulder to shoulder. There and in the bleachers on the Capitol roof, the shivering crowd made the chill air shimmer like a desert mirage. There was something surreal about the scene, and it had to do with more than the eerie hush. It was the sheer impossibility of the event. Everything in Franklin's existence had strained toward this moment, except for one instant that had almost sabotaged it.

Franklin's life after I'd hurried out of the Raleigh tearoom, because to linger would have been suicidal, hadn't been as golden as Mrs. James had assumed, and Mr. Howe had promised, and Franklin and I had expected. I do not know what Eleanor thought it would be, or even wanted it to be. His defeat for the vice presidency in 1920 was his first setback, though he was too canny a politician not to have known that he and Mr. Cox didn't stand a chance. The war was over. The nation was tired of heroism. The people, including women who were voting for the first time, wanted mediocrity, which Mr. Harding called normalcy. Franklin was out of step with the era. But he traveled the country, and made headlines I read religiously, and was young enough to bide his time. Even as I studied the outcome of the election and suffered for Franklin, I imagined Mr. Howe squinting into the future through a cloud of Sweet Caporal smoke and marking the moment when Franklin and the country would be ready for each other.

Two Republican senators had other ideas. The summer

heat hadn't yet begun to cook the air that July morning I picked up the paper and saw the headline.

LAY NAVY SCANDAL TO F. D. ROOSEVELT; DETAILS ARE UNPRINTABLE

I raced through the article. The paper refused to print the details, but it managed to hint at them. The navy had set up a sting operation to stamp out vice in the Newport Yard. It had resulted in "beastly acts," and "unspeakable perversions," and "the use of enlisted men in the uniform of the United States Navy to ferret out unnatural behavior." The article wasn't a news piece. It was an obituary for Franklin's political career.

A week later Livy paid a visit. He'd gotten in the habit of stopping by whenever he was in the area. Each time I saw him his dark eyes were sunk deeper in his face, his dapper clothes a little seedier, his hands more unsteady as he reached for the drink I always remembered to offer him, no matter what hour of the day. Perhaps that is the trouble with occasional friends. The less we see them, the more we notice their decline. Nonetheless, I was always glad to see Livy. He brought news of Franklin. That was something else that made me feel sorry for him. Livy lived on another man's credit.

"I've seen the report," Livy said. "It blames Franklin for everything. Of course, there isn't a word of truth in it."

"Why didn't he defend himself? The paper said the investigation has been going on for months."

"He begged them to let him testify. Senator Ball kept putting him off. Then suddenly they announced the report was ready to be released. And don't think for a minute it was an accident that Franklin had left for Campo. He came racing back. Went straight to the committee and protested that he'd never even seen the testimony of the other witnesses, let alone been given a chance to respond to it. So Senator Ball said fine. Here's the report. Give us your statement by eight o'clock tonight." Livy shook his head and took a swallow of his drink. "It was eleven in the morning. They gave him an empty office in the State, War, and Navy and nine hours to read fifteen volumes of testimony. Six thousand single-spaced pages.

"He worked all day. He and Missy. Miss LeHand, his new secretary. You remember what that place is like in July. Hotter'n hinges. But then Ball double-crossed him again. He and Senator Keyes released the report without waiting for Franklin's response. Even the reputable papers ran banner headlines about 'unprintable details' and buried Franklin's statement next to ads for the new Marmon."

"What will he do now?"

"There's nothing he can do. If he goes on denying the charges, he just keeps them in the news. If he doesn't fight them, people think he really is guilty of 'dereliction of duty,' and 'abuse of office,' and 'gross immorality.' It's the old where-there's-smoke-there's-fire-mentality. And it stinks."

I offered to refill Livy's drink, but he said he'd do it himself.

"You should have seen the letter Franklin wrote Senator Keyes. Ball was the one who lied to him about testifying, but Franklin figures what can you expect from a man who went to public school and the University of Delaware. Keyes is a Harvard man, though. He should know better. That's what Franklin told him. The letter was a corker." Livy took another swallow of his drink, then looked at his glass and frowned. "Only problem is he couldn't send it."

"There would have been no point," I said.

"Not in the long run," Livy agreed.

But we couldn't meet each other's eyes. At that moment we

both doubted Franklin had a long run politically. People who would not cast their votes for a man who divorced his wife to marry another woman weren't likely to elect an official who'd exposed American boys to acts of beastly perversion. I had walked out of the Raleigh tearoom for nothing.

But Franklin could not be kept down. The crush of silent spectators around me now was proof of that. They'd gathered for the reassurance of his smile, and the comfort of his voice, and the infectiousness of his confidence. They'd gathered because he was golden after all.

The short memory of the American people had helped. Three weeks after the headlines screamed of unprintable details, he was back in the news without a whiff of scandal. I still have the photograph that accompanied the article. I'm not sure why I clipped it. I had no premonitions. Perhaps I just liked the way Franklin looked in the picture.

The article told how fifty prominent men had sailed up to Bear Mountain to inspect the Boy Scout camps that took more than two thousand boys out of steaming disease-infested tenements every summer and introduced them to a world of cool forests and wide river and good clean fun. It taught those street-toughened youths, who'd built up resistance to the dangers of the city, how to survive in a different wilderness. There was a line in the article about the scouts demonstrating their knot-tying skills for the former assistant secretary of the navy, and I pictured Franklin giving them pointers on the intricacies he'd mastered in his own childhood. I imagined him roughhousing with the boys, getting in among them, becoming one of them, picking up their baseballs and bats, their slang and their sheer pleasure in the day. I never dreamed there was anything else he might pick up.

Perhaps he didn't. Perhaps the virus, so small it was invisible through even the most powerful microscopes of the day, wasn't lurking at the Boy Scout camp, but in that steamy office in the State, War, and Navy Building, or in the dining room of one of his clubs, or on the hand of a friend he stopped to shake on Wall Street. He could have picked it up anywhere, but I blame the Boy Scouts because of the photograph. Since I clipped that picture, I have seen dozens more of Franklin, as presidential candidate, as governor, as the speaker whose nomination of Al Smith brought the entire Democratic convention to its feet cheering Franklin Roosevelt. But I never again saw a photograph of him standing alone and unaided. Now, when he walked, he had to lean on a cane or someone's arm for support.

There was a stir of movement on the portico. Eleanor and Mrs. Hoover were making their way through the crowd. As they stopped, turned, and walked to opposite ends, applause rippled across the platform and echoed here and there in the audience. The sounds were as isolated and sporadic as gunshots. They made me suddenly uneasy. Three weeks earlier in Miami there had been gunshots. But Franklin had survived the assassination attempt too, though poor Mayor Cermak of Chicago was still in the hospital and not expected to live. According to Mr. Vincent Astor, whom I'd seen since, Franklin's sangfroid had been astonishing. Even after it was all over and he was back on Mr. Astor's yacht among friends, he had shown no fear nor any trace of shock.

Eleanor smiled and nodded to a few people, but she did not look happy. I'd heard she was miserable. She did not want to be first lady. She did not want to give up her own work with the Democratic Committee, and the Women's Trade Union League, and the Todhunter School in New York where she taught several days a week. She dreaded going back to pouring tea, and cutting ribbons, and making small talk. Poor Eleanor. She did not have much of a gift for happiness. But she was glorious in misfortune. During the awful summer of 1921, and in the years following, she'd been heroic.

F. D. ROOSEVELT ILL
OF POLIOMYELITIS

The paper had rattled so badly in my shaking hands I'd barely been able to read it. PATIENT STRICKEN BY INFANTILE PARALYSIS A MONTH AGO. USE OF LEGS AFFECTED. My eye raced through the trembling words. "Definitely he will not be crippled. No one need have any fear of permanent injury."

For the first time in my life I understood the meaning of God's infinite mercy. He had punished us, but He had forgiven us.

The stories began to filter back to me. People said his spirits were high. "My appetite is excellent, and I'm getting stronger every day," he told one friend. "I am still on crutches and cannot possibly play golf for a year or two," he wrote another.

Eleanor was entirely selfless. Everyone said so. I imagined her sitting for hours by Franklin's side, reading to him, writing his letters, anticipating his every need. She would sleep on a cot in his room in case he awakened in the night, and massage his muscles according to the doctor's instructions, and see him through the terrible indignities to bladder and bowel until he was on his feet again. People said she was running herself so ragged the doctors were as worried about her health as his. But I could not feel sorry for Eleanor. I could only envy her.

The platform was filling up now. Vice President Garner, who'd already sworn his oath of office in the Senate chamber, crossed and took his seat. Hatless, without an overcoat, he leaned over and borrowed a muffler from a young man who looked familiar. It took me only a moment to realize it was Franklin, Jr. He was standing with Elliott and John, and I would have known all three of them, even if I hadn't seen photographs in the newspapers. They were tall and fair and fine-looking, with an easy grace. Each of them had something of Franklin in the way he held his head or grinned or waved to someone in the crowd. Anna, who stood beside them with her husband, was lean and long-legged and elegant as a racehorse. The first time I'd met her, I'd wanted a daughter like her. Now I hoped Barbara would grow up to be as lovely. The row of Roosevelt offspring made Mrs. James look even smaller and stouter than she was. She stood, swathed in yards of stiff black fabric and dignity, but her smile gave her away. Her smile was almost laughable, it was so like her son's. She could not wipe it off her face. Unlike her daughter-in-law, she looked extremely happy, though if it had been up to her, none of this would be happening.

"It's almost as if this is what she's been waiting for," Livy said when he paid a visit several months after I'd seen those terrifying headlines about Franklin's polio. "Now she doesn't have to share him with the rest of the world. Now she can take him back to the Place, wrap him in cotton batting, and turn him into an invalid gentleman farmer like his father."

"She can't want that," I said, though I knew she could. Mrs. James resented having to share Franklin with Eleanor. I could imagine how she felt about people like Mr. Howe and the other ill-bred, unkempt politicians who trampled her lawn, and spilled ashes on her carpets, and polluted the crystalline air that Roosevelts and Delanos and a handful of other nice people breathed. Besides, it would not be seemly to have

Franklin out and about. Mrs. James's attitude was not
unusual for the time. People who could afford to hid their
incapacitated relatives away at home. Those who couldn't
locked them in institutions. One way or another, they were
not supposed to live among the ordinary population, calling
attention to themselves, embarrassing others, blighting the
fine sunny landscape of American optimism. That was before
Franklin started Warm Springs and changed for good the way
people like him lived and the rest of the world looked at them.

"Oh, can't she?" Livy said. "Fortunately, Franklin has
other ideas. He has no intention of being an invalid. And even
if he did, Louis Howe wouldn't let him."

"What does Eleanor think?"

"Now, there's the real surprise. Louis has her making
appearances, and giving speeches, and standing in for Franklin
all up and down the state. She's taking to it like a duck to
water."

I could imagine nursing Franklin. That would be second
nature. But no matter how hard I tried, I could not envision
going out into the world, standing up before auditoriums full
of people, subjecting myself to rude questions, engaging in
heated arguments. I would have tried to do it for Franklin, but
I doubt I would have succeeded. The knowledge should have
made my loss easier. It didn't.

Chief Justice Hughes was making his way across the platform now. The crowd was still silent, but I could feel the
expectation mounting. Everyone else was preliminary. We
were waiting for Franklin. And he was getting closer.

He hadn't been back on the golf links in a year or even two,
though he'd fought valiantly and embraced every treatment
imaginable. I knew because I kept track. Hot baths, cold dips,
salt water, fresh springs, ultraviolet light, electric current,

working with gravity, struggling against gravity, leaning on parallel bars at his waist, hanging from parallel bars above his head, massages, horseback riding, and schemes so unconventional he had to laugh at them even as he hoped against hope they'd work. There was no ordeal he did not put himself through, though he never behaved as if it were an ordeal.

"Keep me company while I go through my paces," he'd say, and as he dragged his legs back and forth between two parallel bars, or swung beneath them, or struggled with some other agonizingly repetitive exercise, he kept up a marathon of dazzling conversation designed to distract and entertain his audience.

He did not like to be alone, but he was alone when he made his greatest stride forward. The drive was a short elm-lined stretch, no longer than a quarter of a mile, leading from the house to the main road. As a boy, he'd galloped up and down it a dozen times a day. As a young man, he'd strode it without a second thought. During the years he was learning to walk again, it took him an entire summer to get to the end of it. By the time he reached the big stone gateposts marking the intersection with the Albany Post Road, perspiration soaked his shirt and ran down his pain-etched face. But he had done it. He had made it, Livy told me, to the end of the drive.

After that he took to the sea. "Water got me into this," he said, because when he'd first felt feverish and achy in Campo, instead of taking to his bed, which might have mitigated the long-term effects of the disease, he'd tried to swim and sail and will the symptoms away. "And water will get me out." According to Livy, that was the way he talked. He didn't avoid the subject. And he would not be pitied. He kept up a mask of faintly rueful irony.

He bought a secondhand boat to cruise off the Florida Keys.

The *Larocco* wasn't a patch on the big sleek yachts of Vincent Astor and VanLear Black and his other cruising friends, but it was seaworthy and enabled him to spend long days fishing and cruising and swimming, most of all swimming, because swimming, he was convinced, facilitated walking.

Eleanor hated the life. The childhood disaster at sea still haunted her. The loneliness of the wind-howling anchorages depressed her. Life away from her committees and meetings and speeches bored her. She visited the *Larocco* rarely, stayed briefly, and left the rest to Miss LeHand. Livy didn't tell me about Miss LeHand, but others did.

Most of the time the boat was filled to the gunnels with guests. A group of old Groton and Harvard friends left. A bunch of political colleagues arrived. James and Elliott and Franklin, Jr., and John came to fish and swim and spend time with the old man. But sometimes days and even weeks went by when Franklin and Miss LeHand were alone on the boat with only the hired couple who served as cook and crew. Then Miss LeHand was the one who kept Franklin company while he fished and played solitaire and arranged his stamps. She was the one who shared his excitement when the buoyancy of the water lifted his legs with promise. And she was the one who endured those long mornings when he did not emerge from his cabin until noon because progress was slow, and hope slipping, and he was face-to-face with his damnation.

Mrs. James was scandalized. She thought Eleanor belonged with her husband and Miss LeHand did not. Others were titillated. I was glad. Really I was. I wanted Franklin to be happy.

The portico was overflowing now with cabinet members and officials and Roosevelts. President Hoover emerged from the Capitol, crossed the platform, and stood beside his wife.

The square of his face was set in a dour frown. A young man came hurrying behind him, stopped in front of Chief Justice Hughes, and handed him a black leather-bound book. It looked like a Bible. Knowing Franklin, I guessed it was not just any Bible but the old Dutch translation brought to this country by Claes Martenswzen van Rosenvelt three hundred years earlier. Franklin had been preparing for this day since before he was born. I was glad I had not prevented it. I had walked away, and he had walked back onto the political stage. Literally. He had spent more than a lifetime preparing for the presidency, and years regaining the use of his legs to claim it.

As the young man retreated, I noticed a woman sitting among the Roosevelt clan. I didn't know how I'd missed her before. She was more striking than she appeared in photos, not pretty but what people call handsome. Her face was long and ended in a jaw that, depending on your point of view, was either strong or lanterned. Her features were bold but pleasant. She carried her height with ease. She knew how to dress. Her dark coat, trimmed with a caracul shawl collar, was understated and slimming, though I don't mean to imply that she was overweight. She was wearing something called a "Montijo" hat which dipped low over one eye and curved back on the other side to reveal a stripe of premature white like a streak of lightning in her dark hair. She had an air about her, studied perhaps but no less real, of good breeding. Gossips said that in the years she'd spent with Franklin, the winters cruising off the coast of Florida, the months in Warm Springs after he decided hot medicinal waters were more conducive to restoring muscles than the cold sea, Miss LeHand had adopted his language and mannerisms and manners. That too is a sign of love.

A bugle sounded. The crowd, no longer an aggregate of

individuals but a single living organism, shuddered. The marine band launched into "Hail to the Chief." Faces lifted to the portico. Bodies strained forward. Franklin appeared. The human hush, silent as water, came crashing down in a wave of whistling and cheering and clapping and shouting. On the platform dignified men and women lost composure. Former Secretary Daniels pounded on the wooden floor with his walking stick, and Mr. Bernard Baruch climbed on a bench and swung his silk top hat in wide jubilant circles, and Mrs. Wilson, the late president's widow whom Mama had resented, waved a handkerchief as frantically as if it were a flag. But it was all a blur to me. My eyes were on Franklin. Beneath the silk top hat, his face shone in the winter-gray afternoon like a beacon. His chin was a lesson in optimism. His beautifully cut morning coat could not disguise the muscled shoulders and massive torso. The aura of hope and strength he gave off had an alcoholic kick. No wonder he'd promised to repeal Prohibition.

With one hand he held the arm of a balding young man whose face still retained the traces of the boy I'd known as Jimmy; in the other he grasped a cane. I had known he often leaned on a son or a cane when he walked, but I was troubled to see he needed both.

They started forward. Franklin twisted his hips and hurled his right leg out in a stiff arc that somehow inched him ahead. He twisted again and repeated the movement with his left. His face set, his arm clutching Jimmy's, he twisted and hurled, twisted and hurled. The Marine Band blared its way through "Hail to the Chief," as Franklin heaved himself up the maroon-carpeted ramp. The cane thumped, and the heavy iron braces clanked beneath his trouser cuffs, and my innocence died.

They had lied to me. The doctors who had examined him
for a half-million-dollar life insurance policy and sworn to the
American people that he was in excellent physical condition,
and the photos and newsreels that showed him waving from
the backs of touring cars and towering behind podiums, and
Eleanor and Mr. Howe and Franklin himself had all lied to
me. He could move his hips. He could propel his body. He
could imitate the appearance of walking. But he could not
walk. He was paralyzed.

I saw that now, but the crowd refused to believe it. They
watched him inch along in that grotesque parody of a walk
and cheered and shouted and waved their faith. The sight was
astonishing. The moment was historic. A nation swooning
from disaster was looking to a crippled man to get it back on
its feet.

He let go of James's arm and gripped the podium with one
hand, then relinquished the cane and hung on for dear life
with the other. I wondered where he found the strength.

Standing in the crowd, listening to Franklin tell a terrified
nation that it had nothing to fear but fear itself, watching him
prove it with his damaged body, I knew there must have been
times when he'd feared God had lost faith in him. Worse than
that, there must have been times when he'd feared God had
punished him for what we had done. And I came face-to-face
with my own culpability.

❧ 1918–1940

⚰ Eighteen

"We never saw Eleanor and Franklin Roosevelt in the same room alone together. They had the most separate relationship I have ever seen between man and wife. And the most equal."

⚰ J. B. West, White House usher

"She [Lucy] married Mr. Rutherfurd, not for money but because she felt he needed her."

⚰ Mrs. Lyman Cotton, Lucy Mercer's cousin

How could I not have known? Because I did not want to. And because Franklin did not want me to, any more than he wanted the rest of America to know. I understood that. He thought if they knew, they would not elect him president. But he should have known I would go on loving him.

He never lied about his paralysis. He simply didn't make a fuss about it. He wrote that he was still *stomping* around, and I thought he meant he was walking with a cane. I sat in my cabin on the S.S. *Belgenland* on the way to Europe and wrote back that he and Eleanor and the children ought to make a tour of their own, and if he liked I would be happy to find out about a special chair made to fit into French trains, which Bessie Kittridge's sister had used. I didn't believe he needed the

193

chair to get around. I simply thought it might make touring less tiring.

Later, Violetta's husband Bill, who became interested in psychology, would call it a *folie à deux*. Franklin and I conspired to delude ourselves and each other. It was not difficult. He still gave off an aura of vitality and power. When Bill and Vio's son Carroll died of leukemia just before Franklin's inauguration, and the authorities refused to permit him to be buried in Arlington because the cemetery was becoming too crowded, I telephoned Franklin, and he made another call, and we buried poor little Carroll in his grandfather's grave in Arlington. Is it any wonder I did not think of Franklin as incapacitated?

What of these letters and telephone calls I mention so casually? What of Franklin's promise to Eleanor never to see me again? Yes, I knew about that. And I tried to respect it. That was why I asked Mrs. Polk to break the news to Franklin.

Mr. Polk had served as undersecretary of state when Franklin had been assistant secretary of the navy. The two couples saw each other often. It would not be difficult for Mrs. Polk to find a moment alone with Franklin to tell him something I did not want him to read in the newspaper.

✍ In the weeks after I hurried out of the Raleigh tearoom, I lived in a world made entirely of despair. It was in the rain and the wind and the sunshine, especially the sunshine. It was solitude. It was other people. It was so familiar it was almost comfort. But as I sat on the porch of my cousins' house in North Carolina and watched the smoky autumn dusks give way to sudden winter nightfalls, I discovered I was not made for unhappiness, though I was brutally unhappy at the time. Grief is more difficult to sustain than most people think. Life begins

to insinuate itself. Especially if you are young and healthy and
have loved and been loved. Sometimes on those chilly evenings
on my cousins' porch I imagined seeing Franklin. I knew we
would meet again, despite his promise to Eleanor.

"Lucy," he would sing with the pure joy of my name,
"what have you been up to?"

I did not want to be ashamed of my answer. The question
became more insistent after the summer of 1921. If he could
be a hero in the face of polio, I would not be a coward in the
face of life.

At first it was less a matter of happiness than of the occasional forgetfulness of unhappiness. Violetta came home, and
I realized how much I'd missed her. I also discovered that I
liked Dr. Marbury after all. He had a sensitivity to mood that
picked up on my worst moments and managed to make them
a little easier without saying a word. Perhaps it had to do with
his medical training, or with the fact that he had so many
black moods of his own. But he was happy now with Vio, I
was sure of it, and their marriage filled me with pleasure, and
envy, and a longing so palpable it made my bones ache. I was
extraordinarily susceptible. Perhaps that explains my reaction
the first time I saw Tranquility. The irony of the name struck
me as soon as Winty mentioned it. Eleanor had often quoted
a line from a book called *The Countryman's Year*. "Back of
tranquility lies always conquered unhappiness."

The rumor has somehow spread that I went to Tranquility
as a governess. It makes for a neat symmetry, and a better
story. She went to Eleanor Roosevelt as a social secretary and
won Franklin. She went to the Rutherfurds as a governess and
captured Winty. I hate to disappoint the gossips, but I went to
Tranquility as a guest. Winty wanted me to meet his children.
We both knew he did not have a governess's position in mind.

It was a bronzed autumn day, almost exactly a year since I'd said good-bye to Franklin, two and a half since Winty's wife had died, leaving him with six children. Most people would not have thought of Winty as lonely, but then few people knew him. As we drove through the gates, he pointed out the small stone chapel he'd built for his late wife. Alice had converted to Catholicism, and Winty had promised her he would raise the children in her faith. He still kept a priest to say mass on Sundays and, he added with a mixture of irony and affection that made me like him even more, keep the older boys in line.

He'd put the top of the Pierce Arrow down, and the sun hugged my shoulders and struck the peak of his tweed cap so it cast a shadow over his fine English features. He was American, but there is something about growing up in England, and espousing English ways, and speaking with an English accent that can lend a British cast to the most American face. Perhaps it's akin to speaking French like a Frenchman. It does something to the set of the mouth.

There are many anecdotes about Winty's being mistaken for the perfect English gentleman, but then there are many stories about Winty. For a man who prized privacy, he attracted an unusual amount of attention. There was the contretemps with the American Kennel Club about his fox terriers; and the rumors that he'd inspired more than one of the characters in the novels of Mrs. Wharton, with whom he'd grown up; and the fuss about Consuelo Vanderbilt, who by the time I met him was the Duchess of Marlborough. "Six-foot-two in his golf stockings, Mr. Rutherfurd was no match for five-foot-six in a coronet," the papers wrote slyly after Mrs. Vanderbilt forced her daughter, who was in love with Winty, to marry the duke. A few years ago, when the duchess petitioned for a divorce, the papers called again. But that came later.

The day Winty first took me to Tranquility, he was fifty-two and I was twenty-nine. People spoke of a May-December romance, and I suppose they were right, but they put the emphasis on the seasons, I on the romance.

How can I describe how handsome Winty was? Our house-maids blushed when he entered the room, though he was exquisitely correct and never noticed them. He radiated the easy grace and physical discipline of a born sportsman. His presence commanded attention, his voice obedience, from animals as well as people. Some found him austere. I thought him dignified. They spoke of his formality. I admired his manners. They said he was a snob. I saw him as discriminating. And it was simply not true that he had no sense of humor. He merely chose not to show it to most people. He lived beauti-fully and quietly, breeding his terriers and cattle, running his estate, doting on, though never indulging, his children. He was perfectly happy within the confines of the universe he'd created for himself. He had no need of the approval of others. If he'd had to choose between being loved or feared by the world at large, I suspect he would have settled for the latter. He was nothing like Franklin. That was one of his attractions. If I could not have Franklin, I did not want a pale imitation.

There was something else that drew me to Winty. Like many men who are admired by many women, Winty needed a single woman. After his eldest son Lewis died, he needed me more than ever. That was why we did not postpone the wed-ding. Some people found it unseemly. Poor Lewis had died only a few days earlier, one of the last casualties of the flu epi-demic. But Winty and I saw no reason to sacrifice what little solace he could find to other people's sense of propriety.

Lewis and the other older boys had come home from school the weekend I went to Tranquility for the first time. Winty had summoned them. The four older boys and little Guy and Alice were all on the lawn in front of the sprawling turreted house Winty had built on the family property only a few miles from the larger one where he'd grown up. Of course, being Winty's children, they weren't simply waiting for us. They had put on boxing gloves, divided into twosomes, and were sparring with each other. Heaven help the son of Winty's who couldn't ride or golf or row or shoot. Fortunately, they all could. A few years later, when John, who was the tallest of the group, and all the boys were more than six feet, massive as a stone chapel and gentle as a benediction, entered the Golden Gloves Tournament, the sportswriters had a heyday. They called him a Princeton playboy who'd been born with a silver glove on his fist. They said he didn't stand a chance against the tough street boxers who'd learned to fight the hard way. They predicted he'd go down bloodied and bowed in the first round. But Winty never doubted John would win. He was convinced excellence would out. He was sure Rutherfurd blood would triumph. He was right. John won the Golden Gloves. But all that was in the future the afternoon we found his six children boxing on the lawn of Tranquility.

As he came around the auto to help me out, he told them not to stop.

"That's Lewis and Win." He pointed to the two oldest boys, who were dancing about the lawn, feinting and bobbing and jabbing at each other. "And John and Hugo." He indicated two younger boys, who made up in enthusiasm for what they lacked in technique. "And these two budding pugilists are Alice and Guy."

Alice looked up long enough to give me a shy smile, but it

was the small boy, not more than five or six, who caught my attention. His knees, beneath short flannel pants, were scratched and grass-stained, his face was set in an old-man scowl, and his skinny arms ended in two absurdly large gloves. They were swinging wildly, while his sister kept him at arm's length with one hand on his furrowed forehead. His feet slipped on the grass, and his arms churned the air, and his face flamed with frustration.

As we stood watching, Alice took her hand from his forehead, and he lunged forward. But her arms were longer, and she was more coordinated. Just as his fist moved toward her chin, hers landed squarely on his nose. A burst of red bloomed like a bright anemone in the afternoon sun. His small body staggered backward and sat hard on the ground. His face was a mask of outraged surprise. Blood ran down his upper lip, over his chin, and onto the rumpled shirt that had pulled out of his shorts. But his eyes remained dry. Standing there watching him struggle to keep them that way, I fell in love again.

A few weeks later I asked Mrs. Polk to find an opportunity to tell Franklin that I was going to be married. I didn't want him to learn of it from the newspapers. And I did not think I should write to him.

The announcement did not go as smoothly as I'd hoped. Shortly after I'd asked Mrs. Polk to pass on the news, Eleanor invited her and her husband to tea, but despite the hour the four of them spent together, Mrs. Polk could not manage a moment alone with Franklin. Finally, as they were saying good-bye, she decided she had no choice but to tell Eleanor. "Did you know," she said in a voice pitched loud enough for Franklin to hear, "that Miss Mercer is going to marry Mr. Winty Rutherfurd?"

Franklin started as if he'd been kicked. At least that was what Mrs. Polk told me.

∽ Franklin wrote me, as I knew he would. He sent his congratulations to Winty and wished me all the joy in the world. The form was proper, but out of character for him. He'd always joked that when he'd gotten engaged to Eleanor, everyone had congratulated him and wished her luck, as if he'd been fortunate to snare her, but she would need all the help she could get going through life with him. As a result, he always made a point of congratulating both the bride and the groom, despite what the etiquette books instructed. But in the letter he wrote me, the first communication we'd had since that afternoon I lied to him in the Raleigh tearoom and told him I could never have married him, he congratulated Winty and wished me joy.

∽ I went to live among the enemy. At least that was the way it seemed once Franklin returned to public life. In the beginning the gossip was more about his personal affairs than his politics. Business was still flourishing, the stock market had not crashed, and gentlemen were not yet hurling themselves from windows or fleeing to other countries to escape federal authorities.

"I understand Eleanor is rarely there."

It was an overcast afternoon in the summer of '29. We were four or five women for tea. All of them knew Franklin and Eleanor. Most of them, I had thought, liked them.

"She's relinquished the ground completely."

I slipped a slice of lemon into my cup.

"I heard her bedroom connects with his," another woman said. She was referring to Miss LeHand, not Eleanor.

I stirred my tea in silence.

"I know someone who saw her coming from his room in a nightdress."

I put my cup and saucer down. I did not want them rattling in my hand. "Mr. Roosevelt is the governor of New York," I said. "Miss LeHand is his secretary. Surely you can't expect her to put on a hat and gloves every time he remembers some bit of official business."

A few months later the stock market crashed; Mr. Hoover reassured the people that it was not a panic, merely a depression; and anyone paying attention to what Franklin was up to, and I always was, would have noticed the way he was drifting. He championed the forty-eight-hour work week for women, and as I read about the proposed bill in the paper, I remembered the night he had come home and found me working late in the back parlor of the house on N Street, and told me about the fifty-four-hour bill for women and children, which he said he'd put through, and Eleanor's frown suggested he hadn't. He enacted an emergency relief law for the unemployed. The adjective had become a noun. He urged, and this is what really infuriated the people I knew, higher taxes. Still, a governor is not a president. And many of his measures never passed the legislature. Aside from friends who had apartments in New York City or houses overlooking the Hudson or Long Island Sound, most of the people I lived among thought Franklin was simply a misguided soul who had taken up an unsavory profession and acquired a handful of harebrained ideas.

His run for the presidency changed all that. Suddenly people who barely knew him had half a dozen reasons to hate him. Suddenly total strangers had it on the best authority that he was mad, or dying, or confined to a hospital somewhere, despite pictures and public appearances to the contrary. After one of Eleanor's speeches, a woman asked her whether her husband's illness had affected his mind. The audience gasped, but Eleanor said she was glad the question had come up. His illness had affected his mind, she admitted. It had made him more understanding and sympathetic. The audience gave her a standing ovation.

When Livy had first told me about Eleanor's efforts to stand in for Franklin, I'd tried to imagine myself in her place. But as her life became more public and mine more private, I gave up. I knew what it was like to love Franklin. I had dreamed about what it would be like to be married to him. I could envision nursing him and doting on him and raising his children. But no matter how hard I tried, I could not picture standing in front of a room full of strangers facing questions no decent woman would ask and no nice woman should have to answer.

Eleanor's reply to the rude woman was becoming the official line on Franklin's character. Sickness had humanized him. Hardship had softened him. One or two people—Livy, Eleanor's cousin Corinne Alsop—maintained that I had changed him too. "Before you came along," Corinne said to me one evening in an extraordinary conversation I will never forget, "I always found Franklin without depth. He had a loveless quality, as if he were incapable of emotion. But all that changed after he found you."

Much as I loved hearing it, I knew it was not true. The people who thought Franklin had changed simply hadn't known him to begin with. And now that they did, they were unwilling to admit they'd been wrong.

He was widely loved, and virulently hated. The whispering campaign did not stop once he was elected. The longer he was in office, the more outrageous the rumors became, and the more outrageous they became, the more impossible it was to combat them. Mr. Howe couldn't plant stories in the papers saying that Franklin was not mad or syphilitic or a Bolshevik or a Jew.

I was spared the worst of them. Most of the Roosevelt-haters I knew, and I suspect that included most of the people I knew, held their tongues in my presence. I never made a secret of the fact that Franklin and I were good friends. There was a bit of a scene, however, one morning at the beginning of his second term in the White House. By then he'd ruined American business by reopening the banks, and undermined self-reliance by giving men who were out of work and farmers who'd lost their land government jobs, and betrayed his class by heading off the revolution that would have lined it up before a firing squad. "We are going to make a country," he said to me once, "in which no one is left out." People who had dedicated their lives to the principle of exclusivity could not forgive him his dreams of inclusion.

It was the week of the Aiken Drag, and though Winty and I managed to avoid the worst of the social frenzy during that and the hunt and the horse show—the formal dinners that began too late and went on too long, the card games after that lasted until the hunt breakfasts began—we had a house full of guests, including one of the DuPonts and her husband, who was a vice president in the firm. That was before Franklin, Jr., married poor unhappy Ethel DuPont, though the union did nothing to endear Franklin to the clan.

We were at breakfast when the gentleman from DuPont came striding into the dining room brandishing a newspaper as if it were a sword. "Have you seen what *that man* has done now?"

In certain circles, *that man* was Franklin's name. It was also an epithet.

Every face turned to him, except Winty, who went on eating his kippers.

"He's trying to pack the courts!"

A chorus of men's voices rose in outrage. A choir of women sang a well-modulated accompaniment.

"You know what that means," our guest went on. "Even when we get a Republican with some sense back in the White House, he won't be able to do a thing about all these so-called reforms." The last word curdled in the venom of his voice. "They'll have become permanent."

Winty put down his knife and fork and placed his napkin on the table. I noticed the gesture, but the rest of the table went on berating Franklin.

"It's outrageous."

"He's a madman."

"He wants to be a dictator."

Winty stood. "I do not want to hear about it," he said.

Silence fell over the table. As I said, Winty's voice commanded obedience. He turned and left the room. It was a good thirty seconds before anyone spoke, and then the conversation turned to hunters. For the rest of the week, no one mentioned *that man* again.

❧ I have made it sound as if my life in those years was nothing but Franklin. In fact, it was full to bursting without him. The five children were away at school, but they came home for holidays and occasional weekends, and kept me busy. I always mentioned them in my letters to Franklin.

"We have at last decided to go abroad this summer—sailing in June—11 strong of us. It seems quite an undertaking as the time approaches—but it has to be faced sooner or later and the children are keen to go," I wrote in a letter a few months before the one telling him about the special chair. I also congratulated him on becoming a grandfather. Anna had given birth to a daughter.

Five years earlier, when I'd held my own daughter in my arms for the first time and understood what perfect contentment was, Franklin had written to say he considered himself an honorary godfather. Barbara was born on June fourteenth, and in years to come his observance of the date would astound me. "It is today even more essential that you stop in Washington to visit your Godfather," he cabled her less than a month before the Allied invasion of Sicily. "Thinking of you today. Hope you will come up and see me soon," he wired her a week after D-Day. The lives of millions of men hung on his decisions. The world's problems demanded his attention. And he found time to send birthday wishes to my daughter.

In addition to the children, I had Tranquility in Allamuchy, and Ridgely Hall in Aiken, and the *pied-à-terre* in New York. Life had returned to normal, or at least to what it had been before Mama had received that shocking letter from the lawyer telling her that everything was gone. When I looked back, I saw the lean years in cramped apartments as an unfortunate, but brief interlude. When I remembered the time Vio had given Mama money for food, and she'd come home with flowers, because neither of us could abide a room without flowers, I viewed those years as a lighthearted adventure. But for the most part, I didn't think about them. And I saw no reason to talk about them.

The children and the houses and the constant moving back and forth occupied my life. Winty filled it.

"He doesn't like you out of his sight," Violetta remarked

once when she and her daughter Lucy were staying in the stone guest house that was just a mile and a half from our house on the grounds of Tranquility. I couldn't tell from her voice whether she was envious or disapproving. While she summered with us in New Jersey, Bill's medical practice kept him in Washington from Monday through Friday.

Vio often teased me about my life in those days. She laughed at the French kid gloves I wore to work in the garden so I wouldn't ruin my hands, and at the small plot the men were instructed never to touch so that I could weed when I had the urge—very Marie Antoinetteish, she said—and at the full bathing attire, including black stockings, I wore to take a dip in my own lake in the company of my own sister and daughter and niece. But Winty admired my hands, and indulged my whims, and believed in decorum even while swimming. As I said, he was nothing like Franklin.

Even Bill teased me. One weekend, when he was up from Washington and he and Vio and I were returning to Tranquility along a country road, we passed a stand with silk-tasseled corn and fat tomatoes and phlox and larkspur and cosmos rioting in the late afternoon sun.

"Stop!" I shouted over the wind.

Bill slammed on the breaks, and he and Vio turned to find out what was wrong. I laughed and told them I simply couldn't drive past without buying something.

A woman sitting on an overturned bucket beside the stand stood as the car stopped. Her rough hands hung at her sides. She might have stepped out of a Dorothea Lange photo.

I had planned to buy only a few things, but once I started I couldn't stop. The woman and Bill and a small boy who'd appeared from nowhere stuffed green beans and squash and peaches and white lilies into the rumble seat and the front and back of the car. By the time we finished, the stand was bare.

"Lucy," Bill said as he climbed behind the wheel, and Vio put a basket of peaches in his lap because there was no other place for them, "what on earth were you thinking?"

"I couldn't resist."

"Obviously," he said.

"It was all so inviting."

He glanced at Vio. "Almost as inviting as the acres of fruits and vegetables and flowers you have growing on your own property, which, incidentally, your gardeners are picking for dinner even as we speak."

"That's true," I admitted, "But . . ."

He turned from the road to glance back at me.

". . . now that poor exhausted woman can go home."

Vio and Bill looked at each other again, and shook their heads, and laughed, and I had to laugh too, because the gesture was so foolish. But I was glad I had made it. And I was grateful to Winty for making it possible for me to make it.

∾ Franklin and I did not correspond regularly. He was a busy man. I did not want to make a nuisance of myself. But we did write on occasion. When Mr. Howe died in April of '36, I sent a letter to say how sorry I was. It was not hypocrisy. My resentment of the little man with the huge ambitions had faded years ago.

But the saddest letter I wrote Franklin was dated four years earlier. In January of '32, the same month that he announced his candidacy for the presidency for the first time, his friend Livy, who drank too much, and fell in love too often, and was, everyone agreed, entirely lacking in seriousness of purpose, went into the woodshed behind his house in Brookline, put a gun to his head, and pulled the trigger. In his will he left a thousand dollars to Franklin in grateful remembrance of joyful comradeship.

When Franklin answered my letter, he admitted it was a terrible shame about Livy and went on to tell me about the coming campaign. Though he didn't say so, I knew he'd become disillusioned with Livy's drinking, and womanizing, and sudden quarrelsomeness. Franklin was not alone. Little by little we'd all lost patience with Livy. Little by little we'd come to agree with Eleanor, who'd always known he was a frivolous, feckless man. But now, years later, I think of him walking into the woodshed and lifting the gun to his head, and I know poor Livy was more serious than any of us guessed. That, I have learned from personal experience, is what people always say about suicides.

~ 1940–1945

 Nineteen

"He [FDR] is the loneliest man in the world."

                  Mrs. Edwin Watson

"In 1941 . . . Winthrop Rutherfurd fell ill in Aiken; she [Lucy] brought him to Washington for treatment; and Mrs. Eustis, who liked human drama above all, thereupon tried to arrange a meeting in the White House. Much to the disappointment of Mrs. Eustis, however, and indeed to the President's disappointment, Mrs. Rutherfurd balked at the last minute and only sent her daughter, Barbara, and her stepdaughter, Alice."

        Joseph Alsop, *FDR: A Centenary Remembrance*

Prime Minister Chamberlain assured Ambassador Kennedy, who passed the word on to Franklin, that Hitler was highly intelligent and therefore would not wage a world war; Stalin signed a pact with Hitler; and Germany swallowed Austria and Czechoslovakia and Poland. Winston Churchill replaced the fallen Chamberlain, Nazi troops marched down the Champs-Élysées, and Londoners slept in the underground for fifty-seven consecutive nights and awakened to fire and rubble and empty holes where their homes had been for fifty-seven consecutive mornings.

At home, Franklin ran for an unprecedented third term; and Miss LeHand cried all through the speech announcing his candidacy because she had hoped he would leave office and retire with her to a cottage he'd built on a hill in Hyde Park; and the Republicans threatened to release letters revealing Vice President Wallace's peculiar mystical streak, while the Democrats promised to retaliate with rumors about Wendell Wilkie's mistress, though, Franklin joked in one of our telephone conversations, as long as Mr. Wilkie, whom he usually regarded as a formidable opponent, went around promising voters that he, unlike Franklin, would never appoint a woman to his cabinet, there would be no need for dirty tricks to defeat him.

Franklin went on the radio to explain that if your neighbor's house caught fire, you didn't stop to quibble, but lent him your garden hose to put out the flames before they spread to your own property, and suddenly millions of Americans recognized the need to send billions of dollars' worth of ships and arms and supplies to Britain; and I stood in the crowd and watched Franklin take the oath of office for the third time beneath a cloudless ice-blue sky. The military was out in force, and security was extreme, and everyone said the inaugural atmosphere hadn't been so ominous since Abraham Lincoln had been sworn in eighty years earlier.

The times were dire. The pressures on Franklin were unbearable. He saw war coming, as he had two decades earlier, but now he was not a young firebrand in the administration eager to get into it. He was the administration, and he knew we would not be able to stay out of it. The problem was, he explained to me, he could not get too far ahead of the American people in racing to meet it. "Your boys are not going to be sent into any foreign wars," he'd promised the mothers and fathers of America during the campaign, though he'd been fairly certain they would. The catch, he confided, was by that time the United States would be in the war, so it would not be foreign. And all the while the isolationists in America First, like Charles Lindbergh and Franklin's cousin Alice Longworth, fought his policies, and impugned his motives, and spread vicious stories about him and Eleanor and the children, who were now old enough to get into trouble on their own. The boys were not good judges of men, or of business opportunities. Anna's and Elliott's marriages had ended during Franklin's first term, and James and Betsey, Franklin's favorite daughter-in-law, were separated. Divorce, which had been impossible for Franklin, was turning into a habit for his children.

It was no wonder he began telephoning me more regularly. He left instructions with the head operator, Miss Hackmeister, Hacky as everyone called her, and Miss LeHand, and the other secretaries that when Mrs. Rutherfurd called, she was to be put through immediately. Occasionally that made for an awkward situation, though Franklin didn't see it that way. If someone was in the room with him, he simply spoke French. I often wondered if Miss LeHand spoke French.

Occasionally I worried what would happen if I were put through when Eleanor was at home. It had been more than twenty years since Franklin and I had seen each other. These days Eleanor had her own work, and her own life, and her own friends. There were rumors about that too. First it was the women who were too mannish, then it was the bodyguard who was too dashing, finally it was the young man from the American Youth Congress who was too bookish and left-wing. Poor Eleanor. No matter how much good she did, she couldn't do anything right. At least that was what the people I lived among seemed to think.

But my concern was Franklin. He was, I could tell from his

calls, horribly lonely. "I'm either Exhibit A or left completely alone," he said one night. Eleanor was seldom there. The children were off pursuing their own lives. Mr. Howe was dead.

The White House wasn't empty. Guests came and went constantly. The toniest boardinghouse in town, wags called it. Miss LeHand lived on the third floor. Mr. Harry Hopkins, who'd become as attuned to Franklin's needs and wishes as Mr. Howe had been, moved in with his little girl after his wife died. And there were the royal guests. Franklin's enemies complained about them too. They said his enthusiasm for the titled heads of Europe was undemocratic. He insisted it was merely good manners. When war had broken out in Europe, he'd written to the various monarchs asking if there was anything he could do. First Grand Duchess Charlotte of Luxembourg showed up with her husband and seven children and without a penny, then came Queen Wilhelmina of Holland, who he said had no sense of humor, and after her the Norwegians, who didn't like his informality, and were very pompous, except for Princess Martha, whom he called Godchild.

I had heard about Princess Martha. She was young and beautiful and said to be flirtatious. The newspapers opposed to Franklin's policies wrote about her long stay at the White House, and her many visits to Hyde Park, and how fetching she looked descending from the train in high heels and black silk stockings. The war in Europe hadn't yet made silk stockings a scarcity at home. I was glad for Franklin. Really I was. The princess sounded like exactly the kind of company he needed.

Washington was full of European refugees. Vio wrote that our old friend Marguerita Pennington, who'd married a German officer after we'd left the convent and stayed in Europe, was back, though her sons were still over there, and she worried about them terribly. She was a widow now, but still lovely, and quite flirtatious. "Perhaps it's a European trait," Vio wrote, "like your Princess Martha. Marguerita came to tea and couldn't stop batting her lashes at Bill. But I suppose we must have her back, and even take her under our wing. She is very much alone here."

War was everywhere that spring of 1941, the last one we would know of peace for some time. Interventionists clamored that we had to stop Hitler before it was too late, and isolationists shouted we'd already fought one European war and look at the outcome of that. Fascism and bolshevism and capitalism and democracy. The words flew from mouth to mouth like parting kisses to a passing world. Women whispered them, and men swore them, and Winty and his sons could not give them a rest. The boys debated which branch they should enlist in and when, but never whether. Of course they would all be officers.

Winty worried, though he would not have wanted them to do anything else. But it went against the fine, logical grain of nature, he said one night, for young men to die before old.

A week later he had his first stroke. In a matter of seconds the youthful vital sportsman became an elderly invalid. The arm that had driven a golf ball two hundred and fifty yards had difficulty lifting a fork. The man who had refused to suffer the conversation of fools had trouble making himself understood. The husband who hadn't liked me out of his sight needed me more than ever.

The children urged me to go out. Friends invited me to dinner. Vio begged me to visit to her and Bill in Washington. But I did not like to leave Winty alone. It was a matter not of obligation, but of gratitude. And, of course, love.

Early in June, just as he was beginning to regain the use of

his arm, he suffered a second stroke. The doctor in Aiken rec-
ommended a specialist in Washington. I telephoned Vio and
told her I would take her up on her invitation.

Two days later Winty and I were sitting in the garden. It
was late in the year for us to still be in Aiken, but I hadn't
wanted to move so soon after his stroke. I was wearing a
short-sleeved silk dress and had opened my parasol, but
Winty had a sweater beneath his tweed jacket, and I'd
wrapped a woolen blanket around his legs. It was terrible to
think of Winty, who would have once gone out in frigid
weather without a hat and gloves, were it not for propriety,
shivering in the southern sunshine. But he was comfortable,
and the garden was fragrant, and he enjoyed having me sit
beside him and read from Dickens or Trollope or his old
friend Mrs. Wharton, though he found her a bit too modern
and cynical.

I was reading Mrs. Wharton that day, *A Son at the Front,*
and I didn't notice Grant until his black houseman's coat was
beside me blotting out the sun. He said there was a phone call
for me. I kept my finger tucked between the pages of the book
as I stood and started for the house. I would not leave Winty
for long.

I recognized Miss Hackmeister before she announced that
the president was calling. A moment later the big voice came
surging down the line.

"I understand from Edith Eustis that you're coming to
Washington."

Edith Eustis was Winty's late wife's sister, and a good friend
to me as well as Franklin. In the old days we'd often dined at
her house. She loved people. She simply couldn't resist getting
mixed up in their lives.

"I've checked on the doctor you're going to see," Franklin

went on. "He's a good man." And then, without a break, without a change in tone, "Come see me while you're in Washington."

The comfortable world I'd been sitting in a moment ago lurched off its axis.

"I can't."

It was what I always said these days when people invited me out, but Franklin was not people.

"Of course you can. Come see my White House. Come see what fun I have. Come see me."

I was still standing, and as I looked down at the telephone table, I saw I was holding the book so tightly that my finger marking the place had turned white.

"It'll be grand," he said.

"What about . . ." I began, though I wasn't sure how I was going to finish the sentence. What about your promise to Eleanor? What about my obligation to Winty? What about propriety?

I glanced at the mirror above the telephone table. The sight shocked me. I'd grown so accustomed to being younger than Winty that I hadn't noticed how much I'd aged. I still wore my hair up, but now streaks of gray turned the luster tinny. Lines as fine as spiderwebs gathered at the sides of my eyes and mouth, despite the parasols I'd carried all these years. I'd been careful not to grow stout, but I was not the willowy girl who'd run from the Raleigh for her life, or his.

"Lucy . . ." he began, and I remembered the first time he'd tasted my name, and knew I could not see him. What woman is the equal of her lover's memory?

". . . I'm the president. When I ask heads of state to visit, they arrive. When I invite senators and congressmen, they jump at the chance. When I summon titans of business and lords of labor, they file into my office and sit down with each other. Are you going to be the only one to say no to me?"

"They come to see you out of deference to the office."

"Let's not split hairs. What's good for me is good for the country. And seeing you would be good for me. Say you'll come."

I glanced in the mirror again. I smiled. The lines at the corners of my mouth were signs of a life well lived.

"Yes," I said.

I read especially well to Winty that afternoon. It was not the thrill of the clandestine, though I know for some people it would have been. Franklin loved secrecy, which his opponents called duplicity. Later, when we were in the war, he sent messages to Mr. Churchill and Mr. Stalin and Mr. Chang through the army and received replies through the navy, so only he could see the whole picture. But I had a simpler nature. The reason I read well to Winty that afternoon was because I was happy, and I wanted him to be too. Perhaps that sounds self-serving or ingenuous or lacking in moral nuance, but it's true.

∽ I still had a personal maid in those days. Everyone did. Well, perhaps not everyone, but many women I knew. The war hadn't yet sent domestic servants fleeing to better-paying jobs in factories and offices and shops. Paulette, who had been with me since I'd married Winty, was a genius with hair and kept my wardrobe in perfect order. Her only flaw was her weight. She was huge. In the days before we left for Washington she joked that she was fading away, because I kept her running up and down the stairs between my bedroom on the second floor and the closets on the third with different dresses and suits and hats and shoes. It was not seemly behavior for a woman who had just turned fifty, and I was thoroughly ashamed of myself, when I wasn't giddy with anticipation.

We arrived at Vio and Bill's on Tuesday afternoon. Winty's appointment was scheduled for the following morning. I'd told Franklin I would see him on Thursday afternoon. He'd said that was grand. He had lunch with Chief Justice Hughes and an appointment with Secretary of War Stimson on Thursday. There was a certain irony to that, though neither of us mentioned it. Mr. Stimson was so enamored of probity that he and his wife did not entertain divorced persons.

Vio had fixed a room downstairs for Winty, and their maid Emma had moved to make room for the nurse.

"There's also a doctor in the house," Vio joked, "so I expect you to get out a bit. You've been cooped up for too long. Even the train ride has helped. You look better."

"Better than what?" I was teasing her, but no woman, even one of a certain age, likes to hear that she's been looking badly.

"Better than you were looking last time I saw you. Better than Shoumie said you were looking when she visited you in Aiken." Shoumie was Madame Shoumatoff, a Russian émigré friend who'd painted my portrait, and Winty's, and several of the children, and one of Winty with his fox terriers. "According to her, you've even begun to dress in a more 'mature' style."

"I'm a more mature woman," I said, but Shoumie was right. Hemlines were already inching up, though war restrictions were still in the future, but I'd refused to raise my skirts with the fashion. I saw me as Franklin would in forty-eight hours, an aging matron dressed in clothing so safe it was almost dowdy. He had no taste for what he called war paint, but he'd always appreciated stylish dresses and glamorous hats with substantial brims.

"She thinks it's because you don't want to look so much younger than Winty," Vio said.

"I think Shoumie should stick to her portraits. And you should stop listening to gossip." But I resolved to find an hour the next day to shop for a new hat, one with a substantial brim.

◡◠ We'd come to Washington to consult a medical specialist, and Franklin had said he was a good man, but I did not fool myself. Perhaps Winty could be made more comfortable. Perhaps his speech would improve and increased mobility would return to his right side. But I did not let myself hope for more than that. Winty was seventy-nine years old. He'd had two strokes. The doctor said we could expect more. As we sat in the consultation room with the windows open a crack to the cool damp Washington morning, and listened to the horns and whistles and brakes of the city vibrating with the energy Franklin had pumped into it, I wondered how much of what was being said Winty understood. The doctors agreed that his mental functions were largely unimpaired, though I knew he sometimes became disoriented. I hated to think he couldn't comprehend the doctor's prognosis, but I didn't like to think that he could either.

The doctor finished, and we stood and shook hands. I turned to Winty, who was in his wheelchair. The nurse, who knew his preferences by now, had arranged his tie in a neat Windsor knot, buttoned the coat of his trim suit, and fixed his bad hand on the arm of the wheelchair so the immobility was not noticeable. His eyes, as he looked up at me, forbade pity.

◡◠ I had agreed to go to a dinner party with Vio and Bill that evening, but as the afternoon wore on, I saw how much the doctor's appointment had taken out of Winty. I told Vio I would stay at home and have a tray with him.

"You're burying yourself alive," she said.

"I'm not burying myself. I'm taking care of my husband."

"Winty would want you to go out."

I told her I preferred to stay home, and didn't add that she was wrong. Winty did not want me to go out. He never asked me to stay at home, but I always knew he wanted me to.

There was one other thing I didn't say to Vio. If I did not leave Winty tonight, I would not feel as bad about leaving him tomorrow.

∿ June 5, 1941. Pearl Harbor was six months in the future, but in the past eight weeks almost twelve thousand British civilians had died in air raids. American warehouse workers were on strike tying up millions of dollars' worth of war material for Great Britain and food for our own army and navy. Nonetheless, Washington, and I, awakened to a fervent promise of a morning. Last night's rain had scrubbed the air clean, the paper predicted the sun would come out by afternoon, and as soon as I saw Winty, I knew he had slept well. I was glad I had stayed in the night before.

At three o'clock I went up to my room to get ready. I was sorry now I hadn't brought Paulette along. I could never fix my hair as well as she did. Today I was all thumbs. My new hat didn't sit properly either. The big brim seemed somehow lopsided. Vio knocked on the door, stuck her head in, and met my gaze in the mirror. "You look lovely."

"Not too mature?"

"You could pass as my Lucy's sister. Now hurry. The car will be here any minute."

I followed her downstairs, turned, crossed the living room,

and entered the library she'd arranged for Winty's comfort. The nurse had gotten him into the big Queen Anne chair in the corner and put a light blanket over his legs. She was reading to him, though I knew Winty did not enjoy her reading. "English cannot possibly be her native language." His tongue had stalled on the consonants and thickened the vowels, but I'd understood him.

She stopped reading as I entered the room, and I asked if she'd leave us alone for a moment. She looked relieved. I think she knew Winty's opinion of her reading. He was not a man who hid his feelings. And she hated Dickens.

I pulled the nurse's chair closer to Winty's and took his good hand in mine. "I'm going out for a little while, darling."

He turned his head. His eyes shocked me. The morning before, they'd flashed defiance bright as a neon sign. Do not pity me. Now a milky film had dimmed the light. It took a moment for them to focus on me.

"Lucy," he whispered and stopped.

"Yes, darling?"

"Where am I?"

Pity floated up, the one thing he did not want from me.

"You're at Violetta's and Bill's. Remember? We came up so you could see the doctor."

His eyes crawled around the room, then returned to me. "I don't know where I am." His good hand was clutching mine tightly, as if letting go would be casting himself adrift.

"The library, darling. You're in Bill's and Vio's library."

He went on staring into my face. Gradually his grasp on my hand eased. The confusion drained from his eyes. He lifted his good hand and touched my cheek. A small sibilant word escaped from his mouth. At first I thought it was "Yes." He'd gotten his bearings. Then he repeated the word, and I heard it clearly, though his speech was still slurred.

"Please," he said.

In all the years I had known Winty, I had never heard him plead with anyone. Even me.

∾ "Good afternoon, Miss Hackmeister, this is Mrs. Rutherfurd," I said, though I knew I didn't have to. According to Franklin, Hacky had two gifts. She could track down anyone he wanted anywhere in the world. And she could recognize any voice after she'd heard it once.

"Good afternoon, Mrs. Rutherfurd. One moment, please."

As I waited for Franklin, I hoped he would not answer in French. I did not want to have to tell him this in front of anyone else.

"Lucy," he said, and I knew he was alone. "I thought you would be here by now. Or at least on the way."

I told him I could not come after all. I did not tell him why. The explanation would have been unfair to Winty. It was not the infirmity. Franklin was incapacitated too. It was the fear. Franklin was fearless.

"But you promised." Only a strong man can seduce with the words of a child.

"Perhaps another time."

"Spinach."

It was one of his favorite expletives, and I had to laugh.

"You see, Lucy, you ought to come. For your good as well as mine. No, I take that back. Come for me. I need cheering up today."

It was a surprising confession for Franklin. He admitted being tired. He acknowledged being lonely. He occasionally showed anger. But he never gave in to depression. I should have known then that something was wrong, more wrong than the coming war and the current strikes and the other public responsibilities.

"Please," he said.

‸ Winty looked up as I returned to the study. I crossed the room, took his good hand and his bad in both of mine, and bent till I was on a level with his eyes. I was searching for fear or recognition or, I admit it, permission. All I saw was a scrim of age and illness.

There was a knock on the open library door. "The car is here, Mrs. Rutherfurd," Vio's maid Emma announced.

It wasn't Franklin's fault. I hadn't called in time for Miss LeHand to stop it.

"I'll be back in a moment," I said to Winty. The eyes went on staring up at me. I didn't know if he understood or not. "As soon as I send the car away."

It was a long walk, almost as long as the trek across the Raleigh tearoom through the lobby and out onto the street. My pumps clicked through Vio's rooms, from Turkish carpet to parquet to carpet again. I crossed the hall and opened the front door. The weather forecast had been right. Q Street was a mosaic of gold and green. A black car sat glistening at the curb. A driver stood beside it.

I started down the steps. As I drew closer to the waiting automobile, the driver removed his cap and bowed. "Good afternoon, Mrs. Johnson."

The greeting caught me off guard. I'd forgotten Franklin's flair for intrigue.

"We'll give you a Secret Service code name," he'd said when he'd pleaded with me to visit him at the White House.

"Smith. No, that's too common. Everyone will know it's a ruse. Johnson. Johnson is exactly right. Don't you love it! Don't you just love it!"

The driver opened the back door to the car. "Lovely afternoon, isn't it, Mrs. Johnson?"

I had never masqueraded under an assumed name before, unless you counted that time so many years before when Franklin and I had driven to Virginia Beach. The sensation was unsettling, and faintly heady. I suddenly understood his passion for secrecy.

I agreed with the driver that it was a lovely afternoon and stepped into the backseat of the car. Or at least Mrs. Johnson did.

๔ Twenty

A partial listing of FDR's appointments for June 5, 1941

1130-	To Marguerite A. LeHand's apartment
1140-	To office
1300-	(lunch) Chief Justice Hughes
1530-	War Sec. Henry L. Stimson
1555-1740	Returned from Office to Study White House accompanied by Mrs. Johnson
1740	To Marguerite A. LeHand's apartment

๛ From President's Appointment Log

The car pulled up at the South Gate of the White House. It was the entrance used for visitors Franklin didn't want the world to know about. Usually, he said, the intrigue was political or diplomatic or military. The driver said something to one of the guards, who glanced into the backseat of the car. I felt as if the emotions on my face were as gaudy and vulgar as the makeup Franklin hated.

The car purred through the gates and came to a stop. Another man approached, opened the back door, and helped me out. "Good afternoon, Mrs. Johnson," he said. Franklin was having a grand time with this.

Across the south lawn, the White House, Mr. Howe's gor-

geous hunk of real estate, sat fat and pristine and immeasur-
ably stirring. A row of tall windows, turned opaque by the
angle of the afternoon light, marched along one side. In front
of each stood a man in civilian clothing. Franklin was inside.

I was led through a door guarded by another civilian, down
a short hall, and into an office where a woman in a tailored
suit that was smart but not too smart sat behind a large neat
desk. I had been so busy thinking about seeing Franklin that
it hadn't occurred to me that I would be meeting Miss
LeHand. Only this was not Miss LeHand.

The woman stood and held out her hand. "Mrs. Rutherfurd," she said.

Mrs. Johnson had fled. I was on my own.

"How do you do? I'm Miss Tully. The number-two girl.
Miss LeHand is terribly sorry she can't be here to welcome
you, but she's a little under the weather."

I was surprised. Miss LeHand was Franklin's guardian.
Cabinet members and congressmen courted her shamelessly.
Lesser mortals groveled at her feet. And in view of what she
must have guessed about me, it seemed odd that she wasn't
curious to meet me, but I had no time to worry about Miss
LeHand. My gaze was focused on a door across from the one
I'd come through.

"The president is waiting for you," Miss Tully said and
pulled open the door. I stepped through it. It closed behind
me. Franklin was across the room. I reached out and grabbed
a chair to steady myself.

Though neither of us moved for a moment, he came at me
in half-remembered bits and sweet pieces. The fair hair had
thinned and grayed, and the brows had grown darker and
thicker, but the ocean blue eyes hadn't changed a bit. Freckles

dotted his skin, and a small scar over his left eye showed where a growth had been removed, and the cigarette holder clamped between his uneven teeth shot the sky.

He wheeled out from behind the desk. I gripped the back of the chair more tightly. I'd known he couldn't walk. I'd realized he was in a wheelchair. I was accustomed to wheelchairs by now. But nothing had prepared me for the sight of Franklin in one. The light linen trousers revealed the outline of withered legs as thin as the limbs of any of the undernourished children he'd fed and clothed and sheltered. He had wounded me in the past. He'd told me he loved me, then promised to behave well. He'd proved he loved me, then gone back to his life. He'd forced me to lie to him to assuage his misery and guilt. But nothing he ever did broke my heart like the first sight of his ruined legs that afternoon.

"Lucy!" he cried.

"Mr. President," I said.

He threw back his head and laughed. "*Franklin* would be better. *Darling* would be best."

He was coming toward me now, his powerful arms spinning the wheels of the narrow wooden chair he'd designed for himself, his face getting bigger and closer and more real by the second. As the distance between us closed, the years didn't fall away. I was not a besotted girl, but a grown woman with an almost-grown daughter and an ill husband. He was not a golden boy with the universe in the palm of his hand, but a crippled man with the misery and hate of the world on his shoulders. Only the love was still young and new and strapping. It turned a blind eye on those poor withered legs.

I stayed for more than an hour and a half that afternoon. I kept saying it was an unconscionable amount of time to steal from the national interest, but he kept assuring me it was for the public good. I believed him. I had worried that the reality of the woman I'd become would sully the memory of the girl he had loved. It hadn't occurred to me that the presence of that girl, even in the guise of a middle-aged woman, would take him back to the young man he'd been. When he looked at me, he saw himself striding across a golf course, and whirling around a ballroom, and doing a hundred different things he'd never given a thought to at the time.

He called Mr. Prettyman, and the valet came and wheeled him over specially constructed ramps to a small elevator, and we rode upstairs to Franklin's private study. It was like every room I'd ever seen him inhabit. A large oval space, painted battleship gray, it was filled with ship models, and naval prints, and what must have been hundreds if not thousands of books. The furniture, upholstered in leather and brocade, looked worn and comfortable, and, except for a large cabinet radio in one corner and a pastel of Eleanor looking older than she'd been when I'd last seen her over the door, I felt as if I'd come home.

He gestured me to one of the sofas, wheeled himself to the high-backed red leather chair which stood near it, locked the wheels of the moving chair into place, and heaved himself from one to the other, all the while keeping up a steady stream of conversation about the wing chair, which was a reproduction of one that had belonged to Thomas Jefferson; and the massive oak desk, which he'd had fashioned from timbers of H.M.S *Resolute*; and the portrait of John Paul Jones, which Mr. Howe had bought in a seedy secondhand store for twenty-five dollars and had cleaned up as a gift for Franklin.

"His last name wasn't really Jones, you know. He assumed that after he killed a mutinous sailor in self-defense." Franklin flashed the grin he'd borrowed from the devil so many years ago, and for a moment we were across the street in his old office in the State, War, and Navy, and beyond windows open to the summer night, the world was at war, but we were safe and blissful in each other's arms. Then he took hold of the trousers of one leg with both hands and lifted it over his other, and the horror of what we'd done and how he'd been punished turned my head away like a slap.

A tea tray arrived, and I poured a cup for Franklin, and he asked me about my children. He wanted to know how Barbara was, and whether she had a beau, and when she was going to visit him. He said if he could ever do anything for any of Winty's boys, especially with war on the way and so many men signing up, I mustn't hesitate to let him know. He had, he pointed out, a fair amount of influence with the military, though he wasn't saying he could get a man posted where he chose, and launched into a story about poor Elliott, who, after enlisting in the army and requesting overseas duty anywhere that was warm, was promptly assigned to Newfoundland. As he threw back his head and laughed, he took hold of his trousers with both hands and uncrossed his legs, and this time the gesture struck me as the most natural thing in the world.

We went on that way for some time. He told me wonderful stories about senators and kings and diplomats and scoundrels. Every time I said I really must go, he begged me to stay for a few minutes more, and I agreed, and he put another Camel in his cigarette holder and was off again. We covered dozens of topics that afternoon, except the one that must have been foremost in Franklin's mind at least part of the time we were together. It wasn't Germany's torpedoing of an American freighter in the South Atlantic, or the attempts to get Japan to withdraw from China without provoking war in the Pacific, or the record number of strikes that were setting back crucial war production, though all those crises weighed heavily on him. It was a personal matter, and because he could not fix it or even fight it, he refused to admit it.

Each year the manager of the Willard gave a party for the inner circle of Franklin's staff. The event was usually held at the hotel, but the night before Franklin and I met for the first time in more than two decades, the manager had moved the party to the White House so Franklin could attend. Mr. Hopkins was there, and General Watson, who was Franklin's aide and whom everyone called Pa, and Mr. McIntyre, who went all the way back to the 1920 campaign, and Miss Tully, the number-two girl, and, of course, Miss LeHand. Some of the guests thought Miss LeHand seemed tired and overworked, but then she'd been driving herself relentlessly for twenty years. And she was still brokenhearted that Franklin had decided to remain in the White House rather than return to the private life they had shared while he'd been trying to learn to walk again. She was also taking opiates for her insomnia.

As the evening wore on, Miss Tully urged Miss LeHand to retire early, but Miss LeHand insisted it would not be fitting for the presidential secretary to leave the party before the president. On a point of protocol she was correct, but I couldn't help remembering Eleanor's reluctance to leave Franklin alone at parties so many years ago.

Franklin retired at around nine-thirty. A moment later Miss LeHand stood, cried out, and collapsed. Franklin's physician, Dr. McIntire, and his physical therapist, Commander Fox, carried her to her room on the third floor and sedated her. The doctor suspected heart trouble, or, more likely, another nervous breakdown, like the two she'd had in the past when she'd thought Franklin was slipping away, though there was no reason for her to think she was losing him now. As war approached, he needed her more than ever. Certainly my visit did not change that.

I knew nothing of Miss LeHand's collapse the afternoon Franklin and I sat drinking tea and talking about everything under the sun except her illness. Mr. Early, the press secretary, had made no announcement of it that morning. Nothing would be said of it for some time. Her presence on the third floor of the White House was kept as dark a secret as if she were the madwoman in the attic.

Perhaps that makes Franklin sound callous. As he and I sat in the oval study falling in love all over again with the people we'd become, who were simply wiser and more tender versions of the people we'd once known and loved, the woman who had spent the past twenty years at his side, learning to relish his pleasures, waiting out his despair, and putting every ounce of her energy into making him the public figure she never wanted him to be, lay in her small room on the third floor, sedated but uncalm.

Franklin had paid a brief visit to her that morning. I imagine him wheeling in, cigarette holder cocked at a jaunty angle, voice aching with optimism. He would have kept up a bright monologue. "Good morning, Missy. I heard you had a bit of the collywobbles after I turned in last night. Wasn't the party grand, though? All those old songs Mac sang." He would have managed not to see her tears, because she felt herself slipping and him slipping away. And he would have pretended the desperate clutching of his hand was simply an affectionate squeeze. Better than that, he would have convinced himself it was a sign for him to go.

After I left that evening, he returned to Miss LeHand and spent another five or seven minutes going through the same grotesque charade. For the next two and a half weeks, he continued to stop in her room at odd moments throughout the day until a second, massive stroke—her collapse had been due to a small stroke, not a heart or nervous condition as the doctor had thought, or change of life, as Eleanor suggested—made it necessary to move her to Doctors' Hospital.

His visits became less frequent then. Surely no one could blame him for that. Germany invaded the Soviet Union. Japan marched into Indochina and Siam. Franklin could not leave the White House on a whim. He could not spare time for personal niceties, no matter how much he might want to.

No one could blame him, but some did, even among his closest associates. Heartless, they murmured. Cold as ice, they whispered. But they saw only the surface. They didn't realize that Franklin couldn't bear to see Miss LeHand ill because he'd cared for her so deeply when she was well. He couldn't pay sick calls, because he couldn't admit to illness, his own or anyone else's, unless there was something he could do about it. They shook their heads over the infrequency of his visits to the hospital and ignored the fact that he paid her medical bills, and corresponded with her doctors, and changed his will, leaving half his estate to Eleanor and the other half to care for Miss LeHand, if she survived him.

But even if they were right, even if Franklin was too busy saving the world to spare a moment for a woman who'd given him her life, even if Franklin was willfully blind and deeply flawed, I didn't care. As I'd learned when I was still young enough to think the realization was an epiphany, if you cannot accept imperfections, you cannot love.

✐ Twenty-one

I saw Franklin again at the beginning of August and the end of October and in November. In the past I had measured time by the changing of the seasons and the moves from the Allamuchy to Aiken and back. Now I counted weeks and days before Washington and after it, though the visits were a litany of difficulty and disappointment.

Even with the help of Winty's man and my maid and a nurse and private railroad cars, travel was difficult. Winty was exhausted by the time we arrived, occasionally impatient, often disoriented. I was almost grateful for the last. I hated subjecting him to the grim, claustrophobic offices that reeked of antiseptic and medicine and hothouse flowers. I knew what he would have thought of the men who carried immaculate hands before them like gifts while they hid behind faces frozen

234

into official kindness and uttered words of scientific bravado and hopelessness.

Vio and Bill, whom I'd relied on in the past, were of little help. He was preoccupied. She seemed troubled, though she denied it.

But then Vio's maid Emma would knock on the door and say the car was waiting, and my heels would click down the steps, and the driver would bow and say, "Good afternoon, Mrs. Johnson," and the gloomy offices and morbid doctors would fall away, even Winty would slip away, and I'd be on my way to Franklin.

He delighted in the fact that I was still Mrs. Johnson. He always had loved secrets. And he was tickled pink by the thought that people who knew about me speculated about us. Were we old friends, or was there something more, despite the fact that he was a grandfather and I was a woman of a certain age? But what more can there be than love, which does not grow bald or gray or wrinkled or even succumb to paralysis.

Nonetheless, there were indiscretions. That afternoon in August he told me about a trip so confidential Mr. Hull, the secretary of state, did not know of it. Even Eleanor, who was not in town in any event, had no idea where he was going. The next day he would set off for Newfoundland and what would become known as the Atlantic Conference, though at the time he referred to it by its code name Riviera.

"All very hugger-mugger." He was brimming with delight in the conspiracy, and the coming trip, and the presidency. Franklin loved being president. It occurred to me, sitting beside him in the oval study, listening to the secrets he was not supposed to tell me, that we had done the right thing back in the Raleigh tearoom so many years earlier.

〜 The next time I saw Franklin he was wearing a black armband. Mrs. James had died at the beginning of September. I'd written him, of course, and we'd talked on the telephone. He'd joked and gossiped and told me stories about what was going on in the White House, but the fizz had gone out of his conversation. Others had criticized him for not grieving enough for Mr. Howe and worrying insufficiently about Miss LeHand, as if heartache can be calibrated like a fever, but this time he was wearing his sorrow, like his mourning band, on his sleeve. Even the newspapers commented on his grief. They said he'd shut himself off from the world.

I did not try to draw him out. I certainly didn't try to cheer him up. I simply held him and told him how sorry I was. And after a while, when he started to talk of his mother, I listened.

Much has been said about Mrs. James and her indomitable will. She doted on Franklin endlessly and meddled in his life unconscionably. She intimidated Eleanor when she was a bride and young mother, infuriated her when she was a mature woman, and never forgave her for marrying her boy. She bribed the chicks with gifts and money, undermined Eleanor's authority over them, and told them again and again that they were really her children, their mother had only borne them. She was an incurable snob, a meddlesome dowager, and an extraordinary mother. Her love planted the seeds of Franklin's confidence, and Franklin's confidence enabled him to experiment and fail and start over. Franklin's confidence saved the country and won the war. He knew how much he owed her, even if the rest of the world did not.

Leaving Franklin that day after his mother's death was difficult, but so was the thought of Winty's waiting at home for me.

Some people might find my behavior immoral, but I've never thought kindness was sinful, no matter how thinly it's spread.

∽ I was not the only Rutherfurd, even if I was still masquerading as Mrs. Johnson, who visited Franklin in those days. In June, he invited my stepson Win, who was thinking of enlisting, to the White House, and spent half an hour advising him. In December, he asked Barbara, who was staying with Vio and Bill and making the round of coming-out balls with their daughter Lucy, for dinner.

"Just a family affair," he promised, because I'd told him she was shy. "Mr. Hopkins, you, and me. You'll like Mr. Hopkins. All the ladies do. Though I can't imagine what they see in him. Just remember, though, you're coming to see your godfather."

Four days after Barbara dined with Franklin and Mr. Hopkins, I was sitting in the library of the house in Aiken writing Christmas cards. The day was cool, and a fire crackled in the hearth. Winty was settled in front of it with a blanket over his legs. The radio was tuned to the Sunday afternoon symphony, and for once the reception was adequate. The desk where I sat was in his line of vision. A terrier slept at his feet. He seemed content.

The cheerful tone of my Christmas greetings was strained this year. Rumors of war hung on the tree, and rustled in the wrapping paper, and curdled the eggnog. I'd spoken to Franklin on the telephone after I'd returned from church that morning. He said Eleanor was having thirty-one for lunch, but he planned to have a tray in his study with Harry the Hop, as he called Mr. Hopkins.

"I have a good excuse," he said. "Two good excuses. My sinuses are misbehaving, and the Japanese are doing the same."

I told him he was working too hard and needed a rest, and he laughed and said if the America First rally scheduled in Pittsburgh that afternoon to demand his impeachment had its way, he'd have plenty of time for rest.

As I slid a card into an envelope, I heard loud voices from the kitchen, though it was at the other end of the house. I glanced at Winty. He had no patience with unruly servants. Years ago at Tranquility, one of the footmen had swum over from the servants' side of the lake to the raft where Barbara and her nurse were sunning themselves. The nurse was extremely pretty. I never knew how Winty found out about the incident, but I never saw the footman again. Fortunately, Winty hadn't heard the noise now. His eyes were closed, and the index finger of his good hand was conducting *The Goldberg Variations*. It had always been one of his favorites.

I glanced at the small clock on the desk. It was two-twenty-five. Later I'd realize the servants had tuned their radio to the Mutual Broadcasting System to listen to a football game, and had already heard the first bulletin, but NBC and CBS did not interrupt their musical programs. I picked up another Christmas card and began writing.

The Bach came to an end. Winty's finger stopped. On the radio a male voice announced the two-thirty news.

"We have just received a special bulletin from United Press," the voice began. "President Roosevelt has announced that at one-twenty Washington time Japanese planes attacked Pearl Harbor."

At first I couldn't believe it. Franklin had said war was coming, but certainly not by means of a sneak attack to a place most people had never heard of. Not on a peaceful Sunday afternoon with Winty conducting Bach in front of the fire, and me writing Christmas cards, and the country napping. I thought it must be a hoax, like the broadcast about the Martian invasion that the actor, Orson Welles, had perpetrated a few years earlier.

I turned to Winty to say as much, but the sight of him stopped me. My husband, who never showed fear, who never flinched from pain, whose only show of anger was an adamantine iciness, sat, his eyes wide with horror, the tears streaming down his face. The sight was as terrifying as the news. Even the dog sensed something wrong. Its ears made two alert triangles in the air. A fearful growl rose from its throat.

I was out of the chair, across the room, kneeling beside him in a moment. "What is it?" I asked. "What's wrong?"

He didn't answer. His face, washed by two streams of tears, was immobile.

It is useful to have something to do in a crisis. Most of America spent December seventh sitting beside the radio trying to make sense of the steadily worsening, increasingly confusing news. Vio told me later that it was agony. She hadn't even had Bill for comfort. He'd had to rush out to some sort of medical emergency. But a few of us had our work cut out for us that Sunday. While I rang for the nurse and raced down the hall to telephone the doctor, Franklin summoned the secretaries of state, war, and navy, the chiefs of the army and navy, and, for his own moral support, his son Jimmy, who was a captain in the marine corps. While the nurse and Winty's man and I wheeled him to his bedroom and tried to make him comfortable, Franklin presided over a White House that had turned into bedlam, as officials crowded in, and the NBC Blue Network set up a microphone in the pressroom, which had never been done before, and Miss Tully fled to Franklin's bedroom, which was the only place quiet enough for her to transcribe the news coming in over the telephone from Oahu.

While I hurried to the front door to meet the doctor and tell him what had happened, Franklin was calling Miss Tully into his study to take down a message he intended to make to Congress the following day. He spoke slowly and incisively, she told me later, and dictated the entire message without hesitation, interruption, or corrections. "Yesterday comma December seventh comma nineteen-forty-one dash a date which will live in infamy . . ." While I paced the hall as the doctor examined Winty, Franklin told Secretary of the Treasury Morganthau that he did not want soldiers guarding him, no matter how wild the rumors of air attacks and espionage, especially since the Secret Service detail had already been doubled that afternoon. While I sat in the library listening to the doctor's assurance that Winty was resting quietly, without pain, and there was nothing more we could do except keep him comfortable, Franklin met with his cabinet in what he called the gravest crisis since 1861 and told them about the worst naval defeat in American history.

Later, after I'd said good night to Winty, I went back to the library. It was chilly, but I didn't want to bother the servants, who were still clustered around the radio in the kitchen, to lay another fire. I tucked my feet beneath me, wrapped myself in the blanket I'd folded around Winty earlier in the day, and turned on the radio. I rarely listened to Eleanor's weekly broadcasts, not because I wasn't interested, but because Winty did not enjoy them. He disliked her choice of subjects. He found the sound of her voice grating.

Her voice was still high, but it no longer darted around the room like a bird in captivity. Authority, and tonight grief, weighed it down.

For months now the knowledge that something of this kind might happen has been hanging over our heads and yet it seemed impossible to believe, impossible to drop the everyday things of life and feel that there was only one thing which was important.

She hesitated. I drew the blanket closer and hugged myself for warmth.

"That is all over now," she continued.

At first I didn't realize I was crying. I'd gotten out of the habit long ago. Franklin fled from tears. Winty found them unattractive. But I felt the tears on my cheeks, as silent and futile as the ones that had run down Winty's face that afternoon, and knew a dam was opening. I cried for Winty's boys, and for Franklin's, and for the unknown young men whose names we would read in the casualty lists. I cried for their wives, who faced empty days, unpunctuated by deep voices crying they were home and beard-roughened faces bending to kiss them hello, and long nights stalked by worry so powerful and incessant it became a physical ache. I cried for Winty, imprisoned in the husk of his once-agile body and impotent in the face of the danger his sons would face while he could not. And, though I'm ashamed to admit it, I cried for myself. All afternoon, as I'd moved from room to room, I'd heard snatches of radio broadcasts. "The president has warned . . ." "The president is meeting with . . ." "The president demands . . ."

"To drop the everyday things of life," Eleanor pledged. The last war had brought Franklin and me together. This one would separate us as surely as if he were being shipped overseas.

⤳ Twenty-two

> "As the war continued, Mr. Roosevelt did virtually what he pleased, in public and in private, and in the secure knowledge it would not be on the radio or in the newspapers. . . . That was all very fine, but the President began to put on and take off security like winter underwear. . . . True the pressure of the Presidency is heavy and seclusion a welcome antidote, but Mr. Roosevelt made a fetish of his privacy during the war."
>
> ⤳ Merriman Smith, U.P.A.

The nation reeled into 1942, shell-shocked from Pearl Harbor, certain that worse was to come. On the West Coast, a Japanese submarine bombarded an oil field near Santa Barbara, and people prepared for a Japanese invasion. On the East, German agents came ashore in a village on Long Island called Amagansett and got as far as New York City before the FBI picked them up, and then only because one of them had a change of heart.

The war news grew steadily worse. Singapore fell, and Allied ships suffered a terrible defeat in the Battle of the Java Sea, and in Libya General Rommel crushed the British forces at Tobruk and pressed on toward Egypt. Mr. Churchill was in Franklin's office when they received the news of Tobruk. It was, Franklin told me, the closest they came to losing hope.

242

On the home front people grumbled for more frivolous reasons. The government banned all sales of passenger automo-
biles, then rationed gas, which was not in short supply, to save
rubber, which was, and the number of deaths from auto accidents plummeted. But when the War Production Board tried
to ration girdles, the women of America raised their voices in
protest. They could not support the hardships of war without
their rubber foundations, they said, and the board backed
down. In the last war we'd given up our steel stays more gra-
ciously. In February, Franklin asked the American people to
have a map at the ready as they listened to his first wartime
fireside chat, and across the country stores sold out of world
maps.

On December seventh, I'd sat in front of the cold hearth
crying over Eleanor's speech, because it marked the end of the
life Franklin and I had begun to build together. That was one
thing I knew about war. It drove men and women together
precipitously precisely because it separated them physically.
But a month later, on a bitter cold Tuesday with the wind
howling down Sixteenth Street, Franklin started on his first
blackout trip. As the war dragged on, these top-secret travels,
unreported in the papers, unknown to the public, kept from
many in his inner circle by Miss Hackmeister, who answered
the phone in Hyde Park or Warm Springs or my own Allamuchy as if she were speaking from the White House, became
Franklin's salvation. And what saved Franklin saved me.

At first our meetings were infrequent. Winty was bedrid-
den. I was more reluctant than ever to leave him. But when I
was in Washington to see the children or Vio or Mama, who
was in Waverly Sanitarium, Franklin always made time for
me. Under cover of wartime secrecy, he would arrive at Vio's
house at 2238 Q Street at an appointed hour in an inconspic-

uous auto accompanied by another with several Secret Service
agents. There was no siren, no fuss, nothing to let the neighbors know that the men in one of the autos were armed with
revolvers and rifles and machine guns, and the gentleman
lurking in the backseat of the other was the president.

One of the Secret Service officers would get out of the car,
come up the path, and ring Vio's bell. "Is Mrs. Johnson at
home?" he'd ask dear loyal Emma, who must have known
who was waiting in the car but never breathed a word. Then
Emma would come to the parlor or the library where I was
waiting, hat pinned on, gloves in hand, and say there was a
car for me. I'd go to the door, and the Secret Service man
would offer a respectful arm to escort me to the auto where
Franklin sat in the backseat, a lap robe ready if it was winter,
a thermos of lemonade or orange juice in summer, and an air
of quickened expectancy that made my pulse throb beneath
my gloves. He must have known that, because as the Secret
Service man closed us into the privacy of the backseat, and the
driver pulled away from the curb and headed toward Rock
Creek Park or Virginia or Maryland, he would take my hand
in both of his and draw off the glove and tangle his long graceful fingers with mine.

The roads we drove were familiar. We'd traveled them two
decades earlier, though they'd changed as much as we had.
Franklin was responsible for that. His policies had put men to
work paving highways and landscaping parks and building
schools and hospitals and lighthouses. As we purred along the
roads, uncrowded thanks to gas rationing, he'd interrupt himself to point out a bridge the PWA had put up here, a stand of
trees the CCC had planted there. Once I told him I couldn't
imagine how he kept track of it all, but he said that was nothing, and asked me to name any town in the continental United

States. I chose Allamuchy, but he said that wasn't nearly difficult enough. "Try something on the West Coast."

"Pasadena," I said.

"Now draw an imaginary line from here to there," he said,
and proceeded to list every county in every state the line
would pass through. "Just a little parlor trick," he said when
he finished, "but it works wonders on congressmen and visiting firemen."

Though we drove the countryside we'd traveled during
another war, we were not chasing our youth. The present was
more than enough, certainly more than either of us had
expected.

Our outings were kept from the press and the public, and I
was Mrs. Johnson to the Secret Service and in the various logs
and appointment books that tracked Franklin's every waking
minute, but our friendship was not furtive. The people we
loved knew. At least most of them did.

Franklin continued to send birthday greetings to Barbara
and invite her for tea and dinner when she was in Washington. When I mentioned that Winty's youngest boy, Guy, was
thinking of leaving the University of Virginia where he was at
law school with Franklin, Jr., Franklin had him to the White
House and convinced him to finish his studies and take the bar
exam before enlisting. He saw Hugo and promised to talk to
Admiral McIntire about helping him get sea duty. He had Win
and his wife to dinner. When he found out John and his wife
were going to be in Washington for Mr. Churchill's address to
a joint session of Congress, he gave them two of his last four
tickets. The other two went to the Duke and Duchess of
Windsor, whom, Franklin confided, he found far less pleasant
than my stepchildren. That is not the stuff of which a clandestine affair is made.

Occasionally I went back to the White House with Franklin after our drives. We were like an old married couple. I'd accompany him on his afternoon visit to the medical office, where Admiral McIntire, his physician, treated his sinuses and checked his blood pressure, while Franklin regaled us with anecdotes and gossip and jokes, but never complained about his symptoms or inquired about his condition. In the past he'd been in the habit of going for a swim in the pool grateful citizens had built for him in the White House basement after his first election. Frequently Miss LeHand and other secretaries had swum with him. But the demands of the war interfered with his regular exercise, and he said he'd rather spend the little time we had together alone. That was why he hadn't called in Commander Fox for his usual leg massage that afternoon. And that was why I offered my services. "I'm a first-rate masseuse," I said. And that was why I was sitting on the floor at Franklin's feet when a young man in a navy uniform came bounding into the oval study.

He stopped dead when he saw us. The color rose in his handsome face which looked as if it had been molded from Franklin's. I think he would have bolted if he hadn't thought it was bad manners.

I remained on the floor, though I did remove my hands from Franklin's leg. Franklin tossed back his head and, without taking his cigarette holder from his mouth, threw a wide smile across the room. "Brud, this is Mrs. Rutherfurd, an old family friend. Lucy, you remember Franklin, Jr. Of course he was in short pants the last time you saw him."

Franklin, Jr., said it was nice to meet me, and I mentioned that I'd heard a great deal about him from my stepson Guy, and by that time he'd regained his composure, and the three

of us had a perfectly delightful chat. He even held out his hand
to help me up from the floor.

"I can't imagine why he was so embarrassed," Franklin
said after his son left. "Especially in view of the fact that he's
lovestruck himself. I can't decide whether I should tell him it's
hopeless."

"Are you sure it is?"

"Absolutely. I spent an afternoon with the young lady in
question."

"Did she tell you it was hopeless?"

"She merely drove me around Algiers. We had a picnic
lunch. She and I and General Eisenhower."

I could tell from his smile that he was having a delicious
time making me pull the story out of him.

"Then I can't imagine how you can be so sure."

"It took me less than an hour to get the lay of the land. Ike
and his driver, the comely Miss Summersby, are what the
young people call an item. Poor Brud doesn't stand a chance.
The real problem, though, is going to be keeping Ike from
doing something about it after the war's over. It would ruin
his career."

The times had not changed so much after all. Ordinary
mortals like Franklin's children might divorce at will, but
great men with big dreams, like Franklin and General Eisenhower, walked a narrower path.

∾ In March of 1944, as Allied planes bombed the abbey at
Monte Cassino, because Franklin said monuments could not
be spared when American lives were at stake, and he lay ill
with a bout of influenza he couldn't seem to shake, my dear
husband died in his bed at Aiken. I could not grieve for Winty.

He was eighty-two years old. He had lived a long life, scarred by the loss of a wife and a son, but blessed by the love and admiration of another wife and six surviving children. He had lived away from the public eye and according to his own standards. That is no small achievement. I consoled myself that I had given solace for the losses, contributed to the happiness, and lived up to the standards. That too is no small achievement. I could not even say that I would miss him. I had been doing that for some time.

I took his body to Tranquility according to his instructions. Snow had been falling all morning, though the calendar said it was the first day of spring. We buried him beneath the cold white sheet left by the rogue storm, but as we started back to the house, the snow was already beginning to melt. I could smell spring.

↬ Twenty–three

"He might have been happier with a wife who was completely uncritical. That I was never able to be, and he had to find it in other people."   ↬ Eleanor Roosevelt in *This I Remember*

Interviewer: "You were carrying around one of the best kept secrets in Washington then, as a friend of Mr. Hopkins."
Kerr: "I suppose I was."
↬ Florence Kerr, assistant administrator for the
Works Progress Administration, on the subject of
Franklin D. Roosevelt and Lucy Mercer Rutherfurd

I saw the jaunty blue Ford roadster, its top folded back to the mild spring Sunday, as soon as the train pulled into the Highland Station. Franklin was behind the wheel. Fala's long head was hanging out the front window. The Scottie, a gift from Franklin's cousin, Miss Suckley, was the best-known dog in the country, in the world. He even had a code name. The Secret Service called him Informer, because the sight of Fala being walked beside the train on an off-the-record trip was a dead giveaway of who was aboard. In a few months, when the Republicans would accuse Franklin of inadvertently leaving Fala in the Aleutian Islands and sending a destroyer to rescue him at the cost of millions of tax dollars, the Scottie would

249

become a political weapon. "I don't resent attacks, and my family doesn't resent attacks," Franklin would tell the nation in a brilliantly droll campaign speech, "but Fala does resent them. He has not been the same dog since."

Beyond the station platform, buds bulged on the trees and fragile green shoots broke through the softening earth. It was a week since Winty's death. As the train slowed to a stop, a Secret Service agent reached up to help me down to the platform. I was at the Place at last.

Another Secret Service man held the car door open for me, and I climbed in, and Franklin said it was grand. His hands flew over the specially designed brakes and gears and accelerator, the car shot away from the station, and as the agent in the auto behind us gunned the engine, Franklin laughed. He loved outrunning the Secret Service, but there was more to his pleasure than that. He was exhilarated by my being there. Just as I was dying to see the landscape I'd been imagining in my mind's eye for years, he needed to show it to me. I think he half believed that if I could not love the Hudson Valley earth, and the broad ribbon of river, the old stone walls and woods and even air, I could not love him. He believed people, like trees, took their shape and character and confidence from the land. That was why he disliked cities. He did not think humans could survive on concrete and steel and narrow slivers of sky. And that was why, months later, sitting with his daughter Anna on the deck of a ship steaming toward a great conference with Mr. Churchill and Mr. Stalin, he would gaze out at the Virginia shoreline and tell her, "That's where Lucy grew up."

He turned the car off the road onto a wide drive hemmed by elms. As we headed down it, I pictured him running it as a boy and striding it as a young man, and managed to forget him struggling down it inch by painful inch for an entire summer. We stopped in front of the big low house with the long porch and neat shutters I had memorized from photographs. The Secret Service car came to a halt behind us, and the men leapt out and surrounded us. One of them opened my door, and two others moved to the driver's side. Franklin was still talking. As he called my attention to various details of the house and pointed out the new wing he'd designed himself, one of the Secret Service men opened his door, and another, the largest and brawniest of the group, reached in and lifted Franklin out. And Franklin, talking, laughing, bubbling with pride in his beloved Place and joy in having me there, threw one arm around the Secret Service man's shoulders and let himself be carried up the stairs and onto the porch like a baby. I stood, wanting to look away, knowing I must not, swearing I would not cry. And I didn't.

At the top of the steps, the agent placed Franklin in his wheelchair, and I wrestled my shock and sorrow and guilt out of sight, and he led me into the house. He showed me the long library with twin fireplaces at either end, where I'd once imagined him reading *A Christmas Carol* in the flickering shadows of the candles on the tree to a circle of children, some of whose faces I knew, others whom I could imagine even more vividly. He took me through rooms papered with rioting flowers, hung with old family portraits, filled with pictures and *objets* Mrs. James had brought back from Europe, and cluttered with Franklin's books and naval prints and model ships and stamps and framed cartoons and all the other interests he'd pursued over the years. Everything in the house spoke of Franklin, but I could hear his mother whispering in the background. This is where I gave birth to my boy. This is where I buffed and polished and perfected him. This is where I made him great. Standing in the faintly shabby glow of good things well used and favorite things well cherished, I felt a rush of affection for her.

I didn't notice it until we returned to the big front hall with the wide stairs leading to the upper floors and the glass cases filled with local birds Franklin had shot as a boy and Mrs. James had had stuffed by professional taxidermists. In one corner stood a life-sized bronze statue of Franklin. It would have been the first thing I saw as I walked in the door, if I hadn't been struggling not to look away from Franklin himself.

He noticed my glance. He missed nothing.

"Mama commissioned it from her friend Paul Troubetskoy when I was elected to the state senate. At first it was going to be a bust, but once Troubetskoy got started, he couldn't stop."

Only he had. On some aesthetic principle or prophetic instinct or only whim, the artist had cut off the sculpture at Franklin's knees. The result was chilling. I was glad to leave it behind as we headed for the dining room.

After lunch we lingered over coffee and Franklin's cigarettes, but presently he said he wanted to show me his library. "The monument I've erected to my own glory—according to Mr. Pegler."

Westbrook Pegler was a columnist who, after initially supporting Franklin and being rebuffed for a position in the administration, was making a career of outrageous accusations against him and even more scurrilous attacks on Eleanor. A few years earlier Franklin had had to stop James and Elliott from calling out Mr. Pegler in a fistfight. "Not that it isn't a grand idea," he'd added.

"Mr. Pegler insists only a king or a dictator would erect his own library during his lifetime," Franklin went on, as he moved from dining chair to wheelchair, rolled out of the house, and crossed the porch. "But it isn't enough just to give my papers to the public, which presidents should have been doing all along. I want to gather together in a single place all the materials and documents historians are going to want in the future. Now, isn't that clever of me, Lucy?" he asked as the Secret Service guard carried him to the auto. This time I did not have to fight to keep from averting my eyes. I climbed in the other side and admitted it was.

By the time we came out of his spanking-new library, the sun was hanging low and red on the horizon. Franklin's face had the same glow. I worried that it was a fever, and in fact after I left that evening he would go to bed with a temperature of a hundred and four, but for the moment we conspired to believe it was the effect of the open car and happiness.

"There's one more spot I want to show you," he shouted over the wind. "My cottage."

Sometimes he called it *my cottage*, others *Top Cottage*. The papers had referred to it as his dream house, but he soon put a stop to that. "Dream house!" he told me when he recounted the story. "I've fought like a banshee to keep the price down. It cost less than seventeen thousand dollars. I simply cannot afford an eighteen-thousand-dollar house, Lucy."

But the strangest name for the cottage was one I heard later, when I came back to Hyde Park under different circumstances. I was discussing what would happen to it with his cousin, Miss Suckley, the sweet-tempered if somewhat prim maiden lady who had given him Fala.

"It's so sad," she said, "to think of 'our cottage' passing into other hands."

I said nothing. Even a prim maiden lady is entitled to her daydreams.

"It's beautiful," I said as he pulled up in front of the simple stone house.

"It's one of only three buildings in the nation designed by a president in office." There was pure glee in his voice. "And both the others were by Jefferson. Monticello, and Poplar Forest just outside of Lynchburg.

"I've never spent a night in this house," he said half an hour later as we sat sipping tea and watching dusk darken the big square-paned windows. "But someday I will. After the war, I plan to retire here and write my memoirs. And detective stories. I've always wanted to write a detective story. I've some grand ideas."

He put down his cup and saucer and turned to me. "Do you think you'd like that, Lucy? Do you think you'd like it here after the war?"

⚜ Twenty-four

"Father asked me one day . . . whether I would mind if he invited a very close friend to dinner . . . Mrs. Rutherfurd. And it was a terrible decision to have to make in a hurry, because I realized that Mother wasn't going to be there, you see, and I was sure she didn't know about it, but my quick decision was that the private lives of these people were not my business."

ᴑ Anna Roosevelt Boettiger Halstead

"I pray I don't get caught in the crossfire between those two."

ᴑ Anna Roosevelt Boettiger in a letter
to her husband about her parents

It was the courtship we'd never had. A month after we'd sat in the stone cottage talking about what would happen after the war, I drove from Aiken to Hobcaw, Mr. Bernard Baruch's estate, to spend several days with Franklin.

"Bernie has promised to give you his gas coupons," Franklin had said when he'd telephoned to make plans. "It's the least he can do to make it up to me."

"To make what up to you?" I asked.

"Back in '32, when I was running for president the first time, he called me wishy-washy." Franklin's laughter rolled

down the telephone wire, then he lowered his voice conspira-
torially. "But never underestimate Bernie. He owns at least
sixty congressmen." He laughed again. "And he's a terrible
old satyr. Did I ever tell you about the time during the First
War when Cousin Alice and I eavesdropped on him while he
was paying a visit to the daughter of a German-American
banker whose loyalties were suspect?" And he was off on
another of his stories.

It was half a day's drive from Aiken to Hobcaw, but I had
Barbara for company. Franklin had said he was eager to see
his goddaughter. The plantation itself was isolated. There was
not even a telephone, and Franklin refused to have one
installed for his stay. He relied on a specially equipped railroad car parked on a siding a few miles away.

Marines guarded a turn off the country highway onto a private road. Five miles farther, a Secret Service contingent stood
sentry at the gates to the grounds. A modern brick house
loomed in the distance. Its white-columned veranda paid lip
service to the old South. As I pulled up before it, I recognized
several of the Secret Service agents. One helped me out of the
auto and said he would see that it and our luggage were taken
care of. Another led us across the veranda and into the large
front hall. I could hear Franklin's voice in the next room. It
came rolling out to meet us. Then he was behind it, and I was
shocked.

I'd noticed when I'd seen him in Hyde Park that he'd lost a
few pounds. The result had pleased both him and the doctors.
But this was more dramatic. His coat hung loosely. His neck
was thin. But it was his face that astonished. The flesh had
evaporated, and the bones emerged, and I was looking at the
young man I'd fallen in love with so many years earlier. It was
a sweetly unsettling experience.

He read my expression. "I'm a young man again, Lucy! Look how flat my stomach is." He slapped himself with gleeful pride, said it was good to see me and his goddaughter, and led us into the dining room.

Lunch was festive. Franklin teased General Watson about a remedy for baldness, and young Dr. Bruenn from the Naval Hospital about someone he called the countess spy, and I thought this is what he needs. Then, halfway through the meal, an aide came in and bent to murmur in his ear. His face folded like a house of cards. The rest of us sat waiting.

"Secretary of the Navy Knox has suffered a heart attack," he said finally. "He died a short while ago."

Murmurs of sorrow circled the table, but we were all watching Franklin, concerned about how he was taking it, worried about him. That is the effect the death of one man has on those who love another, and make no mistake about it, I was not the only one in love with Franklin. I have often thought of something Dr. Bruenn said to me when I inquired about Franklin's health. "Like everyone else who works for this man, Mrs. Rutherfurd, I love him."

We finished lunch quietly. The carbonation had gone out of Franklin's conversation. There was talk of returning to Washington. I thought of my own disappointed drive back to Aiken. I would not stay here without him and could not go to Washington with him. The funeral was a public occasion, and like his wartime travels, I was still off the record.

We were getting up from the table when the aide returned and handed Franklin a telegram. He unfolded it and glanced at the message.

"It's from my missus," he announced. "She says she's going to postpone her trip to New York so she'll be on hand for the funeral."

He sat studying the telegram. General Watson and Dr. Bruenn exchanged glances. The rest of us waited.

"So perhaps we won't have to cut things short after all," Franklin said.

"The longer you stay, sir, the greater the benefit," Dr. Bruenn told him.

"We can call a press conference here this evening," General Watson suggested, "and Mrs. Roosevelt can represent you at the funeral."

Without looking at me, Franklin folded the telegram and put it in his pocket. "That's a fine idea, Pa. Mrs. Knox will want my missus there. Everybody relies on my missus."

Rome fell; and the Allies landed in Normandy; and Franklin pushed through something called the GI Bill of Rights, which, he said, would give millions of Americans the opportunity to go to college, and own their own homes, and start their own businesses, and do all sorts of things their parents had only dreamed of. It would, he predicted when he called one evening, change the face of American society. Then, without missing a beat, he went on to say he had another wonderful idea. "I was talking to Anna."

Anna, her husband John Boettiger, their little boy Johnny, and, when they were not away at school, her son and daughter by a previous marriage, were living at the White House. She'd come for a visit at Christmas, and when she'd seen how lonely her father was since Mr. Hopkins and his new wife had moved out, she'd decided to give up her house and job on the West Coast and stay on to care for him.

"I asked how she'd feel about inviting an old friend to dinner," he went on.

"Are you referring to Mrs. Johnson?"

"Mrs. Rutherfurd," he corrected me, and I knew he'd been turning the matter over in his mind and had come to a decision.

For some time now Franklin had been talking about how much Anna and I were going to like each other, but I knew something about mothers and daughters, and the last thing I wanted was to put Anna in an awkward position. I knew a bit about fathers and daughters too. It was entirely possible that Anna might resent something Eleanor swore she had forgiven. But I could tell from Franklin's voice that he was set on the idea, and I didn't have the heart to warn him that this putting together of loved ones was a dangerous business.

"She thought it was a grand idea," he said.

I was fairly certain Anna thought nothing of the kind, but she would not have told Franklin that. She'd moved into the White House to make his life more pleasant.

"Come for the weekend, Lucy. General de Gaulle will be here, but we won't let him ruin things. I'll manage to get away and we'll drive out to Shangri-La. I want you to see my hideaway in the Maryland hills."

I told him I'd love to dine at the White House and see Shangri-La and meet Anna.

∾ He'd acted as if it were the most natural thing in the world. I want you and Anna to meet. But he must have known the situation was not as simple as that. He'd been juggling people all his life. He was always joking about how one cabinet member or politician or general couldn't get along with another. He'd once taken Mr. Hopkins and Secretary of the Interior Ickes off on a cruise to force them to settle a feud that had been raging for months. Some people said he encouraged the petty rival-

ries and pitched battles, but then there was never a shortage
of people saying terrible untrue things about Franklin.

In any event, he must have known I was apprehensive that
night in early July, because instead of sending a car to Vio's to
collect me, he came in it himself. On the way back to the
White House, he regaled me with stories of General de Gaulle,
but as the car passed through the south gate, he mentioned
that there would be only the four of us for dinner. "Just the
immediate family," he said as he swung himself into the
wheelchair.

They were waiting in Franklin's study. Anna was even love-
lier than she looked in photographs or from a distance at
inaugurations. Her legs were long, and her neck was graceful,
and she radiated a silvery elegance that reminded me of
Franklin in his youth. I was certain she had no idea how
attractive she was.

She crossed the room and held out her hand to me before
Franklin even had a chance to introduce us. "I am so glad to
meet you, Mrs. Rutherfurd," she said, then ducked her silky
blond head and added that she guessed it wasn't really a meeting at all since we'd known each other for years.

I laughed and told her how happily I remembered her, and
she introduced the fair young man in the army uniform with
a major's gold leaf insignia as her husband John, and by that
time Franklin was behind his big oak desk mixing drinks.
There was much banter about his martinis, which Anna and
John complained were awash in vermouth; and about Johnny,
who'd been caught throwing stones at Secret Service agents;
and about General de Gaulle, whom Franklin called a nut,
which Anna said was an extremely undignified way to refer to
a head of state, and Franklin pointed out that the general

wasn't a head of state, and he had no intention of receiving him as such, which was why the general's prodigious Gallic nose was out of joint.

I watched Anna's face, all light and animation, and heard the gaiety in her voice, and thought how much like Franklin she was, and how finely attuned to him. She was keeping up the silly breezy conversation because she knew how crucial this interlude was to his spirits. He would become serious presently. In London, V-1 bombs were raining death on the civilian population. In northern France, American soldiers were fighting the Battle of the Hedgerows. In the Philippine Sea, American airmen were flying beyond their range to sink Japanese aircraft carriers. The entire world war, as well as production problems and labor strikes and civilian complaints about consumer shortages, rested on Franklin's shoulders. All he asked was to shrug it off for half an hour. All he needed was that brief intermission to refresh his soul and replenish his resources. As I watched Anna doing her best to give it to him, I realized that she was not as like him as I'd thought. The vitality and fun and thoroughbred elegance were Franklin's, but the intensity and effort and determination to please were pure Eleanor. Anna understood her father better than her mother did. By now even I knew that Eleanor couldn't resist cluttering Franklin's cocktail hour with her basket of letters and memos and problems that had to be solved immediately. In fairness to her, it was one of the few opportunities she had to talk to him. "But doesn't she see," Anna burst out to me months later, "that she's killing him with all that badgering during the one moment he has to relax?" Then she looked stricken, not only at what she'd said, but to whom she'd said it. Anna would do anything for her father. That was why she had invited me to dinner. But she was her mother's daughter too. That was why I knew that night, despite her kindness to me, she was tortured by the act.

∽ A few days later Franklin left for San Diego, where he accepted the Democratic nomination to run for an unprecedented fourth term, and then Hawaii, where for the first time, instead of putting on his braces, which no longer fit since he'd lost so much weight, he had himself wheeled past the beds of the maimed and wounded soldiers so they could see that he was one of them. I missed him desperately and worried about him constantly. When I tuned in to his radio addresses, I listened for sounds of strain in his voice. When I read his letters, I searched for traces of exhaustion. The holiday in Hobcaw had helped, but work was taking its toll again. Before he'd left, I'd noticed a tremor in his hand. One night at dinner he'd repeated an anecdote over coffee which he'd told during cocktails. Anna was horrified and embarrassed for him, but I could never be embarrassed by Franklin. And everyone makes a mistake now and then, especially after a long and trying day. Anna saw the slip as a sign of her father's deteriorating health. I worried about him too, but I had more perspective. I had lived with a seriously ill man. I had lived with a dying man. Franklin was not that. If I'd had any fear he was, Dr. McIntire had dispelled it. "The president is in sound health," he'd told Anna. "As long as he gets enough rest, he has many productive years ahead of him."

∽ The inspection tour would keep him away for a good part of the summer. Halfway through it, on the next to the last night of July, while his ship steamed from Pearl Harbor to the Aleutians for the second leg of the journey, poor Miss

LeHand, who was recuperating at her family's house in Massachusetts, went to the movies with her sister and a friend. In
the newsreel between the double feature, there was a sequence
about Fala, who, the announcer said, was in danger of going
bald, because crew members kept snipping locks of his hair as
souvenirs. The president had had to issue an order against any
more clipping of Fala. The story was intended to be humor-
ous, but Anna told me later that it made Miss LeHand sad.
The shots of Franklin must have broken her heart. When she
returned home, she began going through old photos of their
life together. She was holding one of him in a swimsuit on the
boat they'd cruised off the coast of Florida when she collapsed. Moments later a siren disturbed the peace of that leafy
Somerville street. The ambulance took her to Charles Naval
Hospital. She died the following morning.

I called Anna as soon as I saw the obituary in the paper.

"I'm glad Pa's away," she said. "The funeral would have
been unbearable for him."

I agreed with her. Franklin was not good at grieving. And
what could possibly be gained by adding to his burdens?

"Mother will go in his place," Anna continued. "She's a
rock in these situations."

ᦞ In August Allied troops marched into Paris, and men welcomed them with bottles of hallowed brandy they'd hidden
from the Germans, and girls covered their war-aged young
faces with kisses. A week later Franklin came to Tranquility,
and I brought the best Montrachet up from the cellars and
kissed his newly lean face in celebration of France, and hope,
and the fact that he was in my home.

He'd said it would be simple. On his way from Washington
to Hyde Park, he would have the train pull off onto a siding

for a few hours. I was surprised. Having me at the Place or Hobcaw or even the White House was one thing; detaining the presidential train and keeping scores of people waiting seemed to be asking for trouble, or at least public notice. His trips were off the record, but three reporters traveled with him. They were bound to ask questions. I knew how scandal could spread. I was a widow of no importance. His position was more lofty, and vulnerable.

"I'll tell them I'm stopping to visit an old friend."

"Won't they ask whom?"

"They're hardened reporters, Lucy. They want war news, or political dope, or scandals that cost the taxpayers money. The sort of thing the Truman Committee's been after. Even if they knew about us, they wouldn't print it. It's an unwritten rule. A gentleman's agreement. Personal matters are off the record. Take that Sumner Welles affair a few years ago. A lot of the newspaper boys knew about Sumner's tastes even before he had too much to drink in the club car and went looking for trouble with railroad porters. And just for the record I'll never forgive Bill Bullitt for forcing my hand on the resignation. When those two men get to the pearly gates, St. Peter's going to give Sumner a rap on the knuckles and let him in, but he's going to send Bullitt straight to hell for ruining another man's life. The point is, though, nobody broke the story. People on the inside knew it, but nobody printed it. And no one will be the wiser about this. Think of it, Lucy, in years to come when historians are poring over my every move, someone will notice that while most trips from Washington to Hyde Park left at night and arrived first thing the next morning, on August thirty-first, 1944, the president left at the usual time, but didn't arrive at Hyde Park until the evening of September first. Can you imagine the speculation?

Engine trouble? A sabotage threat? The poor devils will never figure it out."

For days before, strange men looked into every corner of the house, and set up ramps, and installed telephones. The grandchildren scampered after them; and John, who was home on leave, and his wife, and Guy's wife Georgette, and Alice and her husband Arturo rushed in and out; and one of the nannies said, "Heavens, you would think the president was coming."

"He is," I sang.

Everything went splendidly, though nothing went as planned. I'd had a room made up for Franklin, in case he wanted to lie down, but when I showed it to him, he said he had no intention of wasting the little time we had together resting. I'd planned to serve lobster, but it turned out he'd had lobster the night before and would have it again that night at Hyde Park, so I sent word to the kitchen that we'd have cold soup and squabs. I'd placed Franklin at the head of the table, but he insisted he wanted to sit on my right, so we flouted protocol and sat beside each other.

Don't you love it? he asked, and I did. I loved bringing him into the life I knew he was glad I'd made for myself. I loved having him at the table I'd presided over for so many years. I loved watching the faces of my loved ones turned to him as he asked Johnnie about his experiences in the navy, and Georgette about how Guy was getting along in England, and told us stories about the progress of the war and the egos of the men who were waging it. "Patton is a wild bull," he pronounced. "Entirely uncontrollable." I loved showing him through the house, and driving him around the lake and through the fields and forested lands, and listening to his advice on how to keep things running now that most of the staff had gone off to war or left for better-paying jobs making planes and ships and ball bearings.

"You know, Lucy," he said as we drove past the kennels, "most people in this country, especially the rich, still haven't awakened to the fact that life is never going to go back to the way it was in the past. It's going to be a little less pleasant for a handful like you and me, and a lot better for almost everyone else."

Until that moment, I had never fully grasped the power of Franklin's imagination. The people I lived among called him a traitor to his class because they could not imagine what it was like to be poor or hungry or out of work. But Franklin could. Though he'd never been without food, or a roof over his head, or had to work for a living, he felt hunger gnawing in his stomach, and saw the Place being taken away from him, and intuited what it meant to lose a job. And the leap of imagination fueled his outrage.

As we stood near the railroad siding at the end of the afternoon, the lengthening rays of the sun melted our two shadows into one. He gestured to the Secret Service agent and the man approached and wheeled him onto one of the two elevators at the rear of his railroad car. The armor-plated, bulletproof safety of it reassured me. The need for it terrified me. The elevator started. Franklin inched toward the sky.

"It was grand," he called.

"Grand," I answered.

Neither of us said good-bye. We knew it was not.

꙳ We spent Thanksgiving together in Warm Springs, among others, of course. Franklin could not move without his official entourage. He liked having an unofficial one as well. His cousin Miss Suckley was there. She was around

Franklin a good deal, working in his library, keeping him company at Hyde Park or in the White House, turning up at Hobcaw. She was even on the train when he stopped at Allumuchy. She'd taken care of Fala, and Johnnie's twin boys had entertained her. I could not be jealous of Margaret, whom I came to call by her pet name Daisy during that visit to Warm Springs, though there was no doubt in my mind that she was head over heels in love with Franklin. He was fond of her, but affection is not love, and though Daisy was not quite the prim spinster she wanted people to believe, she had an aptitude, almost a genius, for self-effacement. I was sure Franklin found her restful.

His cousin Laura Delano, who was known as Polly, was there that week too. A striking woman given to purple streaks in her white hair, flamboyant lounging pajamas at all hours of the day, and a great deal of noisy jewelry, Polly was anything but restful. They made perfect bookends to shore up Franklin's lonely hours.

I grew fond of both women, and was sorry they had to move out of the main house, which had only three bedrooms, and into a guest cottage to make room for me, but Franklin insisted. Daisy, of course, was a perfect saint and said she didn't mind a bit.

Franklin loved being surrounded by his harem, though occasionally the situation demanded all his political skills. One day, when there were no other guests, I saw him glance around the room as we were about to go in to lunch and realize the problem. Though the meal was informal, one of us would sit across from him and therefore preside as his hostess. I needed no outward sign of his affection, but Polly and Daisy were more jealous of their places in his heart. He did not want to offend either of them. He turned to Miss Brady, the secretary who'd been taking dictation. "Stay for lunch and be my hostess, Dottie," he said with an innocent smile.

A damp gunmetal sky stretched overhead and a cold wind kept us indoors for the first several days of our stay, but on Saturday the sun burned through the clouds and toasted the air. It was a delicious Georgia morning, and Franklin said he knew the perfect place to savor it. "From the top of Dowdell's Knob," he promised, "you can look across the whole Shiloh Valley."

The Secret Service brought around another Ford with hand controls, and one of the men carried Franklin out to it. By then I'd grown accustomed to the ritual. He even made it into something of a game, though only in private. He never permitted himself to be carried in public. But in private he practically surged in and out of the arms of Mr. Reilly, the agent who usually carried him.

Once behind the wheel of the car, clutching and releasing the various handles and levers, he was in control again. He exulted in the power the machine gave him, and the mobility, and the sheer fun of speeding off and leaving the Secret Service in his dust. When he swerved off the road through a field, I heard the screech of brakes behind us, and the shower of gravel, and the deep rolling joy of Franklin's laughter.

We reached Dowdell's Knob, and one Secret Service man spread a blanket on the ground, and another carried Franklin to it, and then they disappeared discreetly. After a moment or two, it was possible to forget they were there.

We talked about everything. By then he'd been elected for a fourth term, and I'd rejoiced in his victory, though I knew it meant putting off that quiet life in his hilltop cottage for another four years. It had been, he said, the dirtiest campaign in all history. Mr. Dewey and his supporters had spread rumors that Franklin was too old, too weak, too sick to run. Opposition papers had gone out of their way to print photos that made him look exhausted and ill. I was sure they had touched up some of them.

"I spent an entire day driving the streets of New York in an open car under an icy downpour to show them how old and sick and tired I was," he told me on that quiet hill. "All the Secret Service men caught colds, but I came through healthy as a horse." He laughed, then grew more serious. "You know, Lucy, of the four candidates I ran against, Dewey is the only one I personally disliked. I admired Wilkie. If he'd lived, we might have started a truly liberal party together. And Hoover and Landon were simply misguided. But Dewey is no gentleman. He went on the radio to admit he was licked, but didn't even have the courtesy to send me the usual message of congratulations. I fixed him, though. I telegraphed him immediately. 'Thank you for your statement, which I have heard over the air a few minutes ago.' " He threw back his head, pointed his cigarette holder at the sky, and laughed again. Then he was off on another tack about the conference with Mr. Churchill and Mr. Stalin which he planned for immediately after the inauguration.

"Top secret," he said. "No one will know about it until it's over. Half the people who are going don't even know where it will be. Shall I tell you, Lucy?" He was leaning back against the log, a tired thinning man with a five-year-old's glint in his eye.

"How else can I send you your birthday gift?"

He leaned over, put his lips against my ear and his hand in front of his mouth. "The Crimea, Lucy. A resort in the Black Sea called Yalta."

He leaned back again and turned serious. "It's going to be a devil of a conference, though. The only good part will be the sea voyage, providing the weather's not too filthy this time of year."

I agreed that a sea voyage would be pleasant, and kept my fears to myself. If the weather was good, he'd enjoy himself, and the German submarines would have excellent hunting conditions. If it was bad, he'd be more uncomfortable, but the subs would have a harder time of it too.

He said he wasn't looking forward to the bartering and bickering. "Winston wants to hang on to his empire, Uncle Joe is determined to take over Poland, and I've got to get Uncle Joe into the war against Japan. The sooner we get him in, the sooner the war will be over. And when it is . . ." He stopped, put a fresh Camel in his holder, lit it, and inhaled deeply. He exhaled. I held my breathe and watched the smoke twist through the clear afternoon. The air smelled of pines. The Shiloh Valley stretched into the distance. "And when it is, Lucy, I'm going to move out of the White House and let Mr. Truman move in. I plan to spend my days steering the United Nations, writing my memoirs and my mysteries, and living quietly in our cottage on our hill. That's what I'm going to do when the war is over."

When the war is over. It was a wish, and a prayer, and a promise. Ordinary people measured their lives by it. Officials outlined the future according to it. Newspaper reporters never tired of asking Franklin about it. When will the war be over, Mr. President? Can you give us some idea, Mr. President? Franklin refused to make a prediction. Even for me. That was all right. I'd waited all these years. I could be patient awhile longer.

～ As soon as I saw the newsreels and photos on Franklin's return from Yalta, I knew the conference had been as exhausting as he'd predicted. His face was lean and hollow-cheeked. The circles under his eyes were dark as soot. The pictures would have been alarming if Anna hadn't told me there were hundreds of others from the trip in which he didn't look nearly so bad. As usual, the papers had chosen the most sensational.

Nonetheless, he clearly hadn't gotten enough rest at the conference. Anna, who'd accompanied him, had written of endless meetings, and champagne- and vodka-laced state dinners that went on long after midnight, and an astronomical number of people jockeying for five minutes of his time. And though they'd stayed in a palace, the accommodations had been less than royal. They hadn't even been sanitary. There were bedbugs and lice and typhus bacilli. Ten years of research could not have unearthed a worse place to meet, Mr. Churchill told Mr. Hopkins, who passed it on to Franklin.

My only solace was that it would have been worse if Anna hadn't been there to care for him. There had been some awkwardness about her going. Eleanor had asked Franklin if she could accompany him, but he'd insisted if she were there, people would feel obliged to make a fuss over her. Besides, Mr. Churchill and Ambassador Harriman were taking their daughters. Anna felt terrible about usurping her mother's place, but she was determined to look after her father. I was glad. Instead of someone pestering Franklin to do things, no matter how important, there would be someone making sure he did not do too much.

Nonetheless, if the pictures were any indication, the conference had taken its toll. He looked tired, and thin, and something else I'd noticed a year earlier in Hobcaw. He looked, in a way, like his old self. That was what gave me the idea.

April 9–12, 1945

❧ Chapter Twenty-five

"I remember saying to myself [after Yalta], 'That Roosevelt man is a wonder. He gets tired, but just give him a little rest and a sea voyage and he comes right up again.'"

❧ Secretary of Labor Frances Perkins

"Now more than ever one must live each day as it comes—but it helps to have a milestone in site [sic] . . . a small home would be a joy—and one could grow vegetables as well as flowers. . . . I know one should be proud—very proud of your greatness—instead of wishing for the soft life—of joy . . . and the world shut out. One is proud and thankful for what you have given to the world and realizes how much more must still be given this greedy world . . . the fate of all that is good is in your dear blessed and capable hands."   ❧ Lucy Mercer Rutherfurd in a letter to Franklin D. Roosevelt

The earth thawed, and life pressed its advantage, and Franklin called daily from Warm Springs to tell me to hurry. On the second Monday after Easter, with the tank of Shoumie's Cadillac convertible filled to the brim with gas bought by our combined rations, and the engine put on something called low mixture which was supposed to give us sixteen miles to the gallon, we set out from Aiken.

Shoumie, Madame Shoumatoff, had not only painted portraits of Winty and the children and me. Two years earlier, after I'd made the arrangements, she'd gone to the White House to paint a small watercolor of Franklin. When I'd seen the photos of him after Yalta, the bones of the young man showing through the mature face like a palimpsest, I'd decided I had to have another portrait, and asked Franklin if I might bring Shoumie along on my visit to Warm Springs.

She was driving, I was beside her in the front seat, and a Mr. Robbins, who would take photos, because Franklin could not be expected to sit for too long, was in the back. Mr. Robbins's real name was Mr. Kotzubinsky, but the judge who'd given him his naturalization papers had advised him to simplify it. Mr. Kotzubinsky had become Mr. Kobbins, until a clerk mistook his *K* for an *R*, and now Mr. Kotzubinsky was Mr. Robbins. Miss Tully said it had not been easy to get him cleared for the visit to Warm Springs.

But now everything was in order, and we were on our way. Shoumie predicted the trip was going to be a great success and cited a good omen that had occurred on her way from New York to collect me in Aiken. She had a superstitious bent, and had told me she'd known about Franklin's trip to Yalta even before I had, thanks to a friend with astrological inclinations. I usually laughed at Shoumie's mystical interpretations, but that morning her prediction struck me as perfectly feasible. It was so in keeping with my spirits. The day before, she'd stopped at the ticket office of the Metropolitan Opera to ask if anyone had turned in a sapphire and diamond clip she'd lost a few nights earlier. Someone had. "Isn't that a good sign!" she called over the wind, and I agreed that it was.

Franklin had said he'd drive to Macon to meet us at four o'clock, and we'd be in Warm Springs in time for dinner. I began to look at my watch at a little after three. At twenty before four, I spotted a sign that said Warm Springs. The arrow pointed back the way we'd come. Shoumie stopped. We turned to Mr. Robbins. He'd insisted on taking charge of the maps, though I'd had reservations. A man who could not hold on to a semblance of his name wasn't likely to be much better at navigating his way.

We doubled back, took another wrong turn, and doubled back again. It was well after four by the time we reached Macon. The old trees cast long shadows in the attenuated rays of the sun. The antebellum houses stood like silent disapproving dowagers. The streets dozed. A man walked with a newspaper folded under his arm. A child rode a bike. A dog trotted behind him. There were no Secret Service agents in sight. There was no flurry that would accompany a presidential presence.

"He's not here," I said.

Neither of them answered.

"We'll drive on, toward Warm Springs."

The sun hung lower in the sky now. The air was growing cooler, but I didn't want to take the time to stop to put up the top on the car. I hugged myself and strained forward in the seat.

After half an hour, Mr. Robbins decided we were on the wrong road again. I told him I was sure we weren't, and at that moment a sign welcoming us to the town of Greenville loomed into sight. As we drove down the main street, I noticed several autos parked at a corner in front of a drugstore. A crowd surged around them. Many of the men were in overalls. The women wore flower-print cotton dresses. It looked like an ordinary small-town gathering, except for a scattering of men in city-sober dark suits and hard watchful faces. The crowd was jockeying and straining to get a view of the open car, but the men in suits kept their eyes on the crowd.

I knew what was going on before I saw him. Then I did see. In the center of it all, sitting in the rear of an open auto, his big beautiful head thrown back, his navy cape draped over his shoulders, Franklin sat drinking a Coca-Cola.

Shoumie parked the car, and she and I made our way through the crowd, and in the noise and exhilaration of greetings, Franklin shifted position to make room for me beside him, and Daisy Suckley made herself small on the little folding seat so Shoumie could sit on my other side, and Fala—I swear it—grinned, and we were off.

That night Franklin was ebullient, as he mixed old-fashioneds at the little card table, and regaled us with stories of Yalta and Mr. Churchill and Mr. Stalin. Shoumie, who was Russian, refused to believe that Mr. Stalin was not the devil incarnate, but Franklin insisted he liked him a great deal, though it hadn't been easy to get to know him. "He sent me lots of caviar, which we'll have tomorrow night, and a case of vodka. I can't offer you any of that, because I left it in Washington. But Uncle Joe is quite a jolly fellow. Even if he did poison his wife." A wicked smile played around Franklin's mouth as he watched Shoumie take it in.

It went on that way for the next two days. Each morning I had my tray, dressed, and crossed the lawn to the Little White House, as Franklin's cottage was known. I was staying in the guest house this time. It seemed only fair to Daisy and Polly, and more discreet as well, in view of all the time Franklin and I had been spending together. A moment later he would emerge from his room, dressed for the portrait in one of his dashing prewar double-breasted blue-gray suits—they must have been prewar because the War Production Board had outlawed double-breasted suits along with cuffed trousers and flap pockets and pleated skirts—and a red tie, looking fit and rested and happy. Mornings were his best time. He tended to tire as the day went on, but I remembered Dr. McIntire's prognosis, and knew that would pass too. "Keep lazy, sir," young Dr. Bruenn kept saying to him, and though Franklin was still doing prodigious amounts of work, he was also getting plenty of sleep. The effect was remarkable. Each morning his color was better, his hand steadier, his face less lined.

Mr. Hassett, the austere secretary Franklin had christened "the bishop," would bring in the mail pouch, and Franklin would read dispatches, and study reports, and sign Franklin D. Roosevelt, Franklin D. Roosevelt, Franklin D. Roosevelt with a flourish, as he chatted and joked and teased Daisy and Polly and me. Meanwhile, Mr. Robbins snapped away with his camera and Shoumie painted. One morning Mr. Robbins said he'd like to photograph me, and Franklin thought that was a grand idea. Then he decided Mr. Robbins should take matching photos of us. "Like those wonderful Dutch portraits of my solid burgher ancestors and their wives." So Mr. Robbins moved a chair to get the right light and background, and I sat in it, and he took my picture.

I still have the photographs Mr. Robbins took that morning. Franklin sits facing the camera. He isn't smiling. It's one of the few photographs I have in which he is not. His serious face radiates all the kindness and generosity and tenderness he brought to the world. The hands, which were shaping an era, lie powerful and elegant on the arms of his chair. In the matching picture, I sit turned a little to the side, a dignified matron in a dark dress. A double strand of pearls circles my throat, and a lorgnette hangs from a gold chain on my bodice. Unlike Franklin, I am smiling. Mr. Robbins called it a Mona Lisa smile, but he was wrong. There is no mystery to the curve of my mouth. The message on my lips is as clear as if I were speaking. I am telling the world how happy I am. That is because of something Franklin had said the evening before.

⌐ The day after Mr. Robbins took the photos I awakened to a morning that cheated all thoughts of war or suffering or death. The sun was a yellow balloon in a jubilant blue sky. When Franklin and I drove to Dowdell's Knob, as we planned to that afternoon, we would shed our hats and coats and sit looking out over the Shiloh Valley into the future. Two nights earlier at dinner, Franklin had made the prediction he'd been refusing to make for months. That was why I am smiling in the photo Mr. Robbins snapped.

Mr. McCarthy, the former minister to Canada, who was visiting because his son was a polio, which was the term those with the disease preferred, had joined us, and Franklin was telling him about a breakthrough across the Weser River near Minden and a major offensive across the Sieg River. It always amazed me that he could keep the entire European and Pacific theaters of war in his head.

"When will it be over?" Polly asked the tired, inevitable question.

Sometimes good news is as numbing as bad. When Franklin spoke, we sat stunned and silent. Each of us was afraid to believe him. I was most frightened of all. I did not want to be disappointed again.

"Next month," he said.

He looked around the table from one to the other of us. His eyes came to rest on me last. I was sitting on his right as I had at every meal. "The war in Europe will be over by the end of May."

The silence shattered. They were all talking at once. Only Franklin and I were silent.

"What about Japan?" Polly shouted above the din.

"When the European war ends," Franklin said, "Japan will collapse almost immediately." He was still looking at me as he spoke.

Now, two mornings later, I threw off the covers, crossed the room, and opened the window. The air was full of pine and hope.

I breakfasted and dressed quickly in a navy blue dress with white piping, which Franklin had admired the last time I'd worn it, and spectator pumps that were stylish enough for the dress but sturdy enough for uneven terrain. The mayor of Warm Springs was giving a barbecue for Franklin that afternoon, but I wanted to be ready for the trip to Dowdell's Knob after it.

I hurried down the path to the Little White House, pulled open the door, and stepped inside. Sunlight streamed through the windows and glazed every object in the room. Daisy was moving furniture about.

"I want to have his chair in the right position when he comes out," she said. "That way we won't have to bother him when Madame Shoumatoff arrives."

I helped Daisy turn the leather chair to get the right light, though she kept insisting she could do it herself. We were just positioning the footrest when Franklin emerged from his room.

He was wearing another handsome double-breasted suit and a ruby tie. His freshly shaved cheeks glowed. I was astonished. His color hadn't been this good since he'd returned from Yalta.

He shifted from his wheelchair into the one we'd moved, all the while wishing us good morning, and exulting in the fine weather, and telling us that he had it on the best authority that

Mrs. Stevens, the manager of the Warm Springs Hotel, was scouring the entire county for the makings of his favorite Brunswick stew for the barbecue that afternoon. "I just hope she remembers to have an old-fashioned for me before it as well."

Daisy asked how he was feeling, and he said he'd awakened with a bit of a stiff neck and a slight headache, but Dr. Bruenn had rubbed his neck and ordered a hot water bottle, and he felt fine now. I told him he looked it. His color was rosy as a blush.

Mr. Hassett arrived with the mail pouch, and we moved the card table in front of Franklin, and he got down to work. As he read and made notations and signed, Mr. Hassett spread the documents around the room to dry. Even with an unsteady hand, Franklin's signature was too bold for a mere blotter. Soon papers covered every surface in the room.

"Now, be careful of my laundry," Franklin said as Polly came in with a bowl of flowers.

Mr. Hassett placed another document on the card table, and Franklin, pen in hand, leaned over it. "Here's where I make a law," he said, and wrote the word "Approved" at the bottom of the bill, "Franklin D. Roosevelt" beneath it, and finally the date. "April 12, 1945."

He signed another paper and told Mr. Hassett not to hang his laundry over Madame Shoumatoff's easel. I could tell from his tone that he was teasing Mr. Hassett, though the secretary's face was serious as the grave. Franklin insisted Mr. Hassett had a dry and ready wit, but around the rest of us the secretary was extremely proper, even faintly superior. If he could have, I am sure he would have guarded Franklin like a jealous husband.

"The bishop doesn't like Madame Shoumatoff's last portrait of me," Franklin said. "He thinks it makes me look too pretty. He calls it *The President with His Capon*. I told him I resent that, and from now on he is to refer to it as *The President Wearing His Cape*." He laughed, and the rest of us, even Mr. Hassett, laughed with him, and his face glowed in the morning sun.

Shoumie arrived and set out her paints, and she and Daisy arranged the navy cape around Franklin's shoulders, while he went on reading. Finally, Shoumie began to paint. Though I was dying to see the portrait, I knew she did not like to have anyone looking over her shoulder while she worked, but when I shifted my position, I discovered I could see the painting in the mirror on the wall behind her. There was something missing in the composition. She must have thought so too, because suddenly she stopped. "It's the hand," she said. "Your left hand, sir. Perhaps you could hold something."

We all began hunting for something for Franklin to hold. Daisy gave him a book. I took a piece of Mr. Hassett's laundry. But Franklin reached for a leaflet on his desk. It was the program for the Jefferson Day Dinner scheduled for the next evening. He'd been working at his speech for it on and off, and had quoted a line to me the day before. " 'The only limit to our realization of tomorrow will be our doubts of today.' How do you like it, Lucy?"

I'd told him I liked it very much indeed.

"Perfect," I said as he took the program in his hand now.

"We'll pretend it's the peace treaty," Daisy suggested.

"Oh, no," Franklin corrected her. "The United Nations Charter." It was his dream. It would be his legacy. He was determined, he'd told me, not to repeat President Wilson's mistakes with the League of Nations.

Polly went into the other room, and Daisy sat at one end of

the sofa crocheting, while I remained at the other watching Franklin work and Shoumie paint. The only sound was the scratch of pen and the rustle of documents. There was not even the tick of a clock. Time had stopped. This was infinite happiness.

Joe, the Filipino mess boy, came into the room and began setting the table for lunch. He moved as silently as a cat, but Franklin noticed him, looked up, and said, "We have fifteen minutes more to work."

I looked at my watch. It was a little before one.

Mr. Hassett gathered up his documents and left. Franklin went on reading. His concentration seemed to be intense. In the mirror I could see that Shoumie, unwilling to ask him to lift his face, was working on the upper part of his brow near his hairline.

Out of the corner of my eye I saw a movement. My head swiveled from the portrait in the mirror to Franklin. He passed his hand over his forehead. It was a gesture I'd never seen him make. His hand fell to his side. It hung there limply.

I was out of my chair in a moment.

Daisy was too. "Did you drop something?" she asked.

He was leaning forward now, the palm of his other hand pressed to the back of his neck, his eyes closed.

"I have a terrific headache," he said. His body slumped forward.

The rest is confusion. Daisy and Polly and I were trying to tilt his chair back, and a voice was shouting into the telephone to get the doctor, and Mr. Prettyman and Joe appeared from nowhere and began lifting him out of the chair. They held him gently, though I could see that he was dead weight, and began carrying him toward the bedroom. Daisy and Polly were try-ing to support his legs, and I started to help them, but something stopped me. Only later did I realize it was Eleanor. She might have abdicated her place in his life, but she would not forgive my presence at his death.

The word went off in my head like an explosion. It could not be that. Please God, it could not, I prayed as I watched them take Franklin from me.

∾ The clock on the dashboard said five-forty-eight. Shoumie had kept it set to Eastern War Time. In Warm Springs it would be four-forty-eight. It suddenly occurred to me to turn on the car radio. I hadn't before because I was in no mood for entertainment. But I was dying for news.

The strains of a popular song came floating out of the silvery grill. Surely they would not be playing dance music if Franklin was dying.

The music stopped, though it was not the end of the tune. The announcer's voice was solemn as a dirge. "We interrupt this broadcast to bring you a bulletin. . . ."

Later Vio's husband Bill told me heightened color is often a warning sign of a cerebral hemorrhage.

↩ Epilogue

> "I can't tell you how deeply I feel for you and how constantly I think of your sorrow—You, whom I have always felt to be the most blessed & privileged of women, must now feel immeasurable grief and pain and they must be almost unbearable."
>
> ↩ Lucy Mercer Rutherfurd in a letter
> to Eleanor Roosevelt, May 2, 1945

> "[If you] cannot meet the need of someone whom [you] dearly love . . . you must learn to allow someone else to meet the need, without bitterness or envy, and accept it."
>
> ↩ Eleanor Roosevelt in *You Learn By Living*

The next day the stunned world read the headlines.

END COMES SUDDENLY AT WARM SPRINGS
Even His Family Unaware of Condition
As Cerebral Stroke Brings Death
To Nation's Leader at 63

The newsreels and photographs did their inadequate best to capture the misery. Thousands of people standing for hours along the railroad tracks, waiting for a glimpse of the train taking Franklin's body home, some sobbing uncontrollably, others silent and disbelieving because this man had been a part of us, the best of us, for so long they could not imagine life without him. The tear-streaked face of the Negro chief petty officer sounding the mournful notes of "Going Home," as the cortege passed. Eleanor standing straight and stoic among family and friends and dignitaries as they laid Franklin's body to rest in the Hudson Valley earth he loved. At the end of the service, the military guard raised their rifles and fired a salute, once, twice, a third time, and after each round Fala let out an outraged bark.

Less than a month later, Mr. Truman went on the air to announce that the war in Europe had ended. Children banged pots and pans, and women cried, and men threw their hats in the air, and I remembered the night in Warm Springs when Franklin had promised the war would be over by May. I was glad he'd known.

Several weeks later I went to Hyde Park. By then Eleanor had turned the house over to the government. By then she had learned that I was with Franklin at the end. She accused no one, though she was furious with Anna.

Franklin was in the Hudson Valley air that morning. The ground remembered his footsteps. The trees dreamed his dream. He was not buried in the rose garden. He inhabited it.

A guard stood sentry at the drive. I stopped my auto. He asked for my card of admission. I handed it to him. Anna had signed it herself and mailed it to me.

"I'm sorry"—he glanced down at the card again—"Mrs. Rutherfurd, but this has to be signed by either Mr. Palmer, the superintendent, or Mrs. Roosevelt."

"It's signed by Mrs. Boettiger." I tried not to sound impatient. I did not want to antagonize him.

"I can see that, ma'am." He was polite, and unyielding. "However, a countersignature by Mr. Palmer or Mrs. Roosevelt, as well as a signature, is required."

"But I've come all the way from New Jersey." I could hear the desperation rising in my voice like a flood tide.

"I'm sorry, ma'am, but there's nothing I can do. Unless . . ."

"Yes?"

"I telephone for a countersignature."

"That would be wonderful. What did you say his name was? Mr. Palmer. Could you telephone Mr. Palmer and explain that I have Mrs. Boettiger's signature?"

The guard disappeared into a small sentry box. I heard my name and Anna's, a few phrases, several yes's. He emerged and stood beside the car again.

"I'm sorry, Mrs. Rutherfurd, but Mr. Palmer says he has no authority to approve your visit. He suggested I call Mrs. Roosevelt."

I sat in the open car. The breeze off the river had died, and the sun pressed down on my head. I asked him to call Eleanor.

He disappeared into the sentry box again. This time he was back in a moment.

"Mrs. Roosevelt says it's all right, ma'am. Enjoy your visit."

Where did she find the strength?

◡◠ A few weeks later a parcel arrived from Daisy Suckley. It was wrapped in layers of cardboard and brown paper. I tore away one after the other until I was holding a small object wrapped only in tissue. I lifted the thin paper carefully. Franklin gazed up at me from the watercolor I had arranged for Shoumie to paint two years earlier. I didn't understand how Daisy had come to have it. I was surprised she was willing to part with it.

I noticed a piece of stationery among the brown wrapping paper.

"Mrs. Roosevelt wants you to have this," Daisy wrote.

Where did she find the generosity?

⌒ The following autumn Vio came to stay with me in Aiken. As I said, I tried to pretend we were two girls together again, though we both knew we were two women alone. Bill had left her. He was going to marry our old friend from the convent school, Marguerita Pennington.

"He thinks she will make him happy," Vio said.

"You made him happy," I protested.

"He thinks she can make him well," Vio explained. "Free him from his terrible black moods. While she was living in Germany, she studied psychology. She sat at the feet of Dr. Jung."

It would have been ludicrous, if it weren't so awful for Vio. I told her it would pass. I predicted he would return. But it didn't pass, and he didn't return, and on an autumn day so golden it was a reproach to ordinary mortal expectations, Vio arose unrested from the nap I'd urged her to take, came downstairs into the rooms still echoing with the music of my happiness, and shot herself in the head.

I heard the report of the gun in the garden. Lying here in the hospital six months later, I still hear it. The morphine they give me does not muffle it. The word *leukemia* which the doctors murmur to the children when they think I am asleep does not drown it out. Prayer does not quiet it. Only the memory of Franklin's voice crying *Grand, isn't it grand* mutes it.

Only the knowledge of the happiness I gave him stifles the scream of Vio's anger and the howl of Eleanor's pain. Only the happiness.

> "Grace Tully wired me when Lucy Rutherford [sic] died. . . .
> She was a wonderful person and it makes me sad that I will
> not be able to see her again.
>
> ↪ Anna Roosevelt Boettiger in a letter to
> Margaret Suckley, October 25, 1948

✑ Acknowledgments

This is a work of historical fiction, and as is always the case with such novels, the emphasis must be on the noun rather than the adjective. I have relied upon history. Most of the scenes come from official records and family reminiscences. Some of the dialogue has been taken verbatim from existing letters. But I have written fiction. Though grounded in the available facts, the Lucy Mercer, Franklin Roosevelt, and other characters who people these pages are the creations of my imagination.

Many people led the way back to these characters and their world. Lucy Mercer Marbury Blunden and her husband Montague Blunden welcomed me into their home and shared a wealth of information and photographs. Moreover, Mrs. Blunden's charm and graciousness gave me an inkling of what her aunt, Lucy Mercer, must have been like. My views are, needless to say, not necessarily theirs, but their stories shaped the characters I have written.

I am also grateful to Arthur M. Schlesinger, Jr., for his thoughts on Lucy Mercer and FDR which inspired my early thinking, and for his second thoughts which confirmed my conclusions. I am deeply indebted to Ambassador William J. vanden Heuvel, chairman of the Franklin & Eleanor Roosevelt

Institute, who provided valuable access to letters and documents and invaluable insight into FDR's character. Geoffrey Ward, whose two volumes are deep and beautifully nuanced studies of FDR, the man, was as generous with information and suggestions for further research as he is perceptive about the subjects in question. Blanche Wiesen Cook, whose two volumes on Eleanor Roosevelt provide a wealth of information, was kind enough to take time out from her own work to talk about mine.

I am grateful to Raymond Teichman and the staff of the Franklin D. Roosevelt Library in Hyde Park and to Linda and Dwayne Watson of the Wilderstein Preservation in Rhinebeck for their guidance and aid in tracking down materials; to Greg Gallagher, a superb librarian, for his inspired sleuthing and unfailing friendship; to Mary Thrash, Nancy Simko, and Steve Layne, for sharing their knowledge and love of life in the Little White House in Warm Springs; to Lesley Herrmann, director of the Gilder Lehrman Institute of American History, for her help and encouragement; and to Mark Piel and the entire staff of the New York Society Library for professional guidance as well as solace and support during the long process of writing this book.

I also want to thank my agent, Emma Sweeney, for her insights into the story and her faith in my ability to tell it, and Starling Lawrence, an editor with the keen eye, sharp wit, and gentle touch every writer dreams of.

All of these people helped me find my way back to Lucy Mercer and Franklin and Eleanor Roosevelt. It is my fault if I took a wrong turn or stumbled at any point.